DIE WITH YOUR LORD

BLUEBEARD'S SECRET

SARAH K. L. WILSON

Sarah K. L. Wilson
Copyright 2022

For the one I love best.
May this be worthy.
Soli Deo Gloria

Book Four

**Fly with the Arrow
Dance with the Sword
Give your Heart to the Barrow
Die with your Lord**

CHAPTER ONE

THE LAW OF GREETING BOUND ME TO HIM. THE Law of Unravelling stole me away. But it was the Law of my own heart that set me now on this careening course toward fate and death and the barest glimmer of hope.

When I was a little girl my mother would cuddle me and my two brothers on her lap before the fire and tell us Wittentales — tales too fantastic and grisly for the mortal world. Tales of creatures who chewed children's bones to dust and belched out nightmares. Tales of oaths pledged that ruined lives and of bargains made which brought fortune beyond imagining and of lovers and fathers and kings who knew not which they were making before fate forced them to dance to the terms set until their feet were bloody. She told tales of trickery so twisty and horrible that it spun the threads of man and changed the entire tapestry, nation falling upon nation, whole kingdoms swallowed in madness or sickness or storm.

When I became a woman, I no longer needed such stories, for despite all my attempts at practicality, I myself, became ensnared within such a tale. And as the weaver of the warp and weft of history brought together the tangled threads of this saga, she wove it with me at the core. Try as I might to buck the pattern, she had only woven my thread back in, and back in, and back in again until there was no untangling it from the course of fate.

I fled through the Wittenhame with my husband clutched to my chest and my heart in my throat. He was no lighter in my arms than a feather, though he was a full-grown man. I held him clutched to my chest, for he made an awkward burden despite his light weight, and even with Wittentree's magic binding us, I was terrified of losing my grip on him.

Ashes fell around us like rain.

At first, I thought they were my imagination, but soon they floated down as thick as leaves falling from the trees in autumn, great black, fluttery ashes with soft filmy edges. And they coated my hair and my tongue and filled the air with the scent of smoke.

"Cataclysm," Grosbeak muttered from where his severed head was tied at my belt, and it sounded as if he were arguing with himself. "But no, it cannot be. T'was to be succession, not the end of all things."

I paused in a sudden clearing on the edge of the tor, my breath sawing through my lungs, my legs trembling as I turned first one way and then another, my long hair whipping into my face and obscuring my vision as I searched for pursuit. They would be just behind me. They would be on my heels.

I was breathless, heart racing, mind hot with fear. If only I could have just one sip of water to cool me. But though I searched the shadows, there was none following. The clearing was empty.

Though I had run for only minutes — fleeing the celebration of Coppertomb's coronation, the festivities and drinking, the dancing and merry-making — there was no sound behind me. The faint screams and distant laughter had melted away, leaving nothing but the chirping of insects, and the soft fall of ash, and a loud ringing in my ears that was, perhaps, my own fear echoing back to me. It blurred and blinded my senses to such a degree that a figure rode out almost upon me before I saw him there.

He was a pale, pale Wittenbrand in a flowing white robe that folded in a fan across his torso. His white hair reached his waist and then fell further still, dry and hoary as it fluttered in the wind. It blew in a different direction than the ash fell, as if he were not subject to the laws of moving air or gravity, though it was peppered in grey and black and melting white from the blowing ashes.

He rode upon a bone horse so pale that it occasionally disappeared altogether and his hands were skeletal bones just as one of mine was. As I watched he flicked his white sword and a pale flame white ran up and down the edge of the blade.

I swallowed, looking up to his face. His cheeks were sunken and his eyes ghastly white pearls. They rolled as he regarded me, his mouth falling open and his tongue quivering there like a living slug.

There was a long moment of silence as we looked at each other and then Grosbeak screamed, terrible and ear-piercing.

I watched myself freeze as if I were watching someone

else, as the figure reached to point a single digit toward me, and just as I was about to scream, too, I remembered something — Bluebeard, whispering poetry to me as he faded, his heart snatched away, his words only for me. I clung tightly to the memory and to the cry that wanted to escape me. He would take neither from me.

I closed my eyes and held my husband's corpse tightly to my chest and thought about that moment and my roaring love for him.

I took a shuddering breath and then opened my eyes.

The white Wittenbrand was gone, and we had been transported to the doorstep of Bluebeard's home. It stood there, bent and odd, squatting on grouse feet in amongst a group of other Wittenhame homes. Here, too, everything was abandoned, ashes falling so fast and silent that they created a blanket of white and grey and black.

Grosbeak's scream cut off and I heard him gasp, panting with exertion.

"Death. Death has come for us. But how did we escape? What manner of monstrosity are you, Izolda, that you can turn back the avatar of death?"

"That couldn't have been death," I said, swallowing down the emotions churning within me. I felt oddly disturbed by the sight of that terrible Wittenbrand. I could not quite name the emotion seizing me and making my hands shake like leaves in the high wind. It was something that combined fear and horror, something that rolled despair and dread all into the mix leaving me sizzling and snapping like fat thrown into the fire. "Were it he, we would not still be here."

In the distance, a horn sounded, biting into my ears

and mind. I jumped. The sound seemed to come from every direction at once. It was long and soulful, eerie and spine-tingling, like the cry of an elk in the forest. It made my mouth dry with renewed fear, as if the sound alone had found and tapped a spring within me. My heart sped, blood pulsing in my ears.

Grosbeak responded with a moan of despair as I reached for Bluebeard's door.

"The Wild Hunt, the Wild Hunt! Our doom falls upon us!"

"That's very dramatic of you," I said grimly as I tried to shuffle Bluebeard in my arms so I could open the door of his home. I'd forgotten about the magic that took you to the door of someone in the Wittenhame if you thought hard about what you loved about them. It had certainly been a boon to us. Bluebeard's head lolled on my shoulder, both precious and terribly tragic. I pillowed it with one hand as one does with a newborn infant.

A good widow would bury her dead husband. I was not good, for I planned to carry him with me.

"Dramatic? I state only the truth, fool mortal girl, so plain as to be nearly gauche. The end has come. Our doom has come upon us. Saw you not the ashes of the sky burning up? Heard you not the horns of heaven?"

"I doubt that was the sky. There's likely a forest fire nearby," I said calmly. "And by the time it reaches us, we'll be elsewhere."

"Indeed," he said with a bite, "For if you have any sense you'll run. We're about to be hunted by the Hounds of Heaven."

"I thought the Wild Hunt took place in the Mists of

Memory," I said, trying to find logic in these prophecies of doom.

"That's only the memory of it from another age, and 'tis bad enough! The real thing will harrow us to our bones. Did you not see Death himself on his pale horse?"

I paused as the door creaked open.

"That was Death?"

"Who did you think it was?" his voice was shrill with fear and drew up higher and higher with every word.

"I thought he was one of the Wittenbrand to whom I had not yet been introduced," I replied smoothly. "There are a great many of you, each more bloodthirsty than the last, I find. But if it was Death, then perhaps we ought to find him again."

"Find Death? Find him on purpose?" Grosbeak was practically squealing. "To what end? Do you think he will be swayed by compassion for your mortal bones as I am? He's not so soft. He's not tainted by an ungainly affection for a mortal. You're too mad for this world, Izolda. You should have stayed with the other mortals and fought their Last Battle with them."

I frowned. "Perhaps I fled from Death too quickly. If we'd followed him, could he take us to where Bluebeard has gone?"

I realized after a heartbeat that the keening sound I heard was Grosbeak. It finally dissolved into words.

"To the Barrow? Are you so lost to sense that you would die with your husband?"

I barked a laugh as I stepped through the door. "Isn't that what the poem says? 'Die with your lord?'"

"It meant with the Bramble King, obviously. And

Coppertomb twisted it so that he could take your husband's heart and offer it to the Barrow and watch him die alongside his lord while the great Lord Coppertomb was crowned the new Bramble King." Grosbeak's words almost tumbled together he was speaking so quickly. "Were you not paying attention? We can't live it twice like a play we enjoyed. You have to sink into these things and soak them up or you'll miss them entirely. Sometimes I despair that you have learned nothing from me."

"You think I should have soaked up my husband's death?" I couldn't keep the censure from my voice. "Coppertomb reached within his chest and ripped out his beating heart."

"And wasn't it wonderful? Didn't it give you a thrill? Lord Coppertomb — or maybe I should say, the new-crowned Bramble King — is a great master of drama and portents and I applaud his excellent ascension. We will be singing the tale of it for centuries to come."

"I thought you said the sky was falling and we were all caught in a cataclysm?" I said wryly, still caught on the threshold just inside Bluebeard's door as my eyes adjusted to the darkness. I was afraid to enter. Afraid of what might greet me within. Would his friends and servants within reject me? Would the fire burn me up or the rooms shift and swallow me?

"I'll admit," Grosbeak said glibly, "a reign shadowed with such portents as Death walking amongst the living and the sky falling in ash is sure to be a short one." He paused, considering, and the fear in his voice was suddenly replaced by speculation and something that sounded very much like delight. "A short but entertaining one. Perhaps I will enjoy it after all."

I gasped as my eyes finally adjusted to the darkness of Bluebeard's home. There was no fire burning. I saw no cats or other creatures moving in the heights above. No raven. No folk. No smells of food or drink. The door swung closed behind me and slammed shut.

I gasped, feeling my way to the mantle. Hollowness rung in every corner of my husband's home. It felt as though the heart of this house had been removed just as his physical heart had been, plucked away by an enemy. I choked on a swell of that swirling emotion I could not name.

"Ooof. Take a care! You are bumping me into furniture!"

I found the tinderbox and a candle one-handed and then sank to the ground, cradling Bluebeard on my lap so that I could work with the tinderbox to light the candle. It took four tries and even then my shaking hands barely managed it.

"Where is the fire?" I asked, my voice forlorn. I had hoped the fire could help to transport us to somewhere safer than this. But beyond that hope, his loss was even greater, for Bluebeard's home felt dead without its blazing heart.

I looked down at my husband's lovely face, flickering in the pale candlelight. Had I bargained for the wrong thing? Was I merely spinning out his torment by dragging his near-corpse everywhere with me? I'd heard once of a mother whose child had been snatched by fever. It had taken four men to hold her as they wrested the child's body from her sobbing grasp. She could not bear to set his tiny form down.

"Dead, I'd wager," Grosbeak's words sliced into my thoughts. "Rotting now like the rest of this mausoleum, if fires can rot. It cannot live now that he is dead. Perhaps the same is true of you. After all, of what use are you in the Wittenhame when you are flesh and mortal bones without a single breath of magic to sustain you."

"And yet, if these mortal bones did not carry you, you'd soon find the Wittenhame considerably less entertaining," I reminded him.

I stood, carefully drawing Bluebeard up with me, and the candle also, so that I could scoop up the silver thread and needle and with great care, I carried my husband to the settee where once we caressed one another and set him upon the plush brocade.

He looked so vulnerable here, beautiful but broken, once-strong, now nothing but a wisp that was once a powerful man. I remembered yet how he came to me from the sea, how he strode over the water and divided out punishments upon his enemies. Now, he was vulnerable as a newborn lamb and cold as one stillborn.

The candle lit nothing more than a tiny pool around us, so that I felt as though I dwelt only in this small patch of lonely house. Perhaps, all that remained was this one settee with this single dead man lain across it. I hitched up my skirts and set his palm on my bare leg so that I could work with both hands. I must keep his flesh pressed to mine or he would flee this life entirely.

With care, I threaded the silver thread into the eye of the needle and then drew his shredded coat and shirt apart so I could see his ruined chest sagging inward where once a heart and rib were found. Nausea washed over me at the sight of his torn flesh and pale skin. I had to take a moment to look away and take deep breaths of stale air to compose myself. When I felt strong enough, I turned back and I drew in a shuddering breath at how very, very dead my beloved appeared.

"The view from here is ghastly. I'll have you know that I am in no mind to help you when you abandon me to the flights of chance," Grosbeak complained in a muffled voice. "You should consider that right now I can see nothing but your skirts and the cloth is not so fine as to require a close study."

"I have to mend my husband's rent breast. Is it too much to ask for a small dose of mercy from you?" I asked him.

"Indeed, it is, for I have none to spare, nor would I be of a mind to offer it to you. You bargained very badly just now and you are without beauty or living hand," he said nastily as I gripped the needle between my thin skeletal fingers and carefully set it through my husband's cooling flesh.

I watched his slitted eyes as I stitched, pulling flesh to flesh with each draw of my needle, bringing back together what was torn apart just as he had done for my back so long ago. I felt those scars from time to time when I bent or stretched. Bluebeard's face, ever lovely, had taken on a bluish cast, the sacred color of the Wittenbrand, and I felt my chest seize as I watched him, the breath freezing within and becoming awkward and tight.

"I fear you fail to realize your predicament," Grosbeak

said and I could tell he was loving this, even with his face pressed into the hem of my skirt. "Let me reveal it to you. You are cast from the Court of the Wittenhame and into this dying house with your almost-corpse husband. He is spending your remaining days on this half-life of his with reckless abandon. The result of which will cost you dear and deny benefit to him. Unless you abandon him, you must drag him with you wherever you go for no gain but the possibility that he may someday serve a purpose once more."

"I find I am very skilled in carrying about dead weight," I murmured as I set the last stitch and tied a careful knot. The wound was bleeding still around the edges. That was not something that the truly dead did. "I have been practicing and practicing with you."

I cut the thread with deft hands — even if one was entirely skeletal — and then lifted my husband up and into my arms again, gathering the up the candle, and marching to the nightingale stairs. They did not sing as I ascended. The house was truly dying with its lord.

If only that were enough to fulfill prophecy and snatch victory from Coppertomb's hand. I huffed an ironic laugh but it was hollow and grim.

I was numb, I thought, above that mystery swell within. Numb to pain, numb to feeling, numb to thought. I stumbled along as if in a dream, hardly caring that I had seen Death face to face, or that some terrible horn had been sounded, or that the sky might be falling, or burning, or something about a cataclysm. I had set my feet and hands to a task and they carried me capably even as my heart and mind were locked to greater thought or feeling. They felt as inaccessible as my husband and just as lost to me as he was.

I had a list. I would follow it. That would have to be enough.

First, see to my husband's care.

Second, gather help.

Third, form a plan to bring him back. I had all of him except his heart. In the Wittenbrand, in this wide land of magic and mystery where bodiless heads prattled on and on, and specters sat for years on your shoulder, neither eating nor drinking, couldn't I find some way to restore my beloved missing only a single heart?

When I reached our bedroom at the top of the stairs, the bed had crumbled to dust, and the flowering vines desiccated. The window to another world was simply gone. In its place was nothing but tumbled stone in a heap. The spring and the warm bath were dry and cracked, the books on the shelves nothing but dust.

This time, I couldn't escape the gasp that dashed from my lips.

"You'll find no succor here!" Grosbeak said, delighted by my misery.

I swallowed, trying to work moisture back into my dry lips. Where could I go now? Even the few resources left to me were crumbling. How could I fight against Death himself and the new king of the the Wittenhame when I had not even that?

I set my jaw firmly. I was being impractical. I still had my husband — as much of him as there was. I still had my health and my mind. I could figure this out.

"Is this destruction only happening to us or to all the Wittenhame?" I asked my Wittenhame guide.

"That, my darling keeper, is the million crown question," Grosbeak said gleefully. "For if it is only you, then you are on a clock, are you not? Mere hours perhaps before you lose any chance of defeating Death and somehow wresting your beloved prince from the grasp of hell. Already his magic crumbles around you, his personality — upon which both house and fire were built — fades and molders in a way that even the sea could not achieve when he languished in her embrace. But if ... and wouldn't this be golden? Or perhaps diamond? What is more valuable in this age?"

"Get to the point," I hissed.

"If all of the Wittenhame is falling, then Coppertomb has lost with his win, and you have won with his loss, tearing down the roof of heaven with your ruination, and collapsing this world and everything in it with your downfall. It is a sleek blow to take your enemy down with you. I did not take you for the type to charge honorably to your own death, but I find it favors you. Perhaps, we can line you and Coppertomb up and let the masses cheer for which of you wears it better."

"I was not me who wrought this, but my husband," I said and my voice was strained with emotion, which was strange since I felt nothing but emptiness.

"Even so, to drag your enemies with you into death is a masterful move. Worthy of the greatest of princes."

"Do you call him such when your camaraderie has faded into animosity?" I asked

"Burdened though I am with a bitterness heaped on

me by the likes of your prince, still I am servant of the truth and bearer of the obvious," he said sorrowfully.

"As am I," a thready voice agreed, and I gasped in relief as the gargoyle on top of the mirror stirred himself.

"Can you help me, mirror?" I begged as it pulled a horrific face at me. "I need fresh clothing for both myself and the Arrow —useful, hard-wearing clothing for our journey — and a sling with which I might carry him skin to skin against me."

The mirror coughed. "Skin to skin is it? How scandalous! I love it!"

"Please," I begged, worried he'd give me nothing useful now. "We must chase after death and go down into the grave."

The mirror laughed. "Usually, I would spit your wardrobe at you, but my power is weakening. Step through me and I will dress you, but come to me naked, for I have only one last gasp of magic within."

Grosbeak laughed, a horrible, cackling laugh. "Yes, put on a show for the gargoyle, Izolda. It's not like you have anything better to do."

"I can't run in these skirts, Grosbeak," I said coolly. "Not while effectively carrying the Arrow."

Carefully, I untied Grosbeak and turned his head to face away as he snickered.

"The virgin bride, undressing her husband for the first time."

"I've seen him naked before," I said acerbically. "I am no blushing bride."

"Ah, but have you undressed him with your own hands?" He asked me as I quickly stripped my own things off. I left my small clothes on. The mirror would just have to leave them as they were.

I was a mess of blood and gore. It would have been nice to clean myself in the ever-warm pool, but with it gone, I would have to settle for fresh clothing. At least the worst of it was on my clothes, though it made for an awkward dance to undress while still remaining skin-to-skin with my husband.

"I'm his wife," I told Grosbeak shortly. "His body is mine as much as his heart is, and I have just as much a right to tend it and care for it."

"You miss my point quite intentionally, virgin Izolda." Grosbeak chuckled grimly.

I found my cheeks growing hot as I began to strip my husband of clothing. It was awkward to undress him while keeping our bare flesh skin against skin but his clothing was ruined and torn. He needed better or he'd catch a chill. I laid a leg against the side of his torso as I wrestled his boots and trousers off. Even so, I was huffing with effort as I cast them aside.

There was no way to easily maintain this position while removing his shredded shirt and jacket. That would take great care to avoid injuring his ruined chest. There was only one way to manage it, and it was while straddling him. I felt grateful both that he was unconscious and could not see my disregard for his privacy over his health, and equally grateful that I'd had the foresight to turn Grosbeak around. I tried to keep my eyes to myself, and I mostly succeeded, but I could not keep them shut tight when, at last, I lifted him to carry him through the mirror.

He was beautiful in my arms despite his grisly wounds

— the palms and side which never healed and the ragged tear I'd stitched together. Beautiful and far too pale. As blue as his holy color, as bloodless as a specter, as gloriously beautiful as a marble statue. I hoped I could find a way to breathe life back into his chest and keep his soul in this beautiful, ruined body.

I stumbled when an emotion returned to me — a deep, aching, sadness that swelled as the swell of the tide brings in the sea and washed over me with just as much kindness as the crashing waves of the vengeful ocean. And just like the hulls men sail out on the sea, so I was smashed to splinters beneath the rage of it.

I shook as I shifted him to my back as one would carry a large child, and bore him through the mirror, my spine straightening only in response to Grosbeak's continued snickers. I would not give him the satisfaction of breaking now.

We emerged through the other side fully clothed and shod. I looked in the mirror and to my relief, Bluebeard was clothed from head to foot in his usual blue coat and shirt, trousers, and boots, but these were clean, warm, and dry, and his shirt and coat had been left unbuttoned. I, on the other hand, had been fitted in a backless jacket and shirt so that his bare torso was pressed directly to my back and a wide band of blue cloth had been slung under his bottom, around my waist, and then crossed over his back and down my shoulders to tie to itself, keeping him harnessed to me. My own feet were buckled into knee-high boots and my legs fitted with fine leather trousers, ready for trouble.

"Thank you, mirror," I said and he winked but the wink was too much. The mirror cracked from side to side and the gargoyle above it froze in place, his mouth forever caught in a taunting twist.

"And now, Grosbeak," I said with careful calm, "we will find your lantern pole and begin."

"Begin what?" he huffed. "More dress up? More wasting time?"

"The beginning of the end," I said.

CHAPTER TWO

In the main room, a lantern pole was hard to find now that I'd taken so many, but I did find a strange one with a hooked crook at the top like a shepherd's staff. This one was shaped like the head of a hissing rooster — a creature both intimidating and somewhat ridiculous. It held two hooks for lanterns in tandem across a wide bar. I hung Grosbeak's head from one of the hooks, ignoring his gnawed ear and the comb in his hair that a mermaid lover wove within the greasy dark tangles. I was used to his putrescence by now. Just one head hanging from the double tree made it swing so that the rooster stared off to the side as if to guard me against trouble on my right side.

"I do not care for this pole," Grosbeak complained. "I am not feed for a wild cockerel. If you ever prove worthy enough to stop running for your life, I demand a better option. A gilded pole perhaps, or a plush cushion on which you shall bear me."

"Do keep dreaming. I hear that hope keeps you looking young and you could use the help," I said absently.

Bluebeard was positioned so that his head rested on my shoulder and almost, I thought I could feel his breath, faint, yet there, against the curve of my neck. I clung to that. We would find a way to retrieve him. Nothing was so lost that it could not be brought back. I had been assured that he was not yet fully dead, even if his heart had been given to the grave and while there was life, there was hope. If he'd had a plan to restore his wives, then we could have a plan to restore him.

"I hope you are not planning something foolhardy, mortal woman," Grosbeak murmured as I lifted my candle and adjusted my grip on the pole. The candle barely lit further than his face and he was wreathed in the kind of shadows that heightened the otherworldliness of his visage. "If you chase after Death, my fun will be over."

"I make all my plans with the sole aim of amusing you," I said dryly, looking around Bluebeard's home for anything else that could help us. I was finding nothing. When I touched most objects, they turned immediately to dust or ash.

It was a strange thing to walk with the limp body of my husband strapped to my back. The weight was so light I barely felt it, but I had to move with care to avoid hitting his limp limbs on the furniture or turning too swiftly and knocking his lolling head to one side. I was learning — however slowly — to move with slow care, as one might when tending an infant.

"If you wish to amuse me, then keep me alive. This dying house will not keep out the Hounds of Heaven now that they are loose in the Wittenhame, and you must run like all the rest, or form a hunting party to hunt the creatures back. There are only two paths in this game. And as you have no vassals except me, running is the only option for you. I'll have you know that while I was the handiest in all the Wittenhame with arrow and spear, that option has been taken from me. It's run or die today, my mortal conveyor."

"Noted," I said, but it was not toward the outer door that I strode, for I was not fleeing Hounds nor chasing specters. I had a clear plan in mind.

I crept through the darkened, dreary house, the scent of mildew in my lungs, and then made my way down the stairs, and heaved open the heavy oak door there.

"Not the Wall of Wisdom!" Grosbeak protested, but I ignored him. It was not his counsel I sought. He'd made it very plain that he was only along for the ride. "There's nothing they can give you that I cannot! Nothing."

"Wise," the word whispered in my ear.

My breath caught. Had that been my imagination, or was it my husband barely whispering to me?

"Wise, stone-faced certainty."

I twisted my head to look at his face and saw only his slitted eyes and parted lips. It seemed that I had his approval — if that had been him whispering to me, and who else would it be? — and the notion put strength into my limbs and heart.

Husband? I asked within my mind. *Can you hear me?*

There was no reply, but for a moment I thought I felt a flash of emotion that was not mine. Tenderness, I thought. Like watching a new foal take to its feet.

I shook my head. That was not the right emotion for dealing with Bluebeard's advisors.

I made my way into the musty gloom below. Without the fire leaping to join us, the room full of the heads of my husband's enemies was a horror. The chair on which he had sat and dandled me on his knee was threadbare and collapsed. The shelves leaned at awkward angles, and for a moment I thought I might be too late — that the heads also would be gone, rotted away to nothing but empty-eyed skulls.

"You should be running," Grosbeak complained. "Do you want to be backed into a corner when the Hounds arrive? Perhaps we can leap into Riverbarrow."

I'd never endanger my husband's home that way. Grosbeak should know better. It was to be the mortal realm for us, or the Wittenhame, or nothing.

"Who disturbs our imprisonment?" The voice that came from the darkness of the shelves was the firm voice of Vireo.

I lifted my candle high so that he could see me.

He began to smile a gleeful, wicked smile when his eyes set on me, but it collapsed when his gaze shifted to my shoulder.

"The Arrow," he gasped. "What has come to pass?"

"Only the beginning of a cataclysm, Death riding a pale horse, the sky turned to ash, the moon to blood, and all that," Grosbeak said, and he seemed to be gloating that he knew this and Vireo did not. I leaned his pole against the shelves and he scowled but kept talking. "Oh, and now Coppertomb is the Bramble King." Vireo hissed at that. "His coronation was scarce an hour ago. And for the confirmation of it, the Arrow had his heart plucked from him and shoved into the grave."

"His heart?" Was I mistaken or did Vireo's eye turn to me for a bare second before returning to Grosbeak?

All up and down the wall, the severed heads stored there murmured their appreciation or apprehension, excitement passing over the faces of those I could see in my candle's light.

"It's all precisely as it was prophesied!" Grosbeak crowed, "and I got to be there for all of it! I was there to watch his heart feed the barrow and watch the triumph of Coppertomb. And now I will get to watch the mortal bride run with the slathering jaws of the Hounds of Heaven snapping at her heels, her bright shrieks painting the midnight with sparkles of terror, and her wet mortal life running out like water from a spring. Do you not envy me?"

"Mortal wife of Lord Riverbarrow," Vireo said very precisely. "As the only one here with hands, you would do us all a favor, if you were to cuff Grosbeak for his insolence. Your pet is terribly ill-mannered."

I cleared my throat. I was not in the habit of cuffing people. That wasn't what I'd come for.

"I'm here to consult with you, Wall of Wisdom, Vault of the Fallen Enemies of the Arrow. Will you hear my question? Will you consult on my riddle?"

"Only if you strike your pet," Vireo said. "Payment for services rendered."

"Hear, hear!" someone else said and I thought it might be Grosbeak's father.

Grosbeak snickered. "She'd never, weak mortal that she —"

Fast as lightning, my hand shot out and I slapped Grosbeak.

"Enough," I said and let my voice ring with authority. "I have no time for more stipulations. Either hear my riddle or ignore my plea but do not waste what little time I have."

"Speak then, mortal," the woman who looked like a mermaid said, her tongue coming out forked and green. Her tangled seafoam hair curled around her. "Tell us this conundrum and we will advise you if we see fit."

"We will?" Grosbeak's green-faced father snickered nastily. "We owe the mortal nothing."

"We owe her for a slap," Vireo said, considering. And his face now, after life had passed, held none of the ill will he had bourn me while he lived.

"She wears his blood," the head with the silver crown said. Her eyes were still closed, her mouth a perfect cupid's bow. "We can deny her nothing while she is sealed with that."

The murmurs quieted. Interesting.

"This is the riddle given to me by Lady Wittentree," I said, speaking clearly so that all of them would hear. *"What once stood in a line, now missing a brother. What was taken for wealth but refined by another? What holds death or life in the gap left behind? What holds endless damnation in similar kind."*

"We've seen how well you do with puzzles, mortal wife," Vireo said easily. "Who can answer where you see not the solution?"

He was taunting me, I knew. And yet, he was partially right because I recognized a part of the riddle. It was tickling something in the back of my mind that I could not quite remember.

A head spoke, interrupting my thoughts and I recognized the square jaw and red curly hair of the seer who had prophesied for Bluebeard. Her glassy eyes were white as snow.

"A tangled path lies now before you, mortal wife of the Arrow, and only one way endures to the end. Turn to the left or the right and the ground will slip out from under you and drag you to your death."

I shuddered but then paused at the wide smiles on the faces of the advisors. They loved this as much as Grosbeak did, reveling in whatever suffering might come to me.

"Have you nothing more useful to say to me?" I asked. "I know already that the way is precarious."

"Nothing," the Seer said. "Any words might steer your course and any steering might take you from the solid path."

"It doesn't sound solid at all, I'll bet you three flies and a gnat she chooses wrong before she leaves this house," Grosbeak's father said.

"I raise you by a tooth that she makes it to the Hound's chase," Grosbeak countered. "She's cleverer than you think."

"But not clever enough to win?" his father pressed.

"Is anyone?" Grosbeak asked. "I once thought the Arrow capable of winning the game, but look at him now? He's a rag doll in the hands of a mortal woman."

"Mmmm."

I clenched my jaw, frustration filling me. I'd counted on this wall of heads to tell me something — anything, that I could find to point the way. I understood Wittentree's riddle to a certain extent. After all, Bluebeard had told me the story about the rib of the sovereign, there in the ground, mined out by evil men. If that wasn't the thing that used to stand in a row then I didn't know what was.

A loud cracking sound startled me and I swallowed, looking up at the dust spilling from the ceiling.

Mayhap, I should have listened to Grosbeak and run. I clutched at my heart with one hand, certain the whole structure was about to fall on us, when I realized it was laughter I was hearing, not the collapse of the house. Not the laughter of the heads, though some were certainly laughing in their cruel way.

When I raised my candle, it lit a flickering pattern of dancing shadow over a face as large as I was tall, jutting from the wall to one side of the shelf of heads. It was almost entirely hidden by tangled roots and squirming beetles, but I still made it out. The old Bramble King was here. It was he who was mocking me with his laugh. He seemed barely there, he was missing his crown, and he gasped between his chuckles, fading a little more with each gasp and then he spoke and he almost spat the words, he ejected them so harshly and intensely.

"*Mist and Memories,*" he spat and the words were echoed by the heads with confusion in their voices.

"Has he gone mad?" one particularly shrill one asked.

"He's nearly dead, of course he's mad. Coppertomb's replaced him. Do you know what you call a replaced king?"

"Has there ever been a replaced king?

"You call him past, you call him refuse, you call him

boring, for that is what he is." I was pretty sure that was Grosbeak's father.

The Bramble King flickered again and then there was a strangled sound and one of the heads fell to the ground gurgling horribly and then suddenly still.

It *was* Grosbeak's father. I raised a single eyebrow. So typical.

"I'd wager that more respect might be due the Bramble King," I said calmly and the great king's eyes flickered to mine for a bare moment. Unlike the others, I knew what his words had meant for I remembered stealing a glance into the Sword's copy of that very book. "Mist and Memories: The Memoir of Lord Antlerdale." My heart was racing. I had an answer from the Bramble King himself.

"Chapter Ten," he said very clearly, a dozen beetles scuttling into his curving lips as he spoke. "Paragraph Thirteen."

And then he was gone and I was left repeating his words again and again in my mind so I would not forget. Chapter ten, paragraph thirteen. Chapter ten, paragraph thirteen.

"Well," Grosbeak drawled. "This has been enlightening. It's not every day you watch your father killed a second time, and this time by no less than the former sovereign of the Wittenhame."

"Is he *former?*" one of the heads asked. "He seemed anything but."

I shivered. Death and life had different meanings here. But I had my clue and it was time to move.

"A word of caution," one of the heads said in a thin reedy voice. I had to lift the candle very high to see a man ancient, with sallow cheeks. "I saw a man living with no heart once, surviving only on magic. Has he spoken to you?"

"Hardly," Grosbeak snickered. "He's decorative now, nothing more. Izolda's trophy husband."

"I'd not discount him yet," the voice said, "and I'd not leave us here when you'll need his advisors."

"She can hardly carry you all around on poles," Grosbeak said dismissively.

But the head was right. I should take them with me.

"The man I saw," the querulous head said, "was as if in a dream, living again other times of his life and unable to grasp what time or space he found himself in at the present. If you speak to him, I caution you to watch for signs of that."

"Thank you," I said.

"You're thanking him for that nonsense?" Grosbeak objected. "Where is my thank you? When have I failed to be useful? And yet I receive no thanks."

"Your thanks is your continued life," I warned him. "And now, I must hurry. We have little time."

"Finally, she understands!" he said with a dramatic eye roll, but his drama was cut off when I took out my golden key, turned it to open the Room of Wives, and marched to the shelves, scooping up heads by the hair, four to a fist, and hurrying to stack them inside the room around the pillar meant for me.

"What are you doing?" he objected. "You're wasting time."

But he had to speak loudly over the screaming protests of the heads.

"This is not what we agreed to!" they shrieked. "We are not prizes for the taking!"

"I have few resources," I huffed, not stopping in my task. "Best not to waste them."

"I would like to file an official complaint," Grosbeak called after me as I disappeared with the rest of the heads. "This is not an egalitarian society! Everyone does not have equal value. I am your pet. *Me!*"

I ignored him, as I ignored the many protests of my husband's defeated enemies and when they were all secured, I marched to where Bluebeard had left Sparrow's head and body, her arms crossed respectfully over her chest. I leaned down and snatched up her head.

Her eyes snapped open. "What is this?"

I ignored her and marched out of the room, trying my best not to listen to the hiss of the garnets as they ran out faster than I could spend days, locked the room behind me, and tied her head by its hair to the other hook on the pole.

"No, you can't do this!" she screamed.

"You are too mad for even the Wittenhame!" Grosbeak agreed, his voice a ringing shout.

"On the contrary. Only the sanest person can deal with complete insanity," I said coolly. "She neutralizes it, removing the poison by her mere presence. Heed me and be wise." I paused. "Also, though you both hate me, I believe I'll find your counsel useful, so it's both of you or neither."

"Neither," they said in unison.

"Both it is," I said firmly, scooping up the lantern pole, and I left the empty room with my candle held high and my jaw set with determination.

CHAPTER THREE

I hurried up the stairs, balancing my double-headed lantern pole in one hand and my single candle in the other. Human heads are very heavy. Two at once would make me strong as a knight in the king of Pensmoore's training if I kept this up. A memory of Svetgin's proud grin when my father told me he'd been accepted as a knight seared through my mind and with it came a sudden vision of the knights of Pensmoore charging onto a dust-worn battlefield with my nephew Rolgrin at their head, a flag unfurling behind his foaming horse — a black horse sigil over a field of green proudly displayed upon it. Blood was splashed over his dark tunic and flashing sword. I blinked away the memory. It was not mine.

Grosbeak muttered a steady stream of curses and I clung to them to steady me. I wasn't in the mortal world right now. I was here in the Wittenhame, fighting for my husband's life and more than just my happiness rode on his slumped shoulders. Fail, and Pensmoore would fail with me. If she had not already.

"Teeth of the Gods! The indignity. Blights and barnacles!"

Sparrow maintained a dignified silence as my old friend painted the air bright blue with his words. She looked the worse for being dead, but her eyes were sharp and she seemed to be thinking very hard. I could only hope she was thinking to our advantage and not to trip me up. What would she give more weight to? Her love of Lord Riverbarrow, the Arrow, my Bluebeard, or her disdain that he'd married me, a mere mortal, in the Wittenbrand way?

My candle guttered as the air shifted and the boards squeaked under my feet. I swallowed down tremors of worry. What I was about to undertake would be an enormous task for one of the Wittenbrand, never mind a mere mortal. And this time, there would be no magical husband swooping in to pluck me free of a trap I'd sprung. Instead, he was counting on me for success.

I must summon all my practicality and common sense for this. I would need every shred of it.

I opened the wooden door at the top of the stairs, running a hand over Bluebeard's crest etched upon it. An arrow with a streak of blood behind it and a bird flying above. It squealed in protest, binding on the floorboards so that I had to carefully thread the lantern pole through the gap and then adjust Bluebeard on my back to squeeze the pair of us through. The house was shifting, falling apart at the seams. It made something uncomfortable lurch in my belly. I had begun to think of this place as home, but like all my homes from the past, this too would fade and fail and leave me without anchor or place once more.

"*Riverbarrow.*" This time, I did not imagine the whisper in my mind. I smelled the mint on the edges of it as I stumbled into the main room, heart in my throat. I paused, lifting the candle as I turned so I could see his face.

"The pearl," he whispered, his short beard tickling my neck and his words making my mouth suddenly dry. He could speak. He still had that much life.

His pale blue cat's eyes met mine, and for a moment I was almost nauseated by the powerful emotions that tore through me from my numb lips, through my aching chest, and down through vibrating thighs to my toes. Need, desire, hope, absolute obsession — how could I disentangle one from the other when they wove themselves all through every root and branch of me with just one shared glance eye to eye?

He wet his lips with a bloody tongue. "Please, sun of my world. Please. "

I could never say no to that "please" and I did not try. Hope galloped in my chest as I hurried to where the painting hung on his wall — the door to Riverbarrow. I saw that yes, there was a pearl hanging from the frame, strung on a single cord of something that looked like hair twisted and braided into a narrow rope. It was a strange hair, indigo in color and rough in texture as if it were made from a blueish green horse. Or perhaps a kelpie? Was this hair from the water creature he both was and wasn't? My eyebrows were rising even as I reached for it.

This pearl? I asked with my mind and he gasped,

almost inaudibly, and then with a look of enormous concentration, his hand lifted slow, slow as honey in the depths of winter, causing little flutters of emotion in my chest. He snapped his fingers and the painting vanished. His hand fell and his face sagged once more into my shoulder, his eyelids falling shut, and his cheek going limp against my shoulder.

I shuddered into the feeling of his heavy-eyed self resting entirely on me. It was like watching something precious as it dropped from a ship into the sea. One could not tear one's eyes away from the fall, but the moment it plunged into the water all would be lost.

I paused for a breath — refusing to give up the fall, if that was all I had left. And for that breath, I savored the press of his cheek into my shoulder, the sensation of his bare, cooling flesh against my back, the way his fallen hand was slung around my narrow hip. And when I breathed in, I breathed in his scent and I brought his air into me, and it was heady as good wine and it swirled in my heart and body in a way that made me gasp. Was that a tear I blinked back? Surely not.

"Put it around your neck you fool girl," Sparrow said in a tight voice that suggested her patience had thinned to a thread. "Don't you see he put Riverbarrow into it?"

The pearl was as large as the end of my thumb and a hole had been bored through it to take the binding of the hair rope. When I held the pearl up, I saw in its depths the same scene that had been in the painting a moment ago — one of the tranquil river and the blowing willows, with tiny golden fairies floating between them — as if the opaque surface were reflecting back what had been wrought in oil and skill. I swallowed and slung it around my neck, tucking the pearl into my jacket and shirt to keep it safe.

"Wouldn't that take an enormous amount of magic, to transfer a whole world like that?" I asked, in awe.

"Were I you," Sparrow said acidly, "I would not make my estimates of the Arrow so low. He always rises to exceed expectation."

I felt my face heat at that and grow even hotter at the knowing look in her eye as if she knew him better than I ever could. I did not like the splinter of jade jealousy that pierced me with her expression. It did not suit me or aid my efforts.

"Oh, yes, this is excellent. Ignore the end of the world to thrash out which of you is Queen Hen," Grosbeak mocked. "Will it be a battle of devil looks or sharp silences? Have no thought to whether you will hurt me in the crossfire. For I am unaffected by the evil eye and I can fill any silence. Have I told you about the writings of Mistress Le Pen? I was indulging in them not long before my head was taken."

His rambling shook me back to the present. He was right. What we had to do was urgent and there was no time for me to worry about where and how my husband's loyalties might be been entangled.

I strode to the frigid fireplace, searching among the stacks of books as Grosbeak rambled on. Antlerdale's memoir must be here somewhere.

"She writes the most scandalous truths, Sparrow. You really should have read them while you could. Delightful, flagrant, violent, and absolutely addictive," Grosbeak said, warming to his tale as I sifted through books in the light of my flickering candle.

These volumes looked intact and solid but they fell to pieces in my hands, bindings splitting apart and pages streaming out and spreading across the floor. In vain, I took up one after another only for them to slide through my fingers and disintegrate. But even so, I could read the titles and none were *Mist and Memory*.

All at once, the tangled roots of the tree that held coats by the entrance gave a terrible creak, and then with a shudder, the tree toppled, cracked, and split into two halves. The top half crashed downward, pulling with it the chandeliers, the candle ends, and the yowling cat that lived within them. He did not look right, his hair falling out in clumps and his tail dragging as he moved.

He hissed at us and then fled through the front door which had been knocked open and left ajar.

We were running out of time.

I lifted the lantern pole and scrambled over the tree when I heard the stones of the fireplace begin to crumble. I was through the door when a terrible crack split the air. My nose filled with the scent of dust and earth, I leapt from the doorway and away, as the house on grouse feet collapsed in on itself in a heap.

"The end of an age," Grosbeak whispered sadly.

"The end of a lot of things," Sparrow agreed, but her voice was more than sad. It sounded like resigned despair.

I stood for a moment, working my dry mouth, shock and worry filling every inch of me.

"I suppose I'll have to find the book somewhere else," I

said, returning to common sense and trying to stay hopeful. We could find this book. Just not here. There was no point fussing about it. I needed to get to work to fix it.

From somewhere nearby, a dog barked and then the horn sounded again, long and eerie, and I bit my lip and tasted blood.

"Run, run, the hunt has come! The Hounds of Heaven flush the prey!" Grosbeak warned, delight in every syllable.

"I need to find Antlerdale's book," I gasped, but I heard the loud dogs baying not far from here and their barks sounded hungry and violent.

The sound stabbed directly into my heart, making it gallop with fear. It was not only myself I was risking here. It was my beloved husband and his entire world slung around my neck.

"And how do you plan to do that?" Sparrow asked coolly, the only one of us unaffected by the baying of the Hounds. She merely seemed merely impatient at not being informed of my plan.

"They should be everywhere," I said, my words laced with anxiety. "Grosbeak said that Antlerdale gave them out like candy. Everyone should have copies, and all I need to do is find the tenth chapter and the thirteenth paragraph."

"I see your predicament," Sparrow said with a lifted brow. Shouldn't she be screaming at me to run, too, or was it normal for her to discuss literature while listening to Grosbeak chant a song that either repelled dogs or drew them in, I wasn't sure which? "And it's a bad one because you can't just grab any copy of the book and look."

"Why not?"

"Because Antlerdale is constantly rereading the book

and every time he does, he changes something and reissues the book. 'Each correction brings us closer to perfection,' I believe he said. So you'll need the original."

"And where is that?" I asked. Was that a snuffling I heard? It was getting closer.

"At his home," Sparrow said calmly.

"So we'll go there, then," I agreed.

"Now. We go now, right?" Grosbeak whined. "Now!"

And then a loud bark made me jump and down the row of collapsed houses, through the ashes filtering down from — yes, Grosbeak had been right — a crescent moon that had turned to blood and was dripping in the sky, leapt a three-headed Hound so large it made me wonder if we were accidentally dragon-fly sized again.

I spun in every direction looking for escape. Not Bluebeard's house. It had collapsed. As had every house we could see. Not the mushrooms, they had fallen, leaving black smears the size of army barracks where they had been.

I could try to run, but I couldn't outrun a normal-sized dog when I was utterly unburdened. I had no hope of outrunning this one.

Before the barking, slathering, short-haired Hound, denizens of the Wittenhame fled. A pair of figures mounted on an oversized fox flung arrows behind them at the beast, but the arrows were the size of pine needles compared to the spittle-flecked dog, and it didn't seem to notice them even when one stuck into one of its six eyes.

No fighting, then.

A group of tiny flying fairies kicked up like a swarm of sand flies, fluttering panicked in every direction. Someone screamed. Some others started to cry out but were cut off.

I spun again and caught sight of a toad the size of a horse leaping past. To my shock, Grosbeak whistled to it and it paused. It was my toad. The one from the joust.

I didn't stop to think, I just leapt onto its back, hoping that Bluebeard would stay tied to me and that I could hold onto the lantern with one hand as I tossed the candle behind my back and grabbed for one of the knobs on the back of the toad. He was leaping before I could steady myself, careening wildly from side to side as the barking grew louder.

There was a crack as something snapped its jaws beside me. I didn't look back, just gritted my teeth and held on for dear life as droplets of moisture that smelled like wet dog and old meat misted over us.

"Teeth of the Gods! Lords have mercy! Saints and scepters!" Grosbeak screamed.

A doggy foot landed right in front of the toad and he froze as a wet nose snuffled down, down. I caught a single glimpse of it and screamed just as the toad suddenly hopped again, brushing against fur edged in flame, and then coming down close to a towering tree and burrowing into a dank hole under a root. The roots ripped at my hair as soft earth cascaded around us. Behind us, the dogs howled their excitement and I heard the distinctive sound of a canine digging.

There was no time to dwell as the toad burrowed deeper and deeper, pressing fresh earth around me so tight and close that I could barely breathe, never mind hear the garbled screams of Grosbeak and Sparrow.

"Use the key, my mad folly," a breathy voice whispered in my ear.

Wordlessly, I fumbled for the key around my neck. I had two. One for the Wittenhame. One for the Room of Wives and in the darkness, I could not tell one from the other, but I pulled out the first one I could find and twisted it in the air.

CHAPTER FOUR

We leapt out into the mist-filled, washed-out passage between worlds. The toad perched half within a steaming swamp, half on a tuft of grass, as the sounds of the terrorized Wittenhame disappeared and were replaced by the cloying silence of the mist.

The light filtering into this strange half-place was so grey that I could hardly tell whether it was a dark afternoon or a very bright night. I only knew by the whisper at my ear. Bluebeard would never speak to me in the day, lest the curse fall on us all. A curse, I might add, that he had never explained to me in full.

"Let my captains guide the toad, jewel of the Wittenhame," he whispered. I shivered at the feeling of his breath on my neck and then his thoughts hit mine in a jumble again. A sudden memory, as vivid as if it were my own, of a young Vireo and a young Grosbeak laughing together as they rode on bundles of straw that had been lashed together with glittering bands of what I could only think was magic to form the figures of horses. The straw animals ran and whinnied just like real horses and I felt a burst of delight that must have been young Blubebeard's, just before young Grosbeak's straw horse leapt over the river and suddenly burst into chaff, the lashings falling apart and dumping him into the water.

I swallowed and my husband's shared memory faded.

"Tell the toad how to get to Antlerdale's house, Grosbeak," I told my friend a little roughly, keeping my voice firm to anchor me. I dared not wander in the past with my husband's slipping mind, no matter how bewitching his memories may be.

"Am I now your carriage driver that you order me about?" Grosbeak protested but in the same moment, Sparrow rolled her eyes and delivered a very passable croak and the toad spun and hopped onto what almost seemed like a beaten trail.

My husband, I said in my mind and the words were sweet on my mental tongue. He was that still.

"I fade," he whispered softly, and his whisper was precious to me. "But I have a memory of a word upon your lips. You spoke to me of love."

I love you, I said in my mind and the words ripped at my heart, shredding the last bits of me and I did not care that it was my responsibility to keep us all on this hopping toad. I shifted so that I could hold the lantern pole wedged under my seat and use my free hand to cup my precious Bluebeard's cheek. *With all my heart I do. If this world no longer holds you then I want no part of it either.*

And in my mind his memories tumbled and fluttered and I saw myself as he did that day that I greeted him, only while that was most certainly my carefully remade dress and long pale face, and while that was the golden bell in my hand, I looked different in his mind's eye — powerful, vibrant, alive in a way I did not recognize from any mirror. And his emotions in this memory were a sharp combination of shock, hope, and dread.

"My true bride," he whispered but his eyes were glassy and his words stumbled and then stuttered. "True. True. Bride."

And then they faded away and in their place his mental channel opened, but it was not words he gave me but rather a strange soaring emotion and with it, the memory of flying on the back of a dragonfly, my arms wrapped around him and the air streaming through our hair. With it came a burst of such true contentment that it made me ache.

My long-dead mother had wanted me to be married and happy. What would she think now if she looked down at me and at my collection of friendly corpses fleeing for our lives, and discovered that this is what a happy marriage looked like for me? Perhaps I was, indeed, never made for the mortal world, ill-suited for good or wholesomeness, as fit for grim adventure as my skeletal hand.

I let my Bluebeard drift, and did not try to wake him. If this was that of which he dreamed, then who would deny him? Certainly not me. Certainly not now. Let him dream. And if I could not call him back to life, then at least he would go to death knowing he was beloved.

It was bare minutes before Sparrow asked me acerbically, "Are you going to sit there all day like a love-lorn girl, or are you going to dismount and take us to the book?"

I blinked back surprise. The toad had stopped in a clearing and when I slid from its back there was nothing here but pale, waving grass.

"Where is it?" I asked, carefully.

"Turn the key and we'll see if it still stands," she said impatiently.

I took out the silver key and turned it, and madness hit us hard as an axe blow. This was not my first time leaping between worlds, but the terrible feeling of being ripped apart and stitched back in a different way, tore through my mind and I was left reeling and sobbing, gibbering into my fist, one hand wrapped behind me to cling to what was left of my husband. I missed him. I feared for him. I was pressed beyond what one heart ought to suffer in this terrible lingering death of his.

I shook myself. I dare not let the madness break me.

The others recovered sooner. I knew because I could hear their voices as though through water and then, when I finally surfaced, they grew clear.

"Different, but still standing," Sparrow was saying. "I always told the Arrow that a few crenelated towers give a place a better martial look than those ridiculous bird's feet. At least his invisible mortals keep the place up nicely."

"Is that what he did with his winnings? Set them to gardening?" Grosbeak snickered. "I hadn't heard that. Waste of slaves, if you ask me."

"I don't even want to know what you'd do with mortal slaves, Grosbeak, invisible or not."

"You really don't. But we should hurry. If he finds us here he'll be furious, especially when he's keeping *her* here. Did you know he had a new captive?"

"When doesn't he? He's a serial monogamist. What happened to the last one?"

"Maybe she didn't fall in love by the time the last petal fell," Grosbeak snickered. "Don't ask me. I think it's a needlessly cruel game and I'm the one who *likes* needless cruelty. It was fun to watch the first five or six times but now it's too predictable. He should shake it up. Pick an older woman maybe. One with some experience with men who can see through his stories. That would make it harder."

"Well, he couldn't guarantee winning then," Sparrow replied. "Besides, few older women have cleavage so firm you could use it to hold the extra copies of your books. Where does he even find these mortals?"

"Could yours? When you had a body, I mean?" Grosbeak sounded speculative.

"Wouldn't you like to know."

"I do. It's why I'm asking."

I cleared my throat. "Discussions about lost bodies aside, I think we have a book to find."

"Sane again, grim mortal?" Grosbeak asked, a strange tone to his voice that sounded both mocking and ... was that actually concern behind his teasing?

A small brown bird circled us and then settled on my husband's shoulder and began to sing.

"As sane as I'll ever be when I'm dealing with you," I said as I surveyed the castle before us.

It was so large that I felt my heart sinking. Sheer walls rose to ridiculous heights topped by crenelated towers at various distances. I counted seven and more could be hidden by our limited perspective. Every inch of the place was disguised by tangled thorny vines and heavy red roses. Someone had taken care to trim wide swaths of tidy grass in every direction leading out from the castle. This lawn was dotted with topiaries clipped into couples dancing or kissing or engaging in other romantic pursuits ... and yet I did not fail to notice the sinister twist to the topiaries. Was I wrong or did that branch twist in such a way that it could be a supportive hand or it could be a dagger in his lover's back? Or how about that one where the two figures could be bathing in a river together — or he could be in the act of drowning her beneath the waves?

"This place makes my skin crawl," I said just as a woman stepped out from behind one of the topiaries wearing a scarlet cloak with a wide red hood and bearing a basket of long-stemmed red roses.

"You don't know the half of it," Sparrow muttered as I strode toward the woman. Perhaps she would know where the book was.

The roses woman was beautiful in the way of Bluebeard's other wives — mortal, but one of those rare mortals of which no flaw could be found beyond their mere mortality.

"Why are all the mortals in the Wittenhame so lovely?" I asked.

"All? I rather think you're the exception to that," Grosbeak snickered while Sparrow spoke over him, "Physical beauty is the only way to disguise the stink of death you all carry. You embrace Death so tightly that you might as well be the specter himself come to call."

I flushed at her description but there had been none of that stink in my husband's memories of me. I could no more help being mortal than they could help being bodiless heads. We could none of us help what we were.

The other woman smiled blankly at me when I finally reached speaking distance.

"Good lady," I addressed her, "I beg you, please lend me your help."

"The castle is not open to visitors," she told me with glassy eyes. She was maybe eighteen or nineteen years old, just the right age to be married in my world.

"Can you help me find a book written by Lord Antlerdale?" I asked politely.

"The castle is not open to visitors." Was she looking over my shoulder? I glanced behind me but no one else was there, just me, my dead husband, and my two bodiless advisors. Nothing to see here.

"They're always like this," Grosbeak said dismissively. "Just ignore her and go into the castle."

"That has the taste of terrible rudeness," I objected, but I walked past her to where the castle doors were wide open. "And how will I enter? Do I not need the permission of the owner to cross? I thought that was true for Wittenhame homes."

"For most homes," Grosbeak chuckled, "But Anterdale's pride opens him up to invasion. He's opened this home to his invisible mortal slaves to come and go and to this beauty to slip in and out and that makes it open to us, too. A terrible flaw and one I expect he did not consider. Look you at the runes carved into the threshold. They bar the feet of other Wittenbrand but allow the feet of mortals."

"And we have no feet," Sparrow growled in agreement.

The gravel of the path crunched behind me and I looked over my shoulder to find the girl following me. At least the Hounds of Heaven had not made it to this place yet, but I dare not linger. They could not be far behind.

"Is this your home?" I asked her, but I did not let up my speed, increasing it instead. The girl kept pace with me.

"It is the home of my beloved beast," she said with a swooning look in her eyes — eyes that still did not meet mine.

"There's a beast in there?" I hissed to Grosbeak. "We should have brought a weapon."

"You can't wield one," Grosbeak said dismissively. "Do you remember the joust? What a disaster. Never in my days have I seen so disgraceful a showing."

"I believe I won," I said coolly but it was not him I was watching in fascination, it was Sparrow who was sputtering through a suppressed laugh.

"You have been in the Wittenhame too long, Izolda," she said once she had control of herself. "How would you describe Lord Antlerdale?"

"Aloof. A detached Lord of the Wittenhame who seems happy to work in the background of things," I said as we passed over his threshold. This place was massive. How would we find one book within it quickly enough? I wanted to shake the Bramble King — figuratively, I'd seen what happened to those who *actually* defied him. Why couldn't he have told us the key instead of giving us this riddle?

Sparrow was still snickering as we stepped into a grand entrance. "Lord Antlerdale has antlers, wife of the Arrow. Though that is no uncommon thing in the

Wittenhame, I believe he would qualify as a "beast" to a true mortal."

The ceiling of the entrance was so high that it rivaled the ceiling in Bluebeard's home. Gilded chandeliers hung in clusters of five or six at various heights, all fitted with hundreds of unlit candles. Tall, narrow stained glass windows lit the room and the light was reflected and amplified by the walls which were made entirely of polished golden mirrors in gilded frames. The floor was a golden-toned wood polished and waxed until it reflected as brightly as they did.

One wall bore a larger stained glass window that clearly featured Antlerdale wearing a crown of red roses and dancing with a faceless woman in a flowing red dress. The place certainly had a theme. And like the others in the Wittenhame, the Lord of Antlerdale seemed glad to lean into it.

I caught a glimpse of myself in one of the golden mirrors, my braid wild and undone, little locks of hair escaping everywhere to wave around my face. There was a streak of blood across my jaw and chin and a smear of fresh earth on my forehead. The grisly lantern pole I held bore two twisted faces, tangled hair failing to disguise the ragged necks where once a body could be found, and on my back was slung a fully grown man who wore a short beard and dead, dead, pale-as-death skin. The mirror had dressed me in a high-necked jacket with a stiff collar and frogging that made me look like a conquering general — if conquering generals wore tightly fitted leather trousers and thigh-high buckled boots.

I was surprised to realize that I looked more Wittenbrand than mortal — more like a conquering power than the wisp of a girl who had been stolen away as an unwilling bride. I looked as though I was here to do the stealing. Good. That was exactly what I was here to do.

Behind me, in the reflection, the mortal girl drew down her hood to reveal her perfect heart-shaped face and rosebud mouth.

"The castle is not open to visitors," she said, her huge dreamy eyes still not meeting mine.

"I'm not a visitor," I said coldly. "I'm the wife of Lord Riverbarrow, the Arrow, and I will have what I have come for and then I will leave, and I think it might be best if we fetch you back to the mortal world when I go."

"We don't have time to save strays," Sparrow reminded me.

"The castle is not open to visitors," the girl said, and what in the world was wrong with her eyes? Now that she was close I could have sworn there was a red hourglass in her pupils.

I shook my head at the incongruity of it.

"The Library is down the hall to the left," Grosbeak said, helpfully. "I was here once for the most delightful party. Antlerdale made visible an entire staff of mortals to serve dinner and between courses he made them fight to the death. The food was less than spectacular, but by the end of the night you could barely dance, the floor was so slippery."

Nausea rolled over me. Would I never stop being horrified by the things Grosbeak had done in life?

"I was at that party," Sparrow remarked casually. "I lost two hundred gold crowns when my mortal fell in the last duel. Slipped on someone's intestines. Lost his footing. Terrible luck."

"You bet on that fight?" I asked, horror in my voice.

"He looked strong," she said defensively. "And his reflexes made him nearly Wittenbrand fast. If Antlerdale hadn't made them fight that round blindfolded, he'd never have made such a disaster of it. He was a prince among mortals I think. Very pretty."

"Ptolemoore," Grosbeak added. "A prince of Ptolemoore. Beautiful for a mortal. A war was launched for his twin sister's hand. I remember the drama of it. Antlerdale wanted the girl for himself but her brother took her place as a sacrifice to him, and Antlerdale put him in the entertainment as punishment for the insolence. Terrible waste, I thought."

"Mmm," Sparrow agreed.

I clenched my jaw, sealing my lips in censure.

"And to think I've felt pity for both of you being nothing more than severed heads now," I said, chastising them. "You deserve no pity at all when you have none for others."

"They were only mortals," Grosbeak said, snickering. "Hardly worth noticing until Antlerdale immortalized them in death."

"The same could be said of you," I snapped. "For your life was nothing before my husband animated your severed head."

I glanced over my shoulder to see how the mortal woman following us was taking all this, but she smiled calmly as she followed me, her eyes never meeting mine, as if hearing that her master made people die in grisly ways was of no more consequence than discussing the weather.

The hall to the library was lined from the polished floor to the high ceiling with skulls. They ranged from skulls so tiny they could only belong to a mouse to one the size of a fishing vessel that could easily have been the skull of a dragon. In that skull, the needle-like teeth were as long as my legs and laid out in three rows and the nose and brow bore bony ridges. I shuddered at the human skulls that accompanied them. Quite possibly one belonged to that poor twin prince of Ptolemoore.

The skulls were bleached and pale, mounted on walls of glittering gold, but I found I could not meet their empty eyes because when I did, it felt as if they were moving to watch me, as if they were as alive as Grosbeak or Sparrow. I had been too long in the Wittenhame to soothe myself with the idea that such a thing was impossible. Instead, the further down the long hall that I went, the more I was sure that it wasn't only possible, it was certain.

"Do these skulls speak?" I asked calmly.

"Not that I've heard," Sparrow said. "But they sing. One night, Antlerdale wrote his own arrangement for their choir. A strange piece that. It involved a great deal of rattling and crashing. I did not find it particularly harmonious."

"He should stick to the written word," Grosbeak agreed. "It's not fair to be terrible at two forms of art at once."

"Not fair to the audience," Sparrow sniffed.

I glanced over my shoulder at my unconscious husband. I did not like bringing him to this terrible place when he was so vulnerable. I kept feeling a prickling in the skin of my nape, as though something terrible was about to happen to him. But what choice did I have? I must follow the clue or give up and I would not surrender for anything less than death itself.

We reached the towering doors of the library and I was grateful to have something else to focus on. I did not care for my friends' grisly stories. They felt entirely too real in this Wittentale of a place.

If the library was anything to judge by, Antlerdale adored books.

The doors to it were heavy wood set with stained glass that depicted roses climbing through the panes as if they were living things rather than fanciful glass creations.

Those doors were open already, standing as high as five of me tall. But I barely glanced at them. My attention was entirely absorbed in what was beyond them — at the swollen library ten of me tall, set with enormous shelves around its circular perimeter, winding ladders and stairs, and stacks of books so mountainous one could never hope to catalog them all, much less read them. As I watched, books took flight — sometimes solitary, sometimes in flocks — fluttering across the library and arranging themselves as they pleased, as if they were caged birds rather than tomes.

And there in the center, in pride of place, was a pedestal. On it, under glass, was a single red rose floating in the air with only one petal left hanging from its sorry stem. Under the rose, heaped in dead petals, was a bound red leather book with its golden title emblazoned across the cover.

Mist and Memories: A Memoir of Lord Antlerdale

I began to smile. We'd found it. That wasn't so bad.

But my smile was cut off when a door at the other end of the library was flung open so hard that the stained glass shattered and rained down and a voice boomed out, "Who in the fires of hell are you?"

CHAPTER FIVE

"I'm the wife of the Arrow," I said coolly, gesturing to the man himself who was passed out against my shoulder. He woke enough to murmur something.

"Tantalizing creature," Bluebeard whispered his breath tickling my neck. I shivered but dared not linger on his sweet epigraph.

Antlerdale paused in the entrance to his own library, gaze flicking from me to the girl trailing me, to the heads on my pole. I had considered antler racks like his to be unwieldy and strange on the heads of bucks. On the head of a man, they seemed like a terrible curse, and maybe they were. One of these curses or geases everyone in the Wittenhame seemed to have, like an annoying skin condition shared by villagers in the same glen. If the antlers were a curse, it was half broken. Or perhaps doubled. Was it more of a curse to have half an antler crown?

I froze. Wait. That had been his bet, hadn't it? His northern estate and one antler if he lost in the game of

Crowns. I felt a chill of cold rush through me at the memory of what my husband had bid. His immortality.

If Antlerdale had lost his antler when Coppertomb won the game and claimed the crown of the Bramble King, then hadn't my husband lost his immortality with it?

It seemed a silly thing to be upset about. After all, he was half-dead and strapped to my back, but I found I was still shaken by the idea that the bids had been paid and collected.

"Antlerdale, Antlerdale lost him a crown," Grosbeak chortled. "Antlerdale, Antlerdale on his way down."

Antlerdale glared at Grosbeak. The crown of antlers only seemed to enhance the width of his shoulders and the fierce beauty of his face as he strode into the room, fury in his eyes.

"Another man's wife has no claim on my library. And her pets have no excuse to mock me within my own walls."

"And a lord of the Wittenhame should not bring a mortal woman to his home," I said, gesturing to the woman behind me. When I caught a glimpse of her, though, my stomach flipped and I felt a little ill. Her gaze was locked on Antlerdale, a look of such admiration in her eyes that I thought she might be forgetting to breathe.

"She's here of her own volition," Antlerdale said, a twisting smile curving the cruel set of his mouth. "And you're a hypocritical little creature to mention it, don't you think? Are you not a mortal standing where you have no right to stand, and speaking to those too high for you to address, and perhaps even ... loving those no mortal ought dare to love?"

His eyebrow rose at that and my cheeks flared hot. This

was different. Different and not different at all and the comparison was humiliating. But it wasn't practical to be embarrassed about bare facts. Facts were cold and hard and did not change and I would not make them different if I had the choice. There was no point in letting my emotions run wild in doubting my choices.

"Is this love, then?" Sparrow asked acidly. "I'm glad I've never partaken of it. It agrees with none of you. You should all see a herb witch and have it purged."

"Talk of love aside," I said in my most courtly fashion. I'd better get on his good side and quickly. "I had heard you wrote a book of memoirs and I had hoped for a glimpse of it."

He barked a laugh, circling me slowly as if he thought I were some kind of threat. Was that because I was standing beside his mortal prize and the glass dome over the rose and book? He could just cross the room to us, and yet he rounded me, looking for an opening. I turned my body to stay facing him as he moved. I had my own talisman to protect. One who was muttering into my ear unintelligibly, his lips occasionally grazing my flesh in drowsy kisses.

"My memoirs are very popular and found in every home. There was no need to come to the source."

"Ah, but I am told that the original is unparalleled."

"Death walks among us. The Hounds of Heaven hunt, and you are here to read about my life?" His cynical snort mocked me.

"You are here, too," I reminded him.

"To retrieve my prize," he said calmly and then turned to the mortal girl. "Why did you let a stranger into our home?"

I edged toward the rose and book while he was distracted.

"Antlerdale, Antlerdale, half man, half beast," Grosbeak murmured, seeming to be enjoying himself enormously. "Antlerdale, Antlerdale, beg for release."

"The castle is closed to visitors," the other mortal girl said to Antlerdale, a tremble in her lower lip. Was she in love with him? She sounded afraid. Was I as pathetic as she looked right now? It made me frown in humiliation.

"Yes, that's what I told you," Antlerdale said in a low voice just as my hand hovered over the glass. "And what do I do when you break one of my rules?"

My gaze snapped back to him. I wouldn't be having this.

"Try to harm her and I'll take her back to the mortal world," I said coolly. "I have the power to —"

My words cut off as a fist crashed across my face, catching my cheekbone and making me stumble back.

"Hit her back! Quickly now!" Grosbeak shouted.

"To your left!" Sparrow agreed, but before I could comprehend that it had been Antlerdale's mortal love who hit me, she was already on me again, trying to swing for my face. I grabbed her wrist with one of mine.

I'm a thin slip of a girl but I've been carrying a human head around for ages now and that builds muscle. I caught her fist easily.

"If you took her back, you'd kill her, didn't you see the Wittenmark in her eye?" Antlerdale said easily, as if he were enjoying watching us struggle. He lounged against a bookshelf, his eyes darkening in a way that made me enormously uncomfortable. "It's the hourglass. In the eye?"

"I see it," I gritted out as I wrenched her wrist, forcing her to turn, and shoving it up her back. Wow. If I only ever had to fight people my own size I might actually resort to physical violence more often. It was effective.

"All the same, I do tire of her." Antlerdale said, lifting the glass dome at the same moment that I said, "Pardon?"

He flicked the last petal off of the rose and with a hissing sound like sand in an hourglass the woman in my grip turned to dust and drifted to the floor.

I sneezed.

That had been a woman. A flesh and blood woman who had been in love with Antlerdale and he'd ended her life with a flick of his finger like she was a beetle.

"Problem solved," Antlerdale said.

"I guess she wasn't properly in love with you," Grosbeak snickered.

"Oh, she most certainly was," Antlerdale said easily. "But it was me who had to fall in love with her before the last petal fell, and honestly, I never do. I think the game is rigged against me."

"That's what I was telling Sparrow," Grosbeak said as if they weren't discussing the deaths of mortal women brought here to play a sinister game they could never win. "I think you should switch up who you take."

"Should I?" Antlerdale asked, eyes fixed on Grosbeak. "What sort of mortal would you recommend? I've taken the most delectable ones, and yet they never seem to tempt me to lose myself."

He was so engrossed in their conversation that he didn't see me move.

I shoved the lantern pole at him, ignoring the startled

cries of its passengers. Antlerdale caught it by reflex, his expression startled. I grabbed the book, flipping quickly through the pages.

Chapter ten, paragraph thirteen.

I flipped like mad to find it. Running a finger down as I counted.

Chapter ten, paragraph thirteen.

I distantly heard the crash and Antlerdale cursing. Distantly heard Grosbeak's loud complaints.

Ten. Thirteen.

The moment I had it, I read it aloud. Maybe if it didn't stick in my brain before Antlerdale ripped it away, then Grosbeak or Sparrow might remember.

"I spoke to the Bramble King and he put a geas on me which seems a cruel demand on a vassal. I will not mention the particulars here," I read aloud.

That was it. The whole paragraph. Frustrated, I ground my teeth.

"Izolda! Izolda?" Grosbeak called. "My view is very poor from here and it's all your fault."

I looked over at him dully and to my surprise, I found Antlerdale frozen and my friends face-first on the ground. Feeling guilty, I snatched up the pole again.

"I find myself impressed," Grosbeak said as I lifted him again and he caught sight of Antlerdale.

"The Bramble King really must have set a geas on him and you've triggered it," Sparrow agreed, but at the words "Bramble King" Antlerdale shook himself and then spoke slowly, clearly, as if the words he said were of utmost importance.

"Sixteen locks with sixteen keys,

From grip of death, vict'ry seize,
Silent brides of silent lord,
Unravel back Time's cord,
Bought by blood and claimed by oath,
Only one holds bitter troth,
One hand living, one hand dead,
She finds the place where hope has fled
Now let her choose what comes last,
Freedom now or holding fast."

And as the last words escaped his mouth something in his eyes turned back on. Released from the geas, he charged at me, his bright, feral gaze locked on mine, teeth in a harsh rictus.

I stumbled backward as his snarl echoed through his body as if this one theft of his will for a few seconds offended him to the very bones, never mind the years and lives and hearts he'd stolen from mortal girls along the way.

The book fell from my hands, tumbling into the glass dome that had guarded both it and rose before I removed them from the pedestal. Dome and book crashed to the ground with a loud crunch as Antlerdale's foot came down on the glass.

"Your mortal life is mine now, child of dust," he said, mouth twisting. "But since you're in my home, let's have a little fun first. I've done some truly villainous deeds within the walls of this castle. I wager a pretty little thing like you comes with an imagination." His smile was terrifyingly lascivious. "Let's play a game. I call it 'Guess the Villainy.' We go to each room of the castle. If you can accurately pinpoint the cruelty I inflicted there, you will be spared experiencing the same, but miss your guess and I'll enact that memory upon your flesh, and drag you by the ear to the next room and the next until you're nothing but a tattered rag that my invisible servants must dispose of in the waste pile. Deal?"

"Grosbeak," my husband's whisper in my ear barely registered and I did not know if it were a plea to my bodiless friend or a command to me.

I cowered back from Antlerdale, a step, two steps, fumbling for my belt knife while I held the two heads angled away from me as if they could save me from his plans to torture me to death. They hovered over the broken glass as I slid back a third step, hands trembling, heart in my throat.

I couldn't outrun the Wittenbrand. I was not fool enough to think I could. And I couldn't outfight him. But I hadn't forgotten the key. Maybe a leap between worlds would be fast enough. I fumbled for it in my neckline.

"Just a little to the right, Izolda," Grosbeak hissed, and he did not sound afraid, not even as Antlerdale backhanded Sparrow, sending her crashing into Grosbeak with a cry, which in turn tumbled him to the right just as he'd asked me to place him.

Elegantly, as if he'd practiced the move a dozen times, he dove with the momentum, and caught the empty rose stem — still hovering there over the pedestal — in his mouth, chomped down hard on it, and sucked it into his mouth with a thick, black tongue.

"No!" Antlerdale shouted, swiveling from me to Grosbeak, hand outstretched, mouth twisting in agony. He froze in midair.

I leapt backward just in time to pull my two advisors

out of harm's way as the great Wittenbrand crashed, his heavy shoulders and chest toppling the pillar. He curled in on himself, twitching and shuddering as Grosbeak chewed noisily. And I watched in horror as his ageless face and immaculate body suddenly aged, passing through middle age, and then old age, and then into something ancient and shriveled and not at all human. With a last scream of anguish, he exploded into a burst of ashes.

I gasped.

"I think I could do with fewer people dissolving into the air," I said firmly, trying to get a grip on my sawing breath and jellified knees.

Grosbeak belched loudly and then made a considering face. "Tastes like ... misery."

"I would have thought he'd taste like roses," Sparrow commented, unruffled by the violence and magic swirling all around her.

"No, it's definitely misery. I've tasted it before."

"What does misery taste like?" I asked, but I didn't get a response. A loud howling filled the air, reverberating the library with such force that books fell from the shelves in a rain of pages and then a great head stuck its nose through the door, snuffling.

CHAPTER SIX

"Shhhh," Grosbeak murmured. "Shhhh."

I slid slowly backward through the other door, hoping the Hound did not enter the library before I had disappeared out the other side. I misliked being hunted like prey. Terror aside, it was slowing me, keeping me from running directly toward my goals. With trembling hands, I fumbled for the key around my neck, ready to flee into the halfworld between the Wittenhame and the mortal world.

"I wouldn't," Sparrow whispered. "You don't have finesse with that. You might miss the inbetween and land us in the mortal world and who knows what might happen then. The Arrow might not have enough magic left to carry you out. Hide, instead."

The Hound snuffled again and snorted. My heart skipped a beat, freezing within my chest. Don't lose your head, Izolda. Don't.

Sparrow made a good point. Whatever was going to save my Bluebeard wouldn't be found in the lands of my people — or at least I didn't think so.

"Wives," Bluebeard murmured in my ear, following the same train of thought I was, or at least, I thought he was. "Wives, my mad folly."

I fumbled in my dress for the other key — the little golden one Bluebeard had given me as wedding present. I turned it in the air just as the dog leapt into the room, landing on Antlerdale's ashes, barking madly with two heads while the third sniffed the air.

I leapt, too, straight into the open door of the Room of Wives, turning the key desperately in the lock behind me. The rip in the air began to close, but the Hound was fast, leaping for the gap, mouths open and slathering. One jaw managed a bite inside the door, snapping shut inches from Grosbeak's face.

Grosbeak screamed and Sparrow cursed as I stumbled backward and the door shut on the Hound, closing him off from us, and leaving us alone with a pile of cackling dead advisors and a ring of sleeping wives looking on.

"Well," I said. "That could have gone better."

"Could it, though?" Sparrow asked. "From where I'm sitting, it went the very best way it possibly could. Grosbeak rather valiantly saved your life and you left with the poem. She repeated it as if to help me remember. And as she spoke the words, I looked around the room at the occupants waiting for us.

"Sixteen locks with sixteen keys."

There they were, fifteen dead wives ... and me. Sixteen keys. But where were the locks they fit into? Hadn't Vireo called me a key once? And hadn't Bluebeard called me his last wife long before he ever fell in love with me? Did he know about this poem? This prophecy or riddle or whatever it was? Had he known it before the Bramble King locked it inside Antlerdale's head to be revealed when the right phrase was read to him?

"From grip of death, vict'ry seize."

I felt cold at that line and I licked my lips because it was exactly, precisely what I wanted.

I have not yet lost, Bluebeard whispered in my mind, suddenly. Surprised, I turned to him but his eyes were closed, his lips forming little almost-kisses when they touched my shoulder like a newborn baby dreaming. *I have won but not won. Victorious but still fighting.*

"What could he mean," I ask, "If he says he's won but not won?"

"Don't ask me," Grosbeak sniffed. "I only live in this world."

"Silent brides of silent lord," Sparrow went on.

And that had been his one demand of me — that we remain in silence, him in the day and me in the night. So small a thing. And yet, if it were part of the key to return him to me, if he had known all along ... I shivered.

"Unravel back Time's cord," Sparrow whispered. She was really getting into this now.

I had no idea what that line meant.

"Bought by blood and claimed by oath,
Only one holds bitter troth,
One hand living, one hand dead,"

Clearly, this was me. Unless there was someone else wandering around with a dead hand.

She finds the place where hope has fled
Now let her choose what comes last,
Freedom now or holding fast."

Well, that seemed simple enough. There would be a choice eventually and anyone with sense would choose freedom. No one wanted to be locked up, enslaved, or tied to a failing cause.

But these things were never so simple.

"I need a moment," I said a little breathlessly. "A chance to catch up to all my thoughts."

"And to solve this riddle," Sparrow said dryly. "In case you've forgotten that the world is ending."

But I hadn't forgotten. I carried her and Grosbeak to where I could set them down to face the other heads piled by the entrance.

"Converse among yourselves," I said. "After all, that's why you're all here. To talk together and find us answers."

"I like the part about one hand living and one dead," one of the heads said. "Perhaps she has a hand in midwifery and another in undertaking."

"Or perhaps one of her hands is skeletal," I suggested, lifting mine and wiggling my fingers. "Do better than that."

"You can't leave us here," Grosbeak protested.

"I can for now." I was already striding toward the other end of the room.

"But we'll miss the romantic part where you two are alone!"

"Yes. Alone is the key to that," I agreed and then I was hustling my husband to the far end of the room and easing myself behind the hourglass of garnets. There were so many in the bottom bulb now that it really was effective cover.

I sat carefully on the ground, making sure both of

Bluebeard's legs were facing the right way and then — with great care — I untied the cloth binding us together and gently eased him to the ground, keeping my bare back pressed to his chest until I could replace it with a palm instead, and lie down facing him.

We couldn't stay here long. Things happened very quickly in the Wittenhame. But we needed this rest, if only for a moment. I had not slept in a long time, and Bluebeard seemed to recover more of his faculties when he had been resting.

Husband, can you hear me? I asked him with my mind. *Remember you may not speak to me in the day, only with your mind.*

Fire of my eyes, his words were strong in my mind, though his eyes remained closed.

Bluebeard, I sighed with my mind as a ghost of a smile raised the corners of his lips.

Your name for me thrills me yet.

It's not your true name, which I remind you I have the right to as your wife, I teased him. I should be talking to him about where to go and what to do. *Can you help me know what to do next? Where do I go to find this rib in the earth?*

But he was still hung up on the request for his name.

What shall you call me? Call me victor, for I have triumphed.

It would not seem so, husband, I said tightly with my mind. *It would seem, instead, that we hover on the verge of ultimate failure. If I lose touch with you, then you will die forever and likely, I will die with you.*

As will all those who depend on me, he agreed, his eyes

opening then, and his cat's pupils widening slightly as they beheld me. *And yet, I have indeed prevailed. It just is not yet apparent to all who observe, and we must see you fulfill your task to realize it.*

I thought that when you won you would fix everything — the lives of the wives you took, the heads on your wall, Riverbarrow. You told me a story about the Divine Sovereign and how the word was set into his chest. Do you remember it? I must find the site where they extracted that rib.

You and you alone, light of my eyes, make my heart glad and my chest swell with pride. He seemed to be drifting again.

Now is not the time to wax poetic, I told him, but my hands had begun to move on their own at his words, they skimmed along his chest and up his neck, cupping his face. *I need direction on how to get there and what I must bring with me.*

I must walk when we go from here. Our hands can be bound together, but I must keep to my feet for this next part. It will take all my energy. I fear I may be incoherent. Do not forget that this heart of mine, absent though it is, belongs to you.

Then let me carry you, I pled. Things were hard enough without making them harder.

It cannot be.

At least tell me where to go. Please.

That also cannot be, for I must remain silent to you in this as well as in truth.

A hint then, a clue. Anything.

The blood of nations. His eyes flickered open, locked on my face as if he was drinking in life just by looking at me.

He reached out, but his hand fell between us, unable to go farther.

The blood of the nations? What is that?

I had not wagered that I would love. He sounded like he was drifting again. *I sought a true bride and married her in our way and I knew this would be best, but I did not wager for these tangles around my heart. I can explain them if I must by speaking of your love of your people and your monstrous way of looking at all things in light of their utility, but I fear my precious bride that words cannot contain the whole of it for I love you in a way that mocks the love of all others, dwarfs their empty promises of commitment and hollows the storehouses of affection they claim to possess, for I love you with a fullness, a depth, a circumference that is too great for mortal mind to comprehend.*

I wasn't going to get a clear answer. He'd fallen off into dreams and rambling.

Then I won't try to comprehend it, I returned dryly. *I'll simply get to work.*

One last boon.

I felt my heart melt at his plea. *Whatever you wish, my Lord of the Wittenhame.*

A single kiss.

I leaned forward so that now my body was flush with his, my heart beating where his ruined chest held no match, and I pressed my lips to his and then parted them, deepening our kiss, and he hummed with pleasure in my mouth and roared with it in my mind. My husband. My precious, dying husband. I did not dare rest much longer. I had to get up and find what he needed so we could bring him back to fullness.

Our kiss took the last of his strength and his eyes fluttered shut, and his breathing grew long and even.

Well, then. I supposed I had a task to perform immediately.

I helped him stumble to his feet and lean on me before binding both of our left wrists together. That way I could still hold the lantern pole in one hand while the other arm supported him. He swayed in my support, but he did not fall, and he did not speak again or open his eyes.

I missed my Bluebeard's wild competence. His flashes of genius and surprise. I swallowed down a wave of hopelessness. I did not dare give in to that. I'd read many Whittentales in my day and how many times had I marveled, awestruck by the bravery of the mortals in the tales who were doomed to perform great tasks for love and home? And we'd all claimed that we, too, would act with such courage if our time came. So why did I now, when I found myself in one, seem so reluctant to rise to the challenge?

Stories are different when they are your life. They sting and press and the discomforts that seem small in a story loom great in life. It took all my courage to stride across the room and approach my bodiless advisors.

"If you were looking for the blood of nations, where would you go," I asked.

"If we're going to leave here, then you'd better disguise the Arrow," Sparrow warned me. "No one likes to see a defeated enemy still walking around."

"Enemy?" I asked aghast.

"He was Coppertomb's enemy," she said and if she still had shoulders I would have guessed that she would shrug.

"And now Coppertomb *is* the Wittenhame because he is its king. So yes, the Arrow is their enemy."

I guided my shuffling husband to one of his wives who wore a thick scarlet cloak, loosened the tie around her shoulders, and brought it down one-handed to drape over his shoulders and head. I tied it in place, though the cloak only went to his knees.

"Happy?" I huffed.

"You will be," Sparrow said with a side-long glance.

"And can someone tell me where to find the blood of nations now?"

"Do not taunt us with such simple queries, Izolda," Grosbeak drawled. "Where else but the place you left your mortal nephew? The field of the last battle? For if there the nations battle, then there their blood will be spilled."

And it seemed so obvious when he said it that I gathered up his pole and pulled out the key and before he or Sparrow could even protest, I was opening the door back out into the Wittenhame.

CHAPTER SEVEN

The Wittenhame had a way of making the everyday seem impossible and the impossible seem everyday. Just when you believed you understood the rules by which it operated it swiveled and spun out new rules and laws. Perhaps there had been no Law of Greeting before Bluebeard needed to acquire sixteen wives in a hurry — well, a Wittenbrand hurry which can be five years or five hundred.

For the first time, a hand reached through the still-widening door, fisted into my hair, and ripped me through the door.

I gasped. I had thought that impossible, but the hand had me now and it drew me inexorably out through the door and into the open.

I was yanked, not into Antlerdale's library, but — to my utter surprise — into the heart of the Wittenhame where the ice and mushroom palace had stood.

I gazed in horror at the dripping icon. It had been reduced already by at least half, water pouring down the sides and flooding out from it to saturate the ground and create standing pools. And where there had once been creatures — human, Wittenbrand, and otherwise, frozen into the glass-like surface, there was now a stinking heap of corpses jutting out from the ice.

Before I could even grasp what I was seeing, an iron fist forced me to my knees, and I lost my grip on the lantern pole as it pressed me downward into a bow. I did *not* lose my grip on Bluebeard's hand, though he fell heavily to his knees beside me into the tainted water at our feet that now soaked through our clothing. His cloaked head leaned heavily against me and I was glad he had not fallen face-first.

I looked up to the hand holding my hair, stomach lurching in horror as around me little scraps of midnight floated down, speckled with bright white lights the size of berries.

Coppertomb stood above me, gloved hand tangled in my hair, a naked sword bared in the other hand, and for a heartbeat, my bowels froze and I trembled, shaking like a leaf in the wind, certain he was about to dash my head from my body and there would be no friendly mortal to carry me around on a lantern pole as Grosbeak had. My story would end right here, on my knees before my enemy.

But no, Coppertomb gripped his sword and shouted, "To me, Wittenhame! Feast your eyes on the prowess of your king!"

He was not looking at me at all, but rather past me as a Hound of Heaven bore down upon him.

A growling snap split the air and then a howl, and Coppertomb released my hair as spittle flicked across my face. I flinched, stumbling backward onto my seat, desperately gripping Bluebeard's hand as I tried to think fast enough.

From the place where I'd dropped the lantern pole, I heard a bubbling sound of submerged heads trying to shout. I couldn't leave them there.

I clawed myself back to my feet, dragging Bluebeard up with me and snatching up my lantern pole. I could live a thousand years and never want to see one of those again. But even as I found my feet, one of the massive heads bore down on me, snapping its mighty jaws.

This was not a time to panic. I braced my feet, twisted my hold on the lantern pole, and then deftly thrust it forward at the same time the Hound opened his mouth wide to swallow me down. I wedged the pole in his gaping mouth, dancing backward. He howled, shaking that head in a very doggy attempt to loosen the pole stuck in the sensitive parts of his mouth.

I leapt backward, drawing my shuffling husband with me, panting in relief, as the swinging heads on the pole screamed at me.

"Have you no care for the dead?" Sparrow hissed while Grosbeak yowled, "A curse on you, Izolda! A curse and four demi-curses! May your toenails blacken and curl for putting me in this thing's jaws!"

I spun, searching for a new weapon, sure I'd be attacked again, but at that moment there was a mighty howl from one of the heads and then it fell, crashing in front of me, as large as a horse, the flesh of its neck severed and blood fountaining out. To say this was the most grisly thing I'd ever seen would be an understatement and I was holding proof in my arms that I was not squeamish.

I barely had time to gasp before a second head joined it and then the third, and this time I leapt forward, set a boot against the creature's black lips, and yanked my wedged lantern pole free.

Huffing and gasping for breath, I balanced it, wrapped an arm around my husband, and surveyed the damage.

Coppertomb stood on the body of the dead Hound, his sword stuck into the corpse like a walking stick and his other hand on his hip as if he were a gentleman surveying his estate rather than a king who had just slain a monster. On his head was the rib crown and on his face was a cruel smile.

"Don't move, Arrow's wife. I have business with you," he said, pointing at me, and then he hopped down from the beast, strode forward, and tangled his fist back into my hair, bloody though it was.

"A manful victory, Bramble King!" Grosbeak congratulated him.

"Is that rose I see around your lips?" Coppertomb asked, a baleful look in his eyes.

Grosbeak licked his lips as if in confirmation. "I may be dead, but I can still bring down the mighty."

"I will not speak to the dead, revenant," Coppertomb said grimly. "If life has no more business with you, then neither do I."

Coppertomb began to move then, driving me before him with his fist as he strode through a crowd of gaping Wittenbrand, his steps proud and firm and his head held high. He was not a tall man, I realized. He was barely taller than me, but he seemed a span higher with the way he carried himself.

I clutched my ruined husband to me, tucked in his scarlet cloak, too concentrated on not losing him or the lantern pole to do anything about the pain of Coppertomb's twisting gloved hand in my hair.

I swallowed down a burst of fear as he marched me forward. "What would you have of me?"

"I will get to that."

The scraps of midnight still rained down over us and between the scraps, Wittenbrand ran and surged, forming shouting groups and chanting hordes. A ragged cheer went up as Coppertomb passed through them. And he flicked the viscous blood from his sword blade in salute as the Wittenbrand crowded around him, calling out their congratulations.

It appeared that they had already been busy here before their king slew the Hound. Banners were lashed to fresh poles and thrust into the sky, mounts were being chivvied into place, armor donned, and weapons displayed.

"Our great king has slain for us a Hound of Heaven! Whosoever doth choose to ride for the Bramble King to dispatch the rest must form a party and swear the oath!" A voice bellowed out and when I looked toward the crier, I saw a Wittenbrand man with long red hair and a cloak woven of nettles standing astride a pyramid made from the bodies of living rats. They did not stand still, but rather roiled and bubbled, churning beneath him even as he spoke to the Wittenbrand gathering at the place that had once been a festival location.

"What manner of madness is this?" I whispered,

tucking the lantern pole under one arm so I could reach out to snatch up one of the midnight scraps floating down from the sky. They coated the ground and the shoulders and heads of those around me, and the bright glowing berry clung to this scrap.

"The sky is falling. And I'd say those are stars," Grosbeak said. "Taste one, Izolda, and tell us if they're stars."

"How in the world would tasting one tell you?" I asked.

"If it tastes like a star, then you'll know it's a star," Sparrow said impatiently. "How else will you know if the sky is falling?"

"And the world is dissolving as snow," Grosbeak agreed.

I was reluctant to put something glowing like an ember in my mouth. I offered it to Grosbeak who gobbled it up and then hissed, steam screaming out of his ears.

"Yes," he panted, face turning cherry red. "It is a star. Tastes just like one."

"Would that have happened to me if I'd eaten it?" I asked in horror.

"Probably worse," Sparrow said dryly. "Because it just fell through his neck. It would have passed into your digestive system."

"I think I'll avoid your food recommendations," I said sourly as Coppertomb dragged me onward. He paid our interaction no mind, but I noticed he refused to focus his eyes anywhere that the small stars twinkled as if their presence bothered him.

She shivers and my skin alights, butterfly tissue, burning bright, Bluebeard muttered in my mind. It worried me that he'd moved to verse. He sounded delirious.

A tiny blue bird landed on his cloaked head and began to trill.

Can you help me find a fast way to flee your enemy? I whispered to him with my mind, glancing at his face beside me. He frowned but did not reply.

"Why is the Wittenhame suddenly falling to pieces?" I hissed and Sparrow and Grossbeak met each other's gaze, eyes wide, lips tightly closed as if they didn't want to tell me.

"Were I you, I'd keep such observations to myself," Grosbeak murmured eventually.

"Why?" I pressed. "Is it not obvious to everyone?"

He made a hmm sound and then Coppertomb leaned in close, "I, also, would not make observations on the state of the Wittenhame were I you, mortal woman. The Wittenhame is mine now as I am her king. Blood of my blood, flesh of my flesh."

I paused.

"Then speak to my riddle, Bramble King," I said boldly. "Was not the Wittenhame whole and merry, fat and flourishing under the former Bramble King."

"It began to fade as he did. Everyone could sense it," Grosbeak replied hurriedly, as if trying to head me off. "Why think you he sought a successor?"

But Coppertomb said nothing, merely setting his jaw and forcing me forward. We were coming toward where the ruins of the ice castle formed a platform of sorts that was ringed with dark-garbed Wittenbrand I assumed were his guards. They were mounted on large black lizards with blunt noses and glittering eyes.

"Speak further to my riddle, Bramble King," I pressed. "Are you not hale as a young warrior and strong as a buck in season? Are you not healthy as a prize bull and more clever besides?"

He stopped, suddenly, turning me to look in his face and his black eyes held a look of death and I remembered, in that moment, that among his kind he was very young and that young men have easily bruised pride.

"You flatter me," he murmured.

"And yet, I speak only the truth," I said as my severed head advisors gasped and then pinned their lips tightly together as if afraid he would punish them for what I said.

"What are you saying?" he asked in a low voice just for me, and his face drew very close to mine.

"Victor but not yet won," I murmured but I did not mean the man in front of me, because if the Wittenhame echoed the life of its ruler and Coppertomb was hale and hearty, what did it say that the sky was falling and the laws of the place dissolving? Could it be that he was not the ruler of this place at all?

Could it be that another ruled? One who faded as I clung to his hand.

"Keep your poison words in your swollen mouth, daughter of dust," he hissed, and then he dragged me up on the platform surrounded by his lizard-riding guards and I swallowed down a burst of horror as something squished under my foot.

Don't look down, Izolda. Don't look down.

"I do love the pomp you've managed, Bramble King,"

Grosbeak said in a honeyed way that made me sneer. He was ever the bootlick.

Coppertomb ignored him, but he tilted his chin up as an announcement was made.

"Gather before your King!" the crier called at the same moment and there was the sound of blaring horns, that were half-trumpet and half-scream, and then the rat pyramid dissolved, and the crier fell from the sky, and there was another ragged cheer as they pressed in toward the platform. Bare bone woven into breastplate stood side by side with bronze scale and boiled leather painted to look like a creature of flame. A spirit of festivity surrounded the martial crowd.

"In a moment, I will address my people," Coppertomb said, leaning over now to look me in the eye. "But first I will deal with you. Right now, before them, so they may witness how those who defy me are humbled. You have stuck in my craw as your pole stuck in the mouth of the Hound and I will have you out one way or another."

He paused and then his hand moved lightning fast and he yanked the silver key from around my neck, snapping the chain and pocketing it.

"No more leaping between worlds for you, mortal woman. None but a lord or lady of the Wittenhame is granted this key, and none but a lord or lady is fit to use it. Two days I grant you." And now his eyes skimmed the scarlet cloak covering my husband's huddled form for the first time since he grabbed hold of me. "Two days to raise your dead, or bury him, for I will not have revenants walking this plane. A geas I place on you now."

My skin tingled as if I could already feel the magic and I

shivered with the cold touch of it. But I would not beg for mercy. I would not ask for leniency. I knew Coppertomb too well to think he'd grant me either.

"Strike a deal with Death. Raise your dead. Or, in two days' time, your hands will bury him under the power of my geas and you will present yourself to me here as my bride for my Coronation Ball."

"Tell me this," I whispered, holding his gaze with mine. "The Wittenhame is thick with women so lovely they could break your heart in twain. Why do so many of you then find the need to steal an ugly mortal as your wife?"

Coppertomb's gaze flicked to my barely conscious husband. "He takes nothing without purpose and treasures nothing without value. If he found you desirable as his bride, then so will I. If he claimed your heart, then I will claim it doubly. If he laid possession to your flesh, then I will mark it as my own."

"I think you have a kingdom to rule," I countered. I did not like how he made my skin crawl or how certain he sounded that he could take whatever he wanted.

Coppertomb watched me, considering. "I will not marry. Nor will I be given in marriage. But you will come here in wedding clothes and surrender yourself to me and all my appetites, and I will see the heart I gave the barrow broken in twain and shattered forever."

He leaned forward, menace in his eye, and said. "Two days," before turning his back to me and addressing the growing crowd.

"Subjects!" Coppertomb called out. "Denizens of the Wittenhame!"

It was exactly the factual precision I expected from

him. And yet, watching him address the Wittenhame, I felt almost as if he were falling apart, too. His eyes were too empty. His gestures overly dramatic. He was a parody of himself.

"The Hounds of Heaven have been called. Death walks among us! The sky falls to the earth and the earth dissolves beneath the fires of heaven!"

There was a cheer. Practically everything in the Wittenhame resulted in a cheer, even the announcement that the world was crumbling.

"What do we do now?" Grosbeak whispered. "Two days is not long enough!"

Fear crept into my bones. How powerful was this geas? Would it truly force me to bury my still living husband under the ground? I felt something tighten within me but I did not know if it was the magic, or merely fear, gripping my heart.

"Our time now has come! We ride against the Hounds of Heaven in the Great Hunt! Boons will be granted to the party that succeeds! Geases placed and the tax of a finger levied on all who fail!"

A finger is too great a tax. Perhaps my husband was more lucid than I thought. *But he would know, for he had to forfeit his.*

Husband, I gasped in relief in my mind. But I couldn't help glancing at Coppertomb's hand caught in a single glove. Did one of the fingers look stiff? Immobile? Like the finger of the glove might be stuffed with wool? I shook my head. It did not matter.

Can you free me from this geas? I must flee Coppertomb.

Patience, wife of mine, Bluebeard whispered in my mind.

There was a great cheer and the Wittenbrand began to chant, "Coppertomb! Coppertomb!"

Hold your patience.

Coppertomb turned and smiled his wicked twist of a smile and in his smile, I felt the barb of the geas on me. "Two days, little mortal. You'd better run."

With the suddenness of lightning, a murder of ravens rose up from around the platform in a roar of flapping wings so loud that they drowned out everything else. They rose over Coppertomb, buffeting him, the rearing mounts, and the startled Wittenbrand as they went. A pale unicorn reared, screaming horsily while a double-headed panther swore and snapped, batting a paw at the black mass. They cawed and flapped, obscuring faces, and figures, and voices, and then all at once they swirled around us.

Stand your ground.

I planted my feet, braced myself, ready to be bowled over by the surging avian bodies ... and was lifted suddenly, into the air in a flurry of squawks and a rain of feathers.

CHAPTER EIGHT

"Well, that was terribly informative," Sparrow said, considering, as we rose into the shredded sky on the shifting backs of the ravens. "Two days, is it?"

Bluebeard reached out and clung to me like a small child clutching a parent in sleep and I leaned into the softness of his embrace, sad because he was not warm and could not guide me. He had carried me far and fast in this Wittenhame, and now soon I must carry him again with my slow mortal feet. He had rescued me again and again, and now I must find a way to rescue him, and I only had two nights in which to do it.

"I believe my husband is the true Bramble King," I said quietly to myself, my thoughts turning inward. Coppertomb was missing the finger he'd bet. He wasn't in a woven cage ... unless it was woven of something I could not see. Disaster, perhaps?

I prodded at the thought and finally spoke in my mind, *Are you the true king of this land, husband of mine?*

I was surprised when he answered. *Did I not gift my heart to the barrow? Am I not a corpse in your arms?*

He had indeed, though Coppertomb had claimed the victory.

Words and claims are powerful geases. And I have set all of my claims on you, heart of my own heart.

I was warmed by that. He had claimed me again and again and I was claiming him, but that aside, he might have given his heart to the barrow, and yet, the Wittenhame was collapsing around us as if it were tied to the man slowly ebbing out in my arms. I drew him in close to rest his head better on my shoulder.

I shifted on the backs of the ravens, feeling their feathery forms bump and lift, fall away and lift again, as they distributed my weight over their small bodies, providing just enough lift to keep me from tumbling to the ground. That I accepted this without balking showed how deeply the Wittenhame had crept into my bones.

"And based on what Coppertomb said," I continued. "I have barely two days to draw back his life."

And if I did not, what would happen? Would this world and my husband with it be gone forever? There was no place left for me in the mortal world. If there was no place here, either, then I was adrift.

"And what? You think that you, a mortal, can wrest the Wittenhame from the grip of Coppertomb, restore life to a dead man, and then dismiss the Hounds of Heaven and Death himself from our midst?" Sparrow asked wryly.

"She's done odder things before," Grosbeak mused.

"Name them."

"Well, she chose to take you along for this journey," he

sniped. "That takes more intestinal fortitude than dismissing Death, I'd say. Surely, you know you're a horror to behold. Your pretty face frozen in the rictus of death and your once fine locks bedraggled."

Sparrow sniffed dismissively.

"I need to work this out," I muttered to myself as Bluebeard slumped further into my arms, pressing his cheek to mine as he shifted so that his chest was to my back again. "The blood of nations, the rib. It's all one big puzzle."

I tapped my lip in thought.

I keep my heart in your chest now, Bluebeard murmured, as though trying to help, but his thoughts were drifting again. *When I was a boy in Riverbarrow, I would fold tiny birchbark boats for the small people and set them to sail. I once folded one hundred in a single day. Can you build me a boat of birchbark for the river of death, Izolda, my heart?*

I am hoping it will not come to that, I said wryly. I shivered. It was cold up here in the winds.

Or perhaps, I will build one for you, and when the world washes away we will float in it together.

Yes, us and a pair of severed heads, what a terribly romantic prospect.

You should speak to Death, he whispered in my mind, seeming to be fading again. *He is not bound as I am. He could speak to you more plainly.*

Husband?

His mind drifted away and he was gone.

I sighed.

"Is it just me, or is this place getting more confusing as it falls apart?" I asked as the ravens bore us further up.

Oddly, a warm breeze met us there, easing the cold from my bones.

I could see between the ravens' backs to the ground below as Coppertomb's subjects formed hunting parties, some hundreds of people thick, but others with as few as four or five people, and began to disperse across the darkened terrain, searching for the Hounds of Heaven.

Sparrow coughed and then swung to look at me.

"Do you truly think your husband is the Bramble King?" She asked me and to my surprise, her tone was reverent.

"I see no other answer to why your world is falling apart," I said plainly.

"Perhaps Coppertomb is merely an epically bad king," Grosbeak countered. "We've had bad kings in the past. Remember the Blood Rains, Sparrow?"

"They were before my time," she said, but her expression was thoughtful.

"It rained blood for three years when the Bramble King was wounded in a joust. A terrible time. Everything was red and slick. I hated it. And then there was the Plague of Frogs. Frogs everywhere. You could barely sleep for them hopping all over you. That was when the Mad Bramble was Lord of the Wittenhame. Is it all that surprising that the world is disintegrating under Coppertomb?"

"This is worse than frogs," I said as I watched one of the Hounds rush into sight beneath us. I wished I could cling to the ravens holding us up and beg them to keep us in the air. If we fell now, we would be torn to pieces.

"Aren't you supposed to have inherited Marshyellow?" Grosbeak asked. "Could you not command them?"

"How would I go about that?" I asked. It would be convenient to have someone, anyone, to command right now.

Instead, I clung to my husband as beneath us, the Hound fell upon one of the hunting parties, savaging its members and flinging them in every direction to break on the rocks and trees, as a dog savages its favorite fetching stick. My belly churned with horror and I barely managed to swallow down my bile.

Grosbeak seemed utterly unaffected by the screams and wails below as he launched into a lecture. "Traditionally to claim a place as prince in the Wittenhame, there's a seven-day trial of combat and wit followed by five days of feasting. Or, if you are named directly by your predecessor, then just the feasting. At the end of the five days, if the feast was enjoyed, your people come and bow before you, you eat a handful of earth, and it's done. You're sealed to the land and the land to you."

"I don't have five days."

"Then I suppose you don't have Marshyellow."

I shrugged. "I don't have the hand anymore. Marshyellow was tied to the hand, not to me."

There was certainly no time for things like that right now. I was far more occupied with trying not to be ill as I watched immortal beings torn asunder beneath us. That could have been me if Coppertomb had not neatly severed the three heads of the one he'd destroyed.

"We mortals think you are immortal," I breathed, "and yet never have I seen such death as in the Wittenhame."

"We enjoy ourselves more," Grosbeak agreed. "Not everyone can handle our level of passion and pleasure."

"I don't think it's that."

"Perhaps it's the jokes then. I think they go over your head."

"Should I be trying to make the ravens take us somewhere?" I asked, searching for any distraction from the horror below.

"Make them!" Grosbeak hooted. "The arrogance of the mortal wife to think she can harness the birds. They came for their lord, the Arrow. They'll not leave until he dismisses them."

I swallowed. That might be a while. Or it might be immediately. Bluebeard was drifting and fading too much to be conscious of where he was and what he was doing.

"If we only have two days then we must be clever in our next move. I am done with being tossed about on waves made by others. No more fleeing from Heaven's Hounds or angry Lords and Ladies of the Wittenhame," I said firmly. "We can't afford to waste any more time."

"Yes, no more slow kisses when you think you can't be seen behind the hourglass," Sparrow agreed dryly.

Grosbeak laughed. "No more flirting with Coppertomb and getting geases placed on you."

"You can hardly fault *me* for the actions of a lunatic," I said stiffly.

Grosbeak snickered. "Don't play coy maiden with me, Izolda. You know how this land works."

I swallowed. I did know. And that was why my heart was racing. Two days was not enough time. And our ravens were already fading in strength.

Can you ask your ravens to take us to Wittentree, beloved? I asked my husband with my mind.

In reply, he sent me a memory again. This time of him in a cloud of birds laughing and leaping with them. When he jumped, they jumped with him, carrying him down, borne on their wings. When he called, they came in a rush of song and then he sang with them and the sound of his singing shattered my heart.

I was still gasping when he sent me another image — but this was no memory. This time, he drew me with him, taking me by the hand and I was in the gown I wore when he married me and carrying my marriage sword and I looked twice as lovely and twice as terrible as I'd ever been in life.

I sighed as the image dissolved. If he'd caught my message, he was too delirious to respond. His mind, it seemed, strayed wide and far. I was touched that it seemed to swirl around me, drawing me into his dreams and memories as flawlessly as if I were really there. I wished I had the time to sit with him in these fancies, to see the world through his stained-glass view, to imagine with him what a future for us could look like if he were not mostly dead and I were not limited by mortal restraints.

"There's another one," Sparrow said tensely, and I ripped my attention back to what was happening below us.

A skirmish was unfolding across a bare, rocky hillside dotted with moss. Five Wittenbrand — mounted on what looked like over-sized mountain sheep — were circling a single Hound of Heaven, but though they charged with barb-tipped lances, they were no match for the Hound. As we watched, the Hound scooped up one attacker in his jaws— ignoring the lance that plunged into his eye and stuck there — and flung the screaming Wittenbrand over the side of the hill where he fell and fell, splashing into a lake below.

"Is he dead?" I whispered.

"Hard to tell," Grosbeak said, invigorated by the display. "Look, Sparrow! It's Klopfen the Bold! He's circling for the flank. And is that Wittentree I see preparing a charge?"

"It is," Sparrow said tensely. "Something is odd about this. The Hound that Coppertomb fought was not so wild."

I opened my mouth to ask her to clarify but my stomach pitched forward as our flock of ravens suddenly began to descend, at first slowly, and then quicker and quicker, little caws of exhaustion escaping them as those holding us flew away, delivering us to the backs of others, and still others, and then fewer and fewer, until we landed on a clump of moss with nothing but a single floating feather still remaining of what had been our escort and a pitched battle playing out barely a half-dozen steps from where we'd been set on the rock.

Wittentree, Bluebeard murmured in my mind.

Yes, very good, I agreed but inside something was gibbering.

CHAPTER NINE

I found my feet, gasping, Bluebeard still pressed to my back, an arm of his wrapped around my waist. His head pillowed on my shoulder. He pressed deliriously against me, his mouth making little kisses along my shoulder blade as his mind wheeled free, either quoting poetry or making it up on the spot.

A terror to the Wittenhame, one mortal girl by oath claimed, she careth not that they be lords or ladies famed, and so I draw my eyes to her and tuck her deep within my breast, why find me now my wandering heart when I have hers to make a nest?

If I had the time, I'd sit and record it and gaze into his strange, beloved eyes as he told it me, but we had been dropped just steps from a battle and that had me somewhat preoccupied.

I focused my eyes and tried to take in what was happening, bracing the lantern pole in front of me.

"If, in the cockles of your limited mind you have conceived of a plan to plant us in the jaws of one of those things again," Grosbeak snarled at me, "then I am compelled to remind you that not only am I your last living friend, but I also saved your life by macerating the rose that held Antlerdale's curse, taking the death of a prince of the Wittenhame upon myself on your behalf."

"Did you inherit Antlerdale, then?" I asked but I was only paying them half a mind.

I was counting. Four remaining warriors. One was Wittentree, one was a Wittenbrand warrior I did not know, though her fierce demeanor and multiple braids made her look like kin to Wittentree. The other two were very familiar to me. No longer dressed as mirror images, they were still Frost and Yarrow, the pair that once guarded Marshyellow and who I commanded to drown him in the sea. I had thought them dead with him, but I was wrong, it would seem.

"Only the living may inherit, though were I alive, I would make Antlerdale so strong that I could challenge the Bramble King himself."

"Your bragging does not benefit you," Sparrow huffed. "And you are not her only friend."

"Are you calling yourself my friend now, Sparrow," I said absently. "I had not thought you would stoop so low."

The Hound was not faring well against these five. It took a snapping leap at Wittentree, only for her relative to chop its hamstring with her double-headed axe. The dog let out something that sounded like both scream and whine before attempting to leap forward again, its hamstrung foot dragging behind it.

I edged backward, trying to keep an eye on my footing and the battle both at once.

Sweet torment close yet far away, her voice would still my longing. But it's her silence I must crave, or spoil all our hoping. Attend your ears and bend your lips and place on me a blessing, then tangle me in strings of love, hark to my song confessing.

Bluebeard, shhh, I begged him with my mind. He was distracting me too much. And who raved in verse, anyway?

The way my breath seemed to tumble at his soft, soft kisses and the knowing that as he slipped in and out of consciousness it was ever me on his mind, was just too much. I had a battle to keep out of and a talking head to verbally spar with and I couldn't do that when I could barely think — which was what his poems did to me.

Shhh, he agreed in my mind and I rolled my eyes. He was going to be the death of me, too.

"You will admit I am friend to you in action if not in heart," Sparrow said coolly.

"I will," I agreed, still watching the battle. I thought it best to remain out of it. I was no warrior, but as I watched, I wondered if these were allies working together, or enemies forced into partnership. They did not seem too concerned with the safety of one another.

"Also, you should take two steps back and one to the left. Right now, I would wager." Her voice was so clipped that I scrambled to do as she said, and we stepped out of the way of a sudden swing of one of the Hound's heads, neat as you please.

I panted a heavy breath. "Should I be fighting, too?"

"Spare us that!" Sparrow spat. "Leave it to those who are good at it."

"And there's Yarrow with a strike!" Grosbeak said

happily. "Klopfen rounds to the flank again, and yes! Another heel chop! Excellent, excellent work!"

"Grosbeak's always enjoyed a good gladiator match," Sparrow said to me, as if confiding. "He served as the Bramble King's champion for a season of entertainment once. I did not care for his loose form or dramatics, but everyone said his costuming was the best."

"What is a gladiator match?" I asked as Wittentree dove under one of the snapping heads and deftly slit one of the Hound's throats while her kin — Klopfen? Ran up its back and hacked at the place where the spine met the shoulders.

"A fight to disfigurement between two competitors for the amusement of the crowd," Sparrow said.

"And how is that different from everyday life in the Wittenhame?"

"There are more attentive spectators," Grosbeak grinned. He was preening. "And we dress up."

"What did Grosbeak wear?" I asked as Frost and Yarrow rode circles around the flailing Hound, keeping it pinned. I wasn't worried now about the outcome of this battle. The Wittenbrand were winning easily and when they were finished, I would beg an audience with Wittentree. I simply had to be patient.

Patience, Bluebeard agreed.

"Why do you ask what he wore?" Sparrow seemed to be suppressing amusement.

"I wore the greatest costume the world has ever seen," Grosbeak said. "It fit me to perfection, flawless in every way, unblemished, unmarred, perfectly balanced, and colored."

I rolled my eyes but I was following the fight still,

waiting to time my greeting until the last head fell. "Of course it was. Tell me, did you dress as a creature of the sea, or as a pouncing lion?"

And then, out of nowhere, one of the Hound's heads snapped, catching Wittentree in its jaws and shaking her savagely. I felt the air whoosh from my lungs as I froze, unable to do anything to stop it. Klopfen smashed her axe one final time, severing the spine, and the creature collapsed, a broken Wittentree still in one jaw. I could not seem to close my mouth or to swallow the horror of what I was seeing.

"I was entirely in my own skin, obviously," Grosbeak said. "No other costume could be so lovely."

"Pity you lost it, then," I quipped quietly, but horror was rushing through me. Wittentree could have helped. Wittentree could have told me where to go!

I scrambled forward over the rocks, rushing toward where she lay torn and bloody, still half pinned by the jaws of the mighty Hound. Klopfen collapsed, exhausted, on its neck, her breath heaving in her lungs. As I drew near to Wittentree, Frost and Yarrow continued to circle, as if they thought the threat was not yet passed. I hoped they were wrong. I hoped that this was safe, because safe or not I was going in.

I hurried forward, careful of my footing on the rocks. Before me, the Hound of Heaven stank of death and wet dog. Its heavy jowls were thick with bloody fur and when I edged by its paw — as large as a small cow — I trembled.

The Hound bled out across the stone and who would have thought one creature could have so much steaming blood in it? That was three of them I'd seen killed now. How many more could there be?

"Why do they call them Heaven's Hounds," I muttered, "when they seem like denizens of hell?"

"I thought you knew, mortal menace." Grosbeak snickered. "The Wittenhame *is* hell. Anything that comes here to rip us apart must be heaven-sent."

"Then I suppose I am an angel," I said.

Drift from heaven, fall to ground, make my breath catch, my heart pound.

You should have been a poet, husband. I say in my mind, with a sigh. *When they cut you, you bleed poetry.*

"An angel of death, perhaps," Grosbeak said, his voice thick with scorn. "Where you go, misery follows. Dismemberment, terror, and death are your vanguard, and a sickening sense of misery your rearguard."

"Always with the flattery," I murmured, but I did not mind. His verbal sparing kept me sharp as I eased myself down around the still twitching corpse of the massive Hound to where Wittentree was pinned.

The teeth of the Hound clamped firmly around her torso, impaling her three times across the waist and hip. The jaw was locked in death, pinning her in place. Blood swelled in blackening bubbles from around the teeth embedded in her. She drew in a pained breath and the blood bubbled more, seeming almost to boil.

"I find my body loathes this trap and pains me as consequence," she said, her breath rattling in her chest.

That was unsurprising.

She still had the beauty she'd bargained for from me and it softened her lips and cheeks, but could not soften the sharp knowing in her golden eye or the glassy blindness of the pearl one. Her face was so pale it nearly matched that iridescent orb, and blood leaked harsh and scarlet from her ears.

"I do not favor death by dog bite. It has little to recommend it."

I crouched down beside her and she held out a hand to me. I took it before I realized it was my hand she was offering me — my living, flesh hand.

"Bargain with me, now at the end," she said grimly.

"How is this the end?" I asked, taking the wiggling hand in my skeletal one. It felt so foreign that it was strange to think it had ever been mine. "Are you not Wittenbrand? Can you not heal from this as you heal from all else."

She snorted. "Your perspective is wrong. Look up over your shoulder."

I turned and looked behind me just in time to see Yarrow skewer Klopfen on the end of his lance. Her mouth formed a silent scream as Frost took her head with a single swipe of his razor-sharp sword. Oh. So they *were* enemies, then.

"Treachery," I hissed and Wittentree laughed.

"Of course. Dear Coppertomb does not bear rivals well. It was only a matter of time before he set his Hounds on us — literal and figurative. I find it only shocking that he acted before we could witness the final glory of his Coronation Ball. I predict it will be poorly attended."

"He betrayed you. He broke the rules of the game." I felt breathless as I stated the obvious. Behind me, Frost and Yarrow were very thoroughly ensuring that Klopfen was completely dead.

"It's nice to know I was worth a betrayal in the end. But I have matters to set right so listen now to me, mortal girl, before they come for us. A bargain I would make with you for that hand you hold in yours."

"I don't want it back," I said firmly.

"I think you do," she countered. "And I require a boon from you."

"What do you want?" I asked, but Yarrow and Frost were carefully sliding down the back of the Hound and circling toward us and I could feel them closing in.

"Rouranmoore," she gasped, reaching out her other hand and opening it so I could see her token pressed within her palm. "Take the token."

I took it and stashed it in my belt pouch. I did not have enough hands, not even — ha, ha — now that my living hand was returned to me. I put it in the belt pouch, too.

"I have given my heart to that place in a way I did not think possible for an immortal Wittenbrand. Almost, I understand your specter husband and his fool plan of marrying himself to the land. Almost."

I made a humming sound that I hoped would tell her to get to the point. Yarrow whispered in Frost's ear and they both grinned wickedly at us, as if savoring the moment before they struck. Did Wittentree know she had the power to stop them because she possessed my old hand? Or, at least, I thought she did. I must indeed bargain with her for the hand and fast.

"All the nations crumble — all but Pensmoore now, and I have considered why that may be and made some inquiries."

"All that in mere hours?" I asked dryly.

She waved a hand, "It's been longer in that mayfly world. I have come to know that you are one with the land of Pensmoore. Now, take on Rouranmoore, too, that she may thrive when I am past."

I cleared my throat. "You love Rouranmoore so well?"

"Make the bargain with me. Your original hand back in exchange for a tie between you and the mortal land of Rouranmoore. What you do for Pensmoore you do for Rouranmoore. How you anchor one, you anchor the other."

"The hand I'll take, and I will give you as you wish, but you must give me one thing more," I said in a hurry as the circling pair drew in closer to us. Frost shook the blood from his blade as if preparing to take more and Yarrow tossed his lance aside and drew out two daggers. I must be quick. "I must know how to find the place from which the Sovereign's rib was mined."

"A fairy story. A tale for mortals." She coughed and blood bubbled up, red and bright, almost pink as it foamed at the corner of her lips.

"Give it to me anyway," I demanded. "I must find the place at once."

She gasped, barely able to get her words out. "A bargain is struck."

"A bargain is struck," I agreed and then I tapped my living hand in the belt pouch, about to use it to dismiss Frost and Yarrow but before my mouth had opened to order them back, something beside me shifted.

I glanced down to see that Wittentree had used her silver key to open a door to somewhere else — the mortal world? — and with a power I didn't expect, she grabbed my coat, yanked me forward, and threw me — from a flat back and using only her arms! — through the doorway. I barely held on to the lantern pole, grateful that Bluebeard was clutching me with his own strength as I tumbled through the door.

Her words were nearly swallowed up as madness struck me, bowling me over, and sweeping me away, but I caught the edges of them as I reached for the hand of my husband and clung to the pole that carried my two bodiless friends.

"Look to Death."

And then she was gone from my mind, shattered into fragments as I fought against the tug of madness and a harsh gibbering in my mind. My eyes rolled back in my head, sounds faded into hysterical shrieks, and I struggled against the tide of insanity to keep a grip on myself.

I am Izolda, I reminded myself. I am not insane. I am merely traveling between worlds.

And then I caught a glimpse of something, maybe something my mind conjured in the throes of madness, or maybe something real. It was hard to tell and either way, I did not like it, because the image I saw was of Wittentree dying, ripped to pieces by the teeth of Frost and Yarrow.

CHAPTER TEN

"No!" I gasped as my mind emerged from the madness of the gate between worlds. "No, no, no!"

Had Wittentree thrown me into the mortal world? After years spent in that place, I felt as though I should be able to identify it at a glance, but I was indoors, which made it hard to tell. Or at least, I thought I was indoors. The high vault of the ceiling was dark, the walls carved in precise lines and angles. There were no furnishings in the room we were in except for a single dark-wood chair such as you might find in a banqueting hall. Though lamps had been lit on great stands around the room, they flickered slowly as if afraid of dancing too wildly, and made it difficult for my eyes to adjust enough to see what lined the walls. Something trickled in a divot along the center of the rocky floor. A drain, perhaps?

"I hate this place," Grosbeak complained.

"So do I," I gasped and then I turned around and vomited, barely missing Bluebeard's boots.

"See?" Grosbeak said triumphantly. "It even makes mortals ill to have to be here."

"It's over," I said piteously. "It's done. There's no hope for any of it now!"

Sparrow stared at me with a line between her eyes. "Is she always like this or has the way through broken her?"

"I like this pitiful Izolda," Grosbeak said, not seeming overly concerned. "I have heard rumors that mad mortals are almost as clever as the Wittenbrand. It might be an improvement."

"Or, she might give up and then I'll never get my body back," Sparrow said grimly. "Your attention, Izolda Savataz," she demanded. "Look at me and end this piteous moaning."

I snapped my mouth shut and looked at her.

"That's a beginning," she said firmly. "All is not lost."

"There's no way we can get to the coronation in time now," I gasped. "Too much time passes here! It could be years that we've been gone already."

"Get back where?" Sparrow asked curiously.

"Or ..." Grosbeak let the word hang in the air.

"Or only a few days," I admitted, "But I do not have a few days. I do not have even a few hours! And all this for the most cryptic and useless of answers."

"Well," Sparrow said. "Not entirely cryptic."

"I hopped once from the mortal world and when I returned to the Wittenhame, I was two days in the past," Grosbeak said easily. "I bought myself drinks in the *Hop and Tarry.* Talked for hours."

"How is that possible?" I gasped.

"I'm an excellent conversationalist."

"We're not in the mortal world, Izolda Savataz," Sparrow said grimly as my eyes adjusted to the light. "Tell me, what do you see in those alcoves?"

I took a step forward, and then another, and then I was walking toward the vaults cut into the wall with horror in my belly. On the shelf nearest me, was a collection of tiny bones stacked in tidy rows right up to the top of the shelf.

"Phalanges" was engraved on a bronze plate under them.

Someone had labeled the shelf beneath it "Prussian Blue" on another bronze plate, and that shelf was entirely full of paint chips that looked as if they had been meticulously removed from something.

The next bore the engraving "Poisons" and had a collection of bottles and jars of various shapes and sizes, arranged by size and place on the spectrum of colors.

I shivered. I was already afraid to meet whoever had made this vault. What kind of mind would take the world apart like this?

The next shelf was labeled "Hearts of my Enemies" and here there were, indeed, dried and preserved hearts ranging from one smaller than the last knuckle on my pinky to one the size of my head. They were arranged, again, by size and someone had neatly pinned a note with an inked date to each one.

I swallowed.

Another shelf was labeled "Small Ceremonial Daggers." The blades were no larger than my hand and as small as my fingernail. Small indeed. I did not bother availing myself of any of them. With both my hands occupied, a weapon would be of little use to me.

"What are you doing here?" a voice asked menacingly.

I jumped with a barely cut-off squeal, as a hand clamped on my shoulder and spun me around.

"As I was saying," Sparrow said dryly. "This is not the mortal world. This is Coppertomb's home."

And it was the master of the house I was facing eye-to-eye.

"I give you two days and you plan to spend them in my vault?" he asked me in a dry tone. One eyebrow rose and the low light made the golden dust on his cheekbones stand out brighter than it normally was.

"I thought you were hunting the Hounds of Heaven."

He waved a hand. "I have vassals for that. I find that you are growing to be more trouble than the worth of your prize."

"Will you put my heart on a shelf, then?" I asked him, boldly.

"It's rather less cruel than a shelf of animated heads, don't you think?" he asked me. "Isn't that what your beloved husband has? A shelf of his conquered enemies, still there to consult at will?"

How did he know that? His eyes sharpened as if he'd seen the confirmation in my eyes.

"Everywhere I go, there you are. In my way. In my business. Do you not yet see how it is you and you alone who has brought the Arrow of the Wittenhame to his knees and to his final end?" I risked a glance over my shoulder at Bluebeard. His eyes were shut, lips slightly parted, and squished against my shoulder. "His weakness for you left him open to my blow. And all your meanderings enmeshed him in the plots that sought his life. And now, when it is all over, you desecrate his corpse by dragging him ever onward."

Coppertomb clicked his tongue in censure.

"Then why don't you kill me?" I pressed. Because why hadn't he? He was always here accusing, thwarting, placing geases on me, but never directly acting. "Why don't you dry my heart for your shelf? Why don't you take my husband from me." He was silent, and my eyebrows rose of their own accord as I pressed. "He protects me yet, does he not? You cannot touch me with more than your accusations."

"That doesn't mean that I can't hurt you," he said, and he reached out and plucked Sparrow's head from my lantern pole. "Will you bury your husband and bow to me if I take from you your friends and advisors?"

"No," I whispered.

"Really?" He tilted his head to one side. "What if I threaten their afterlives? There's no returning from fire," he said, striding over to one of the bright lamp holders.

"There's no need for that!" Grosbeak said shrilly.

Sparrow, on the other hand, had her jaw set in a grim line.

"I thought you had a kingdom to rule," I said sharply. "Have you nothing better to employ you than taunting me?"

He raised a single brow. "Have you not seen how the sky falls? The rotting husk of your husband rots my reign. I must see him buried and his works burned to ash or risk watching the Wittenhame rot with him."

And then with a flick of his wrist, the lamp beside him flared up to bright flame and he tossed Sparrow's head within it like he was tossing a bean bag for a harvest game. Her scream echoed through his vault and then she hit the flame and went up like a dry field put to the torch.

A cry ripped from my lungs, too, and I stumbled forward, only to feel hands dragging me back. Bluebeard's eyes were still shut, his head still resting on my shoulder, but somehow, he restrained me as Coppertomb flicked imaginary lint off his clothing.

"A reminder that I am the Bramble King and I have told you to bury your dead. Do it now, or see more losses."

I couldn't tear my eyes away from the remains of Sparrow's flaming head. Sweat broke out on my brow and tears stung my eyes. I hadn't liked Sparrow much, but she was owed so much more than this.

Trembling, I turned to Coppertomb. I still had enough strength to spit in his direction.

"If you were truly the Bramble King, then you wouldn't need to keep reminding us of it."

"Ooooh ... direct hit!" Grosbeak crowed but Coppertomb strode forward two steps, tilted my chin up, met my eyes, and said coolly.

"Two days. There's a shovel in the corner. You can bury him here in my crypt if you must. You won't be going anywhere else. When I leave here, I will bar the entrance to you. Think on what I've said. I could spare you. I could return you to the mortal world when the coronation is complete, if only you do as I request. And my request is so very reasonable."

"I think that you make promises you have no power to keep and threats you have no ability to carry out," I said but even to my own ears, my voice was weak and terrified.

He snapped his fingers and left in a burst of smoke.

"Needless dramatics," I muttered.

"Coppertomb is a delight," Grosbeak purred. "He never misses an opportunity to puff and display. Puts a peacock to shame. And to think he was not even a lord in the last game and now he is Bramble King." He sighed happily. "The Wittenhame is the best place imaginable."

"Tell that to Sparrow," I said bitterly.

"Fortunately, I won't have to," Grosbeak said easily. "I no longer have a rival for your ear and affections, and I find that is exactly as I prefer it."

With a sigh, I made my way to the lamp, but there was no sign of Sparrow within the dancing flames. Not even the ashes or the dust of her passing. It was as if she never was at all. And I would be the same unless I could solve this last puzzle.

CHAPTER ELEVEN

There was only one door to Coppertomb's vault and when I tried it, it was locked just as he'd promised me. I looked at every shelf, at the strange drain in the floor, at the items cataloged, and behind them, I even examined the plain chair. There was no way out.

"Trapped, trapped, trapped," Grosbeak said, laughing wildly, and then every so often he would murmur another "trapped!"

If Tanglecott was the fairy godmother in a Wittentale and Bluebeard was the tortured lord, and Antlerdale the monster-turned-lover, then Coppertomb was the witch who tricked children into ovens and gnawed on their bones. The careful linear way he'd laid things out and the horribly specific way he labeled them, made me feel like I was inside the mind of someone who did not see living organic things at all, but only parts held together by muscle as a model is held together by wire. I could see a mind like this taking us apart and putting us back together again and the idea of it rattled me.

I was searching a shelf of rib cages looking for a door behind them, when I noted they were sorted differently.

"Why catalog two sets of rib cages?" I murmured to Grosbeak. I needn't have spoken. The bronze plaques spelled it out.

"Human Rib Cages" one said and the other "Wittenbrand Rib Cages."

"Because they're different, but noting that won't help you out of your trap, trap, trap," he sang.

Different?

I looked from one to the other and then back. They looked much the same. I counted on the human side. Twenty true ribs and four floating ribs. That was normal. Even I, a lower noblewoman, had enough learning to know that.

I turned to the Wittenbrand rib cage and paused. Oh. Sixteen true ribs and eight floating ribs. How odd. But something about it bothered me and kept on bothering me as we searched.

"There's no way out. You might as well bury him and see what happens," Grosbeak reminded me.

"I thought you were my ally now," I told him.

"Your ally. Not his."

With a huff, I set him on the chair and then crossed to the other end of the vault and eased my stumbling husband down so he could lay with his head pillowed in my lap. Maybe if he could recover enough energy, he could focus and help me figure this out. I had considered myself a clever puzzle solver, but I was stumped. I needed a hint. And his hint about the blood of nations was not enough.

Why was everything blood for these people? It was too

much.

Blood and phalanges, hearts and ribs.

Ribs.

Sixteen ribs.

I froze.

We had to go to the place where the rib had been mined, right? And the poem was related to that. Sixteen locks and sixteen keys. Sixteen ribs. Sixteen wives.

My husband, can you hear my mind? I whispered to Bluebeard as I stroked his hair. He nestled in closer so that his face was pillowed against my belly.

Mmmm.

You cannot tell me what to do.

Mmmm.

But perhaps you can listen and tell me if I am right.

My beloved Izolda. I wasn't sure if that was encouragement to go on, or a sigh of despair. *Spirit of my spirit, heart of my own heart, fall what may.*

I licked my lips and drew little circles on his back and shoulders, flooded with an overwhelming sense of affection for him as I whispered with my mind.

It's all connected, isn't it? I asked him. *The Legend of the Sovereign and the world existing within his breast, the rib the people stole and the sixteen ribs of the Wittenbrand ... and your wives. Sixteen, right? Fifteen for the unmarred ribs and one more for the stolen rib. That's why all the rhymes and prophecies keep coming back to the one wife, the one of sixteen, the one rib. You're repairing the sovereign somehow. Is he also the Bramble King?*

My clever, sweet love, my one true wife, he murmured in his mind as his free hand found my waist and clung to me.

I held him close, my mind racing, my heart all in tangles.

What will happen to us? I asked him plaintively. *Are we to be sacrifices to the earth?*

Never. It was always my plan that my fifteen wives be restored to their time and place.

Fifteen ribs from all different lands. I paused. *The blood of nations, am I right? These wives of yours are the blood of nations.*

I wanted to ask "but what about me?" But I was too afraid to think the words. Because what if I was to be the sacrifice? What if I were to somehow take the place of that final rib?

The poem had left a choice to the last wife. A choice of freedom or ... something else. Maybe I was supposed to choose that something else.

Worse yet, what if he meant to dial back time and return *me* to my original time and place? Would I marry Lord Danske and care for horses? Would I be happy in that simpler, firmer, happier life? Or would part of me always remember this wild nightmare that had become a dream, that had become my home?

I was just like my father. I loved wild things. I loved them too much. I loved them so much I was spending my life away for glimmers of them.

"I choose you," I whispered to Bluebeard. "If there's a choice, then you are my choice."

I was your stolen true bride, I whisper in his mind. *But I mean all the vows. I find I cannot be Izolda without her Bluebeard. I cannot thrive while you languish. I cannot be hale while you are apart from me. Does it diminish me that*

I am only whole when you hold my heart? Then I will be diminished. Does it pauper me to give my whole heart to you, dead though you are? Then make me a pauper, spend every waver of my fool heart. For I am ever yours and I refuse any choice that does not have you at the end of it.

He shuddered, an intense, powerful shudder, and then with an act that seemed to take all his strength and will, with jaw clenched and teeth gritted, he pulled himself up onto his knees, and his wild cat's eyes opened and his gaze met mine as he murmured in my mind.

Never have I loved until I loved you. I have sought you through lands and worlds, looked for you through the rush of time, bought you with my blood, delivered you with my pain, and I will put my mark on you, and claim you forever. There is no time to come where I am not Izolda's, or where she is not mine, and I say it by the power of my true name.

And then he whispered his name in my mind and I gasped at the gift of such an intimacy. I would tell it to no other. I would keep it forever as my most precious secret held tight to my heart. And in the moment of my gasp, he leaned forward, and his soft lips fluttered against mine for just a moment.

Hold fast, my clever wife. This is your battle to be braved.

And then he slumped once more to my lap, falling like a tree cut by an axe, and left me sighing and hungry for more as I broke his fall.

Well then.

There was only one thing to do. I must bring all his wives out and together we must find the source of the rib, unlock the sixteen locks, and free my Bluebeard from death.

CHAPTER TWELVE

I urged my beloved back onto his feet before I could change my mind. His dark eyes shuttered closed, but his muscles flexed as I drew him up. I twined my bone hand through his hair, as I positioned him against my back again.

Stay strong, my husband, I whispered to him in my mind. *I will not abandon you. Do not abandon me.*

I opened the door to the Room of Wives before I could talk myself out of it — Coppertomb could not snatch this key. I felt certain that was true. Had he the ability to take it, he would have stripped me of it, too.

I stepped inside even as I heard Grosbeak calling out, "You'd better not be going where I think you are! You'd better not be leaving me here!"

With a sigh, I went back for him. "If you insist on coming along, you'd best be helpful."

He sounded appalled. "Name for me, oh mortal soul, whence I have been anything but helpful."

I marched into the Room of Wives and past the heads I

left in a circle, ignoring them and their curses and snarls. Some of them had rolled over and I wondered if that was intentional or if I had somehow damaged them.

Grosbeak stuck out a tongue at one of them and I shook my head. I should have left him.

"Cursed mortal, return us to our last resting place!" the one with the silver coronet said. "You have no right to own us or make us your slaves."

"I have the right of marriage," I disagreed. I held my head high with determination. It would take more than the objections of a few corpses to stop me now.

"Do not think you can treat us thusly and yet still our council keep!" another cried.

"Then to whom else would you pour all your acid words?" I shot back. I was used to talking heads spouting lies. I carried one around with me daily.

I thought I might need them, and despite their barbed words, I thought that they might need me, too. Bluebeard kept them for a reason. If the wives were the blood of mortal nations, could these advisors be the blood of the Wittenbrand, too? I did not know, but even if I hadn't yet worked out the reason for keeping them, that didn't mean there wasn't one.

There were exactly thirty heads there by my count. That was two for every wife but me. I had two, but only one of mine yet survived.

With my jaw gritted determinedly, I made my way to the hourglass at the end of the room and reached inside for a fist of garnets. It was hard to take them with my bone hand, though, and in the end, I was forced to pluck them one by one, and hold them in my jacket pocket. Thirty.

Two for each wife. If we didn't succeed in two days, we wouldn't succeed at all. Strange to think that I held a month of my life in my pocket.

Strange, but not worth wasting time to consider. I marched to the first of Bluebeard's wives. Margaretta.

Because we had worked as partners before, I chose her first. I wanted someone who wasn't crazy and who probably wouldn't try to kill me. I needed her to be on my side before the others awoke.

"Oh! Oh, dear! It's you!" she squeaked when the two garnets were in her mouth. "So. you survived!"

"I'm good at that. To date, it's my only specialty," I replied. "I need your help."

"We're not opening another door, are we?" she asked me primly. "Oh dear!" She suddenly seemed to notice our mutual husband draped across my back. His scarlet hood was down and his beautiful face easy to see, though his eyes were closed in restless sleep. "That's not ... ? Oh dear. It's the very Lord of the Wittenhame who stole me away as his bride!"

"Yes, thank you for recounting that," I said dryly.

"Well, what is he doing here?"

"He needs our help," I said simply and I let her look for a long moment into my eyes before she grudgingly screwed up her face into a determined scrunch.

"I don't think the others will like it much. Their journals were not happy ones. You're waking them, right? I see you have more garnets between your fingers."

"I was hoping you could help me explain this to them," I told her, licking my lips nervously. "I'm not sure if you've noticed, but I'm not really a people person. Most of the people I knew in life are dead now. And my only remaining friend is hideous."

I shook Grosbeak's pole.

"Excuse me? Hideous? That is not how you speak to one you call friend."

"See?" I said.

"All of my friends are dead now, too," Margaretta said sadly.

"And yet you remain enormously likable," I said dryly. "Come, let's wake this next bride."

"I don't know about likable," Grosbeak groused. "Edible, perhaps. She's very edible looking."

The next bride was Tigraine. I stood well back. If she was going to slap someone in the face I wanted it to be Margaretta and not me. I'd already received my slap last time I woke a bride. But to my surprise, when Tigraine woke, her eyes snapped open but then quickly narrowed and she looked carefully around the room without so much as moving.

"Now that is the face of a mortal queen," Grosbeak said delightedly.

"Princess Tigraine," Margaretta began, a little breathless but Tigraine held up a single finger, still assessing until her eyes met mine and she nodded in understanding.

She pointed at me.

"You're the current bride."

"I prefer true bride," I said calmly.

"Apt." She tilted her head to one side. "I always wondered what manner of woman he might choose were he choosing simply for himself. I did not anticipate you."

I clenched my jaw. No one did. They saw only what they wanted to see. The exterior.

"Nor did I," Grosbeak confided. "I would have expected someone more like *you*."

"That's why you're dead," Tigraine said scathingly. "Clearly, you were not one of nature's thinkers."

I liked her already.

"Likely, you'll live to reassess that, mortal princess," Grosbeak said in a threatening voice.

"I rarely find the need to reassess," Tigraine said. "And yet, this true bride has finally done what I did not have the fortitude to try, and what I secretly hoped one of us would do."

"Kill her husband?" Margaretta asked wide-eyed.

But Tigraine was shaking her head. "She's waking us, isn't she? You're clearly a princess of Pensmoore, Princess ...?"

"Margaretta?" Margaretta squeaked and then added a hurried, "Yes!"

"You're going to help her end this nonsense?" Tigraine pressed, her eyes locked on mine.

I nodded.

"Oh, yes!" Margaretta enthused.

"Who better to finish this than his wives? It's always women who have to clean up the messes, is it not?" Tigraine said, hopping down from her plinth. "Tell me, bride of Lord Riverbarrow ..."

"Izolda," Grosbeak said. "Her name is Izolda Savataz of Pensmoore, though she also goes as the 'Mad Princess'."

Tigraine nodded gravely. "Tell me, Mad Princess. What would you have me do?"

"I want you to help me unlock the door to death."

She nodded grimly. "A worthy goal. I will ride with you."

"Great," Grosbeak said, rolling his eyes, "Now, let's repeat this nonsense another fourteen times, shall we?"

We woke the wives, one by one, explaining the need to keep the garnets in their mouths. We started with Coriannian, the bride who had first intimidated me with her majestic demeanor and powerful figure. She turned out to be incredibly meek, following Margaretta around like a very large lost puppy.

Ki'e'iren was the last — the bride with the snow-white hair and the thick golden belt. She watched me with suspicious eyes and she was not the only one who threw constant worried glances at Bluebeard where he was drooped on my shoulder.

"Is he really dead?" she asked me, eventually.

"Mostly," I said. "His spirit lingers."

"There is a wound in his side that is crusted and ugly," she said calmly. "He did not have that when last I saw him."

"He received that for me," I said with bright cheeks.

"What else did he receive for you?" she asked. "Has he lost his ability to restore us to our rightful places as he promised?"

"I ... don't know," I said and her lips thinned in censure. "But we will restore him and then he can fulfill all his promises."

"What promises has he made you?" she asked me. "Are you to be restored to your time and land?"

I swallowed, but I was saved from answering by the cackling of Grosbeak.

"You may well ask what promises she has received, for he has poured promises into her ear as an advisor pours honeyed wine for a king. He has strewn her path with promises as a maiden throws flowers before the bride. He has laid them like cobbles and woven them like reeds, built them up like stones in a wall and —"

"I rather think that is enough," I said grimly. "We hear your words, revenant."

But as if Grosbeak's words had provoked a memory in him, Bluebeard mumbled into my neck, "As long as rivers run and moon shines."

With a gasp, the brides drew back.

"Yes, it's somewhat unsettling to watch the dead speak," I told them grimly. "But he is not so dead that we cannot restore him. So, work with me. Join my cause. And then you will receive all he promised you."

"We weren't told we would have to do more than lend our patience and I find I have no depths in me which long to give," Ki'e'iren said, putting her hands on her hips, but to my surprise, Tigraine slapped her hard across the face.

Ki'e'iren froze, mouth open, eyes lit with inner fire.

"You aren't the only princess here, so stop acting like you are," Tigraine said, leaning in close to make her words more threatening. "Would you risk the futures of the fifteen of us for your own pettiness?"

"It is possible that I would," Ki'e'iren said, snapping her mouth shut and flexing her hand as if she would slap Tigraine back.

I felt as though I was back on my parent's holdings,

keeping the mares from biting. I shook Grosbeak's pole between them.

"Nnnnrggh," he muttered.

"Enough, I beg you," I said before forcing my gaze to run over all the wives as I spoke. There was Givanna, the poet, and the lovely redhead I'd so admired, and Margaretta's hopeful face. "Think carefully on what you will do. I know not what perils may lie along the way or what will happen to your bodies, or chances of returning to your lives, if harm befalls you. But if we fail, you'll remain here, cold and untouched, insensible until time fades away or the magic unravels."

"How will you bring a man back from death?" Tigraine asked, making her way to my bodiless advisors. "And what will we do with these?"

"I thought we might take them with us," I said grimly. "Why should I be the only wife with a Wittenbrand advisor?"

"We do not wish to go anywhere," the head that looked like a mermaid spat.

"All the more reason to take you," Tigraine said, picking her up by the hair and inspecting her.

"Ewww, they're all dead!" Margaretta said, scrubbing her hands on her dress even though she hadn't touched any of them. "I don't like touching dead things."

"You say that now," Grosbeak purred. Was this him being charming? "But you'd sing another tune if you tried it."

"No," Margaretta said primly. "I do not think so."

"And can these advisors advise?" Ki'e'iren asked. "Do

they know how to find this place where a rib is missing and broker a deal with Death?"

"If we knew, we would have mentioned it by now," the head with the crown said.

"Perhaps you can bargain with Death for the knowledge." Tigraine's eyes were on me as if watching to see what I might do. It was a practical suggestion, though I would have no idea how to go about doing it.

"He *does* walk among us now," Grosbeak said with a leer for Tigraine. "Why not try the princess's suggestion."

"You do not amuse me, revenant. Keep your charms to Margaretta," Tigraine circled the heads.

"Oh please, no!" Margaretta said, her hand clasping her own throat.

I cleared my throat. "Is there a way, advisors of my husband, to call Death to you? I cannot bargain with what is not here."

"The dead see him," one of the heads said in a bored tone.

"Can you see him, then? Dead as you are?"

"The *newly* dead," that head corrected.

"Or those dying," the head with crown agreed. "Not possibly dying, but dying in truth. The man who lingers long on a gut wound may indeed see Death. I've witnessed that myself. Or the woman bleeding out after childbirth may hear his footsteps, or the victim of a poison with no antidote may converse with him. All these might earn the chance to bargain with Death while still living."

"Well, I'm hardly going to kill someone just to draw Death near," I said wryly. "Perhaps there is another way?"

There were murmurs but they sounded discouraging and I looked from face to face. The head with the crown sniffed, and Margaretta crouched in front of her, staring, eyes wide.

"Back up, girl-child. I can see right up your skirts."

"Eee!" Margaretta skittered backward, kicking one of the heads in her haste. It, in turn, knocked over the next and the next, and it took me a moment of scrambling with the help of the wives to set them all straight again and calm down a frantic Margaretta.

"I think that maybe you should stay here with me," I told her grimly, but as she made her way to me, something pricked my side under the arm where I held Grosbeak.

I startled, heart racing. It felt as if a hot poker had been driven under my skin for just a moment, and now uncomfortable heat spread out from that spot like the fingers of a fire.

"What —?" I started to say and I turned to see Ki'e'iren holding one of those tiny pinprick daggers in one hand and a bottle in the other. I had been too distracted by Margaretta's antics to see that she had swiped them from the shelves of Coppertomb's home.

"Neverseed, isn't it?" she said, sniffing the bottle. "Smells like aniseed and lemon bore a love child together."

I swallowed. I wasn't sure if it was panic or the poison she'd stabbed me with, but my head was suddenly swimming. Everyone froze, silent, eyes wide.

"Fool," Grosbeak breathed.

"Doubly fool since all our fates ride with her," Tigraine said and it was her face — suddenly dead pale that made me panic more. She straightened slowly.

I was poisoned.

"It's a long-acting poison," Ki'e'iren said breezily. "She gave us two days. I'm giving her the same. If she's careful, and doesn't overexert herself, she might even make it to three days. Wouldn't that be nice?" Her smile was saccharine. "And she was the one who wanted to see Death. I've granted her wish, have I not?"

And as she gestured, I saw that she was right, for a pale figure on a pale horse was riding through the wall of Coppertomb's vault and straight toward me.

CHAPTER THIRTEEN

"Bargain with me, Death," I said through lips made thick with fear as I walked through the open door and out of the Room of Wives into the Coppertomb's vault.

They were arguing behind me, but I dare not let that distract me, just as I dare not let fear control me. I had asked to bargain with death. I had received my wish. Later, I could dwell on the terrible consequences of this wish.

"I really wouldn't bargain with Death, Izolda," Grosbeak hissed. "You don't know what you're getting into. Other Wittenbrand might take a hand, or a few years of your life, or your free will, but Death always plays for keeps."

I planned to play for keeps. I would be a hypocrite if I thought he wasn't playing the same game.

"BARGAIN?" Death asked, the words sliding over his white slug-tongue. He sniffed the air as if he could smell something about me in it. And his words were strange in my mind, seeming to be both there and not there at the same time. Final, and yet ephemeral. "WITH ME THERE ARE NO BARGAINS."

A little shiver of fear ran up my spine. Death smelled like a grave and his very nearness turned my stomach.

"Good, no bargains," Grosbeak said hastily. "No need to catch the eye of Death."

Terror made his voice quiver. It made my blood sing with possibility. Finally, I was talking with someone who might get me nearer to what I needed. Finally.

"Are you not of the Wittenhame then?" I asked. Sweat was beginning to form on my brow. "Do you no longer take joy in bedevilment, or set your heart on the trickery and trappings of the great ones?"

He paused and his long filmy hair swirled around him like the head of a blown dandelion. He looked around the room with pearlescent eyes and then back to me and he seemed transfixed by something over my shoulder — my husband, I thought.

"DEATH BOWS TO NO MAN."

"No one is asking you to bow."

He backed up a step as if threatened.

"DEATH HAS BUT ONE SOVEREIGN."

My heart was beating in my ears. He was going to flee. I could feel it.

"No one is asking to rule you. I would only bargain with you, Lord of Death. "

A cold wind blew from him and he swayed with it, his horrific scent tangling through the breeze. I had to clench my jaw firmly to keep from gagging.

As he swayed, he rattled a little, and I realized his long white robe was sewn all over with tiny skulls like beads, and so were the reigns of his bone horse which stamped now, pawing Coppertomb's floor and casting its dead gaze to me as it flickered in and out of sight.

"WHAT DO YOU ASK OF ME, DYING MORTAL?"

"I would have my husband's life back," I said boldly. Best to ask for what I really wanted first.

"THAT I CANNOT GIVE YOU."

"Then I would that I could reach the place from which the first sovereign's rib was plucked and through the door into your realms, that I might go and retrieve him myself."

"YOU WILL COME TO ME WHETHER YOU BARGAIN OR NOT. THE DRAUGHT OF THE NEVERSEED STEALS YOUR LIFE A BREATH AT A TIME, AND THOUGH YOU TARRY, YOU WILL COME."

I shifted, swallowing uncomfortably. I did not have time right now to deal with the knowledge that I had been poisoned. And yet, a little butterfly of panic burst free each time I thought of it.

"I wish to enter your lands while still living."

"THE PRICE I WOULD ASK FOR SUCH IS SO MUCH MORE THAN YOU CAN BEAR."

"Name it."

"A PIECE OF YOUR FLESH GIVEN WILLINGLY. AND YOU WILL WALK THE PATH OF PRINCES. FAIL AT ANY POINT, AND THE BARGAIN IS STRUCK DOWN."

"What is the Path of Princes?" I asked, nervous now.

"Don't do it," Grosbeak whispered. "You can't succeed at that."

I heard feet behind me. The wives had not stayed put. They had followed me out into the vault.

"The Path of Princes is the way of the song," one of the heads said imperiously. "You know the one."

And then she began to sing and the chorus was taken up by the others.

Fly with the Arrow,
Dance with the Sword,
Give Your Heart to the Barrow,
Die with your Lord

AND IF EVER YOU be broken,
And gasp on the ground,
Hold up your fine token,
And join with the sound.

SING FOR YOUR SOVEREIGN,
Bow to your Dream,
Make Haste for the Fallen,
Rise in Esteem.

AND IF EVER YOU be broken
And gasp on the ground,
The word may be spoken,
And salvation found.

"I've done half those things already," I said boldly.

"I rather expect he'll want you to do the rest of them then," the head said, sounding bored. "Not that we care, really. Many have tried to follow the Path of Princes, but who can follow it utterly?"

I cleared my throat, trying to ignore the murmurs behind me.

"I will need you to lead me as my guide," I told Death.

"YOU WISH TO FOLLOW WHERE DEATH HAS TROD?"

"You don't!" Grosbeak shrieked. "You don't. There will be no bargain with the mortal, Death. I am sworn by blood and honor to defend her and I will not fail in my charge. Stop this insanity, Mad Princess!"

"I must make this bargain," I said firmly. "I must, if I am to succeed. So that is the bargain then? I will give willingly a piece of my flesh and follow the Path of Princes but if you betray me, then I will receive back my flesh and be restored to my life. And for your part in this, you will guide me on the Path of Princes and bring me to the gates of your kingdom and to the place where the first sovereign's rib was snatched and if I fail to do all you have required, then you may leave me with no obligation remaining and you shall have my companions with me, for there will be no way out for any of us then."

Grosbeak cursed quietly and the murmurs behind me were unhappy.

Death seemed to pause a very long time before he finally said, "A BARGAIN IS STRUCK."

"What parts have you already fulfilled?" Tigraine whispered over my shoulder and I saw that behind her, the wives followed in a line, each carrying the heads of the fallen, though Margaretta looked like she might have been struck by a cruel Wittenbrand and then frozen that way, her face was so horrified. And Givanna was pale as Death himself.

"I have flown with the Arrow out of the tower of Ayyadgaard," I said and I made it a declaration for Death to hear, too. "I have Danced with the Sword at the Petal Ball. I gave my heart to the barrow when I declared my love to my dying husband and it is to my own heart that I choose to journey, for there my Bluebeard must be. And now, with the backstab of Ki'e'rien, I am now dying with my Lord. I called for Mercy to Wittentree, when I was broken and gasping on the ground, and she gave it to me. And salvation was found in the sound of my token when the sea set my husband to war against the Sword."

"Yes!" Grosbeak agreed. "Yes, she has!" And then he paused. "But I thought that poem was for the finding of the Bramble King."

"It's the Path of Princes. Of course it gives us a king," one of the heads whispered noisily.

"But she's not the Bramble King," Grosbeak hissed back.

"Maybe it has more than one use," the head whispered.

They were making me even more nervous. Or maybe it was the poison running through my blood that made me feel like my heart was rushing too quickly.

Death bowed to me, an acknowledgment of what had transpired, but I heard Tigraine whispering behind me and I had to bite my own lip to remain calm as she listed what I had yet to accomplish.

"*Sing for your Sovereign,*

Bow to your Dream,
Make Haste for the Fallen,
Rise in Esteem."

"But how do you do any of that?" she asked in a whisper. I really did think she was on my side. She sounded invested and ambitious, as if it were she and not me who must accomplish this.

Death, on the other hand, was smiling, his pointed teeth forming a terrifying grimace. He was too pale. Even his lips and the rims of his eyes were white as snow. He held out his hand and brandished a dagger in the other and I knew exactly what he wanted. A pound of my flesh.

"No! Not more of her!" Grosbeak said in horror.

"Now you're on my side?" I asked wryly.

"I have always been on my own side, but you won't be able to carry me if he takes another hand," Grosbeak said miserably.

"He won't have to." I made my voice hard as flint. "Your flesh," I said, and I reached into my pocket, produced my living hand, and offered it to Death.

It made an independent rude gesture, but Death took it and bit it. I did not know how to feel about the blood that stained his teeth when he smiled again, or how he snapped his fingers and the hand rose up and floated near his shoulder, following him as he turned and began to ride toward the locked door.

And I heard my husband's voice in my mind again, *For as long as earth has bones and death has teeth, that long will I be husband to you.*

This time, when I shivered, it was with more than just

fear. There was a preciousness mixed in that shiver that I dared not deny.

"Time to march, little army," I said over my shoulder to the other wives, and then I turned the golden key in the air, closed the empty Room of Wives, and followed Death through the now open door of Coppertomb's home.

No doors, it seemed, were barred to Death.

CHAPTER FOURTEEN

IF I HAD BEEN ASKED TO GUESS AT WHAT Coppertomb's home would look like, I could not have guessed it would look like this. The vault, odd as it might be, was in keeping with the rest of his home. We passed in silence up a long, drafty, stone staircase made entirely of hard stone lines and copper edges. Ever-dancing lamps burned in bronze cages, giving off the feeling that something alive was inside each one and suffering.

Margaretta began to cry somewhere midway up the steps and I heard Corinnian trying to comfort her with kind shushes as the heads they carried mocked them.

"You're not made for the Wittenhame, softlings."

"We most certainly are not," Corinnian agreed with a scold in her tone. "No one should be made for this terrible world."

"Your leader is. Her who married your husband last. She has a skeletal hand, a head for bargains, and a will of iron," the head replied loftily and I marveled that it would describe me in such glowing terms when I was no Wittenbrand.

"Yes, she's awful. Just like her horrific husband," one of the other brides said and there was something hot in her voice that I could not identify. "I'd like to know how she tripped him into her bed. None of my tricks worked on him." Ohhhh. That's who she was. The one with the scandalous journal. "But she might get us out of here and besides Ki'e'iren already poisoned her, so she won't be around for long."

"She's going to just die when she hears what you're saying," Grosbeak said, trying to twist on his chain so he could look back at them. "Aren't you Izolda? Just die. How ever will you live under the criticism of such fine specimens of womanhood?"

"I suppose I won't," I said dryly. "One of my sister brides has made sure of that."

"Well, you can hardly expect me to fault her for taking proper advantage of a situation," he agreed. "I only wish Sparrow had lived to see it happen. She always appreciated a good twist."

"Mmm," I agreed.

We'd reached the top of the long staircase now and found ourselves in the open air in a strange depression in the earth. A long, shallow-grade spiral began at the edge of the depression and slowly looped round and around to the top. The edge of the step was hammered with copper so that the line was easy to see, and all along the wall edge of the ramp were the figures of Wittenbrand carved of stone in a never-ending line. They had tortured, twisted features, each face a different mask of pain, and they carried stone torches. Their bodies were completely identical and I had the most terrible feeling that they might come alive at any moment and attack us.

"That was his home?" I asked, confused. "But where does he sleep?"

"Perhaps on one of the shelves," Grosbeak snickered. "Did you see one labeled 'Coppertomb?'"

I shook my head. "How does he eat?"

"He eats the hopes and dreams of others."

"Where does he keep his fine-pressed clothing? He always dresses to the most exacting standards. I expected libraries and luxuries."

"And no doubt they are here — somewhere — but also knowing Coppertomb, you likely have to find the right horrible face among these five hundred and twist its ear, and then go extinguish the right torch, and then the whole depression rises a thousand spans into the air, and a palace is beneath, and we discover we only ever saw the attic, or some such," Grosbeak said, unconcerned. "He's hardly the type to keep his secrets where anyone can see them. There are likely a thousand mortal slaves in there keeping his copper-thread clothing pressed and clean, and the finest morsels on his plates, but he'd never reveal that to you. He's a Wittenbrand of secrets deep as the earth."

As we reached the bottom of the spiral of earth, Death turned and beckoned me, and then his horse stepped as though it was planning to walk up into the sky rather than up the spiral. One hoof rose, and then a second, and by the time a third flickering hoof stepped up, I realized it was —

indeed — stepping into the sky and as we followed, our feet stepped up with him.

The murmurs of fear behind me made my spine stiffen as if their fear granted me courage. I would not be weak when my husband needed strength. I would not let nerves or fright from heights make me whimper or waver. I was grateful for these others for existing, for they showed me how I could be and how I must not allow myself to be.

I followed resolutely, my hand firm on my husband's, my skeletal hand still gripping Grosbeak's pole. And if I paid more mind to my husband's sleepy breath upon my neck than I should, who could blame me? These moments of stolen intimacy were all I had, and though I was willing to die for him, I was not willing any longer to live without him.

"You're sweating, Izolda," Grosbeak said, a little flicker of excitement in his eyes. "It may well be that I shall watch you die with my own eyes."

"You seem unnaturally excited by the prospect," I said grimly and he was not wrong. My heart was acting strangely, fluttering in ways it should not, and the world felt too hot.

"You were privileged to be there for *my* death. It is only fair that I be there for yours. I am already preparing your funeral speech."

"How prudent," I murmured. "You'd hate to be caught without a quip."

We marched up into the sky and for the first time, I saw the Wittenhame spread out below and around me. It was night — I thought — though the moon hung very low and was the rich, deep color of clotting blood. What stars remained, clung to the lower edges of the dome of the sky, as if it had begun to crumble from the center and had worked its way lower and lower until soon it would reach the land. Beneath me, the trees and lakes, hills and streams, and estates all trembled slightly. Not as an earthquake might shake the ground, but as if it were breathing just as in the tale Bluebeard had told me.

It did not breathe evenly. The breath that moved it fluttered and snatched in an untidy rhythm and it took a few moments before I realized it was perfectly in time with the uneven rhythm gusting onto my neck.

I swallowed. Coincidence? Or was my husband the Bramble King and was the Bramble King also the sovereign who held the whole world within his chest?

I felt — small — beside the incomprehensible feeling of that. Small, and grateful to be small. What would it be like to bear all the world upon your chest? What would it be like to be more than a man, to have nothing to shelter you, but to be the shelter for others, to have nothing to succor you, but to be the dwindling succor for both your friends and your enemies?

The very thought was too great for me. It made my mouth dry and my brow glisten.

Or, perhaps, that was the poison working through me.

Death marched us lower, and as the ground rose to meet us, all I saw in every direction were Wittenbrand dressed for battle. I blinked, remembering the Hounds, and sure enough, there were twelve heads laid out around a throne on a dais, but though the crowd was battered and bloody, they were forming up once more into ranks and types. This time, I saw more types of Wittenbrand than ever before — winged and with hooves, with vines tangled around eyes, and thorns jutting from faces, with strange bark-like skin and hollow luminescent eyes. The very smallest rode on great creatures made of twisted moss or grasses, and the mermaids and men clung awkwardly to shambling sea-weed beasts.

"Underfolk," Grosbeak muttered dismissively.

The underfolk — if that was truly what they were — carried little cages with strange flickering or swimming or screeching creatures. They had upon their backs great packs of bright silk or tough leather, stuffed and crammed full and tight. And hanging from belts were trinkets and tools I could not name. Strung in antlers or around necks or over shambling backs, were chains of gold and diamonds, of rubies and drilled coins, of tiny glowing butterfly wings — thousands of them — or dried hearts, or locks of hair tagged and cataloged.

This did not look like a hunt so much as ... what?

This reminded me of something.

I gasped. It reminded me of the countryside of Ayyadmoore when war raged there and her citizens poured out of towns and cities and flowed out to the countryside in puddles of refugees that became streams, and streams that became rivers, until every last one who did not fight was fleeing on foot with whatever they could carry.

I looked back up at the moon ... or was it the sun? I could no longer tell. And that explained it.

They were fleeing the Wittenhame. Even I could see that. But where would they go and why were so many of them bristling with weapons and armor?

Death led us down and into the midst of the loud

horde and as we arrived, those around us stilled, eyes widening as they beheld Death walking in their midst and then widening again as they saw the procession behind him.

I glanced over my shoulder to see my fellow brides following with eyes set forward, faces pale and drawn, the severed heads they'd brought with them were raised like talismans. I liked to think that even the Wittenbrand would find them a terrifying marvel.

Silence swelled out from us as we slowly passed through the ranks and many of those we passed made signs of warding with their hands. How strange. To be the horror to horrors. To be the monstrosity to monstrosities.

I found I rather liked it, dying though I was. I had never hoped to be well-esteemed, but I had hoped for a little respect. I was being granted it to a degree I could not have imagined.

"I thought I caged you, little mouse," I heard Coppertomb say, and the ground under us rolled with a growl that I also heard faintly in my ear as my husband's breath gusted over my neck.

"Your cages have holes in them, Coppertomb," I said calmly, locating him and then watching as he moved to pace beside us. He was on a horse. A regular, mortal horse. No big cat for him or strange shambling seaweed creature. Not even a skeletal horse from a different plane like Death's. Coppertomb's horse was plain and brown and smelled of the stable. A nice palfrey I would have chosen for myself were I to take a pleasure ride. She snorted at me, a big horsey snort, and my heart lurched a little with a wave of sadness. I was dying. I would not give my affections and time to a horse again. I thought of Prince, long dead now, and how I loved to feed and care for him. This mortal horse with the big earthy eyes was warm and strong as he had been, and I missed the feeling of warm mortal flesh and warm mortal dreams pale as they were.

Coppertomb laughed — a sound that was more fit for the barrow than the dance floor when it came from him. "It will matter not. This world passes away and without the key I took from you, you will pass with it."

"And how will I meet you at your Coronation Ball if this world is passing?" I asked him coolly.

He leaned down so I could see the twist of cruelty in his mouth and smell the strange spice of him — a little too like the poison I'd been nicked with — and his black eyes narrowed.

This close to him, my breath felt like it was sucked from my body. My mortal mind could never get over the intense beauty of the Wittenbrand. Even Coppertomb, cold and lifeless as both copper and the tomb, was utterly gorgeous, his copper-tinged short curls clinging around his slightly-pointed ears, his cheeks sunken which only made his bone structure more noticeable, his rich, full lips pouty even when he wanted to be firm and his eyes glittering black gems you could lose yourself in while he laughed pitilessly and ensured you never found yourself again.

He was still wearing that single glove on his left hand. Was it only my own wishes that made me think he was disguising a missing finger?

"There is a very rich world waiting for us to pluck it like a berry," he said in a voice smooth as wine. "And pluck it we shall. We wait only for Bluffroll's army before we breach the gap and pour over your poor mortal cousins, seize their homes, snatch their children to serve us, their fields to feed us, their estates to house us, and their courts to entertain us. I could go to Salamoore, of course, where I am honored as a saint, but seeing you here getting so friendly with my home, makes me think I'd be happier learning the intimacies of yours. If you manage to escape this world, you might find me in the Court of Pensmoore ... or Rouranmoore? I feel that place in you, too. How odd. From whatever court I choose, I shall reign over all the mortal world, and if I find any living that share your blood, I will use them as human footstools — and no, that is not figurative. Scurry, scurry, little mouse."

And then he was back up in the saddle and wheeling his palfrey with a haunting laugh.

"You should be honored," Grosbeak said with a tone of delight. "The Bramble King himself has chosen you as an enemy. You could rise no higher than that!"

"I rather think I could," I mused. "I think I could be married to the Bramble King."

"You'd have a time of it," Grosbeak said, watching Coppertomb go. "If I had to guess I'd say he plays as cruelly in the bedroom as he does anywhere else."

"I'm not referring to Lord Coppertomb. I speak, rather, of the true Bramble King."

"Keep telling yourself that. Poison, they say, makes one lose all sense as it kills. I don't know if that's a blessing or curse for you Mad Princess."

"You'll have to advise me on how to navigate insanity, Grosbeak. You've been doing it so barely-adequately ever since I met you."

"I'll take that as a compliment, however it was meant," he said with a toss of his head. "Lords of Viscera," he cursed suddenly. "Are some of your fellow wives crying? How disgusting."

I glanced over my shoulder to see that most of the brides of Bluebeard were, indeed, silently crying. And why would they not be? I had just walked them through a living nightmare, and it was only the beginning. The exceptions were Tigraine and Ki'e'iren. One of whom was watching the Wittenbrand as if she might leap and rip their throats out at any moment, and the other was watching them with what looked somewhat like jealousy. My husband, it seemed, was no judge of women, or he would not have selected such a viper to put in his vault.

I would have to be very careful with these two at my back.

"Well, if you aren't motivated to succeed yet, there's no helping you," Grosbeak said happily. "Your husband is nearly gone for all eternity, you will soon follow him, and Coppertomb will dance on the backs of your kin. Improbable as any win for you would be, it is your only chance now."

"And yours," I said acidly. "As you have been grafted to my fate."

"It's a sacrifice indeed. Never say I have not been for you the most excellent of friends."

"You have certainly not been the most excellent of friends," I replied.

"Oh, well, it doesn't count if you add unnecessary words. That's just deflecting from the meaning, which proves you cannot resist my charms."

"Tell yourself whatever you must to get through the next two days," I said. "And then you will see, one way or the other."

"So much hope," he said, smacking his lips. "I like this look on you, Izolda. It's nearly brilliant. Do keep it up."

CHAPTER FIFTEEN

We found Bluffroll's army along the way as we followed Death through the heaving, disintegrating world that had once charmed me utterly with its vibrant intensity.

"Who are they?" Margaretta had whispered in a tiny voice.

The head she was holding replied sagely. I thought it was Vireo's voice. "The army of Lord Bluffroll. Called, it would seem, to savage the mortal lands on the behalf of the Bramble King and to take for him the many kingdoms and sew their bodies and lives into the earth that they might feed a new age. Would I were not dead, that I might march with them."

"You would go with them? To destroy the mortal world?" Margaretta always sounded like life had surprised her all over again. "He said he was going to make the royalty of Pensmoore his footstools!"

"All the more reason to go. Have you ever had a prince as a footstool?"

"I ... no, of course not!"

Vireo laughed. "You might like it. Even the blushing bride Izolda found she had a taste for our ways once she was inducted into them."

"By *your* treachery," Grosbeak reminded him.

"And I'm not even asking to be repaid," Vireo agreed. "I'm a generous soul."

I did not speak, merely followed our silent guide through the ranks of the army of Bluffroll. They looked like him — green of skin, with pronounced lower incisors that peeked up through their lips. Male or female, all were built large and broad, their hands so full of weapons and their backs strapped so generously with them, that they resembled porcupines. Their armor was fanciful, created with swirls of metal, turtle shells, some kind of scales the size of saucers, and webs of woven gold and something black that looked like lace made of spiderweb, but could have been broken dreams for all I knew.

Some rode on lizards like the men who had surrounded Coppertomb before the hunt for the Hounds of Heaven and all watched us pass through their midst in owlish silence.

"What was the point of the Hounds of Heaven?" I asked Grosbeak. "They showed up, raging and howling and shredding, and then were quickly dispatched. Why come at all?"

"They're a portent. Portents must portend. They can't very well remain sleeping comfortably beside the fires of hell when there are warnings of the end of the world to give, now can they?" he snapped.

"I thought they were Hounds of Heaven, not hell."

"Heaven, hell, what difference is it to me?"

"As a dead man who may eventually find himself in one or the other, I would have thought a great deal."

"And there you would be wrong, for I have bet all the coins of my soul on this one afterlife with you and I will not taste either of the other options. Don't die, or you'll make me regret that."

"I'm dying already," I said grimly. My racing heart stuttered as if to emphasize that. The tips of my fingers were numb.

"For now. Unless you can talk your way out of it."

"You can't talk your way out of death by poison or it wouldn't be used so reliably on unwanted government ministers."

"Ha. That's a good one. For someone with no sense of humor, you occasionally surprise me."

"For someone without a shred of human decency, you surprise me, too."

"Do not go soft on me. We don't have time for that."

We found Bluffroll in the center of his bustling army, gathered around a table of maps with what had to be his generals. Death stopped in front of him, staring down his long pale nose.

Bluffroll's eyes narrowed and then darted quickly down to me and procession of wives carrying heads and then back up to Death.

"You've no business here. Either of you," he said calmly.

"Can I bargain with you not to go where Coppertomb leads you?" I asked, hopeful. I would spare my people if I could. And Wittentree's. I'd promised protection for them as well.

"You cannot. Be glad to keep your head after such an insolent offer."

But there was an edge to his tone that I caught. I lifted my chin.

"Ah, so you know then that you are the last living competitor who worked against Coppertomb for the throne of the Bramble King," I said calmly. "I saw his assassins eat Wittentree alive."

His jaw clenched but he merely spat. "I'm no Wittentree, mortal, and you will not sway me with pretty warnings. I care not whether you live or die. Be off with you."

I stared at him a long time and then I said, "I march to Death's lands with only these mortal brides and our severed heads as my army. And together we will draw back the heart of the Bramble King and restore the Wittenhame, while you and your shining army go down to unleash your frustrations on innocent mortals. I have learned just now that even those of powerful build and stern jaw may have craven bones and runny coward hearts."

Bluffroll reached into his collar and pulled out a long double-looped string on which hundreds of thick ragged pieces of dried meat had been strung.

"Tongues," he said with a lift of his brow. "I collect them. Yours is of poor size, but the sizzle of it might make it worth a place with the others."

There was a general murmur of laughter and a few glances at me, but the generals looked away quickly every time they caught a glimpse of Bluebeard's face resting against my shoulder. While I'd been distracted a hummingbird had built a thimble nest just over his ear and its prospective mate was trying to lure it with a side-to-side dance.

Interesting. So much life seemed to center around this man they all named dead.

But perhaps they understood in their bones that he was their true sovereign. For they dared not cross him even when they thought him dead.

I swallowed.

"I can smell the Neverseed on you." Bluffroll leaned back in his small camp chair. "You'll be dead before we see another moon. And what are you doing here? Are you trying to walk the Path of Princes by following Death as you do? A dying wife with a dead husband clutched to her like her last remaining coin? Good luck with that."

"I am, in fact, doing just that," I said coolly, "and you would do well to help me with it, for when I succeed, you will be as much under his rule as any other Wittenbrand."

Bluffroll's eyes flicked from Death's pale face to mine and back and he leaned back, drawing a dagger and pretending to trim his nails, but I saw by his quick glances up at me that something about my actions worried him.

"There's no way a mortal can walk the Path of Princes."

"What if I don't walk it for myself? What if I walk it to fill full the Arrow's purpose?"

Bluffroll swallowed. "I have no quarrel with the Arrow."

"And yet you plan to sack his mortal lands."

Bluffroll jammed the dagger into the table before him.

"They were only his for one play of the Game. He won't be attached to them."

"And yet, he seems to be attached," I said. "What do you think will happen if I bring him back from the barrow?"

Bluffroll looked up at the crumbling sky and then casually caught a goblet that moved across the table as the earth shook again. He glared balefully at me.

"Tell me this, little buzzing bee. Can death be turned back? Can a broken glass be mended? Can time restore my beauty?"

"You had beauty?" I asked, doubtful.

His laugh was a harsh bark. "Some things cannot be reversed."

"And if they can be?"

He considered and then pointed at Bluebeard. "Then my head will decorate his wall."

"It doesn't have to end so," I warned.

"Doesn't it? It feels to me as if the great tides of fate have been tugging on us all, surging us where they will, and if we are shattered on the rocks then that is as the song has been written and who can deny it?"

"As keeper of the singing flowers," Grosbeak whispered to me so loudly that everyone could hear. "Bluffroll is a master of song and music. His flowers can bring the rain or turn back the tides."

Bluffroll inclined his head in acknowledgment of Grosbeak and said, "But they cannot turn back this tide. It will roll in and bear away the last of the Wittenhame." He looked around him sadly. "And I shall do all that I can so that my kin will not suffer unduly in the depravations of the pale, miserable, mortal world."

"This does not have to be," I warned. "Bargain with me. Do not harm my lands and I will carve a place for you."

He smiled sadly. "While your audacity enchants me, and your misplaced confidence tastes of citrus and cinnamon, I will not make a bad bargain with you. I have tongues to collect, souls to harvest, and slaves to take from the ranks of the mortals. No hand will turn back what I unleash."

"Then we are enemies," I said grimly.

"I cherish the knowledge of it."

To my surprise, his answer felt more like a prospective lover accepting a memento from his beloved than a dark Wittenbrand Lord making an enemy, but that was the Wittenhame.

"The game is over, Izolda Savataz, wife of the Arrow. The chips have been wagered and lost. I've already lost my favorite two stallions, Coppertomb came to collect three of my consorts — and they were not the three I wanted to wager — and my foot aches from where my toe was taken from me. That's a loss, mortal woman."

For the first time, I could see the bitterness. But I shook my head as I followed Death from the war camp of Bluffroll, and I wondered if the mortal world would wash out the violence and delights inherent in the Wittenbrand, or if the Wittenbrand would set the mortal world ablaze. I rather thought both would be true and in the mingling, they would bring out the very worst of each other and dull the best parts.

"I can see you thinking," Grosbeak murmured. "And if your thoughts are that you and your Bluebeard have been each other's undoing, then you are correct. Star-crossed lovers doomed to die tragically. The woman who trips up the great man and brings him down. The pair that marry for love only for their children to savage the world and squander their inheritance. These occur again and again in stories for a reason, and you are playing out the piece before us like a pantomime."

I gave him a long look.

He laughed. "Don't stop. The entertainment is worth the price of admission."

"Your life?" I asked incredulously.

"I think you'll have to stop teasing me about that," he said smugly. "Now that you are dying, too."

CHAPTER SIXTEEN

It was only once we finally left the army behind that we found the place beyond them — Bluffroll's Estate — and it was to there that Death led us.

"Whistleroll," Grosbeak said. "It's what he calls this place."

"I need to stop finding myself astonished by what I find in this land," I breathed.

"It would certainly save time."

Bluffroll — thick, heavy, gauche Bluffroll — lived in an estate made of spun glass and crystal. Its towers rose fancifully high, twisting in sugar-spun shapes that seemed impossible and utterly impractical and yet stole my heart away the moment I saw them. His home was spun of the palest lavender and rose glass as if formed by the clouds at sunrise. It was whimsy and fairy dust and the exuberant joy of spring meeting the delicate wings of a butterfly.

"Whistleroll," I gasped. "It seems nothing like him."

"Well, how would you know? You've barely spoken to the man. We are not how we look on the outside. I would have thought a plain thing like you would realize that by now."

"Consider me chastened," I said coolly, but I felt the other brides behind me relaxing as we drew closer to this estate. It had none of the terror of the other Wittenbrand homes. No hideous dead things gathered or displayed, merely very impressive gardens, all flowering at once though there was no possible way that all these flowers could be in season at one time. Lilacs bloomed alongside roses, which in turn bloomed alongside peonies and orchids. Perhaps these enchanted flowers were permanently in bloom. Their scent was heavy in the air, making each breath thick with perfume, though the ground continued to heave and roll and the flowers with it, timed to my husband's lurching breath.

When we were close to the tower, Bluebeard doubled over, sliding down my back, and coughed a terrible, wracking cough, and as he coughed the ground shook so intensely that one of the glass-spun towers of Whistleroll came crashing down in shattering pieces, tinkling and sparkling as it collapsed.

I drew in a shuddering breath. I was losing him.

I do not know why you must walk, my husband, but I fear you need help now, I told him in his mind and he certainly did. He could not seem to rise from his bent state and his breath was so shallow I could barely hear it, his eyes shut tight. With a sigh, I crouched down, set Grosbeak on the ground, and then maneuvered Bluebeard onto my back, slinging one hand under him to hold him in place even as I lifted Grosbeak's lantern pole again. I was bowed under Bluebeard, even though he was not heavy. Somehow, he seemed to make me bend beneath the figurative weight of all he was. But it was no matter. I would never let him go. Not now, not ever.

Another tower fell as he coughed, clinging to me as if to salvation. I felt his bare chest heaving and clenching against the bare skin of my back.

He was getting worse. Time was running out. We had to make haste.

I blinked back hot tears that insisted on welling up even when I willed them away.

I turned to look back over my shoulder but the other brides were silent, though their lips formed words and their eyes were wide. Margaretta pawed at her face, panic rising in her eyes and then Corinnian turned to run, only stopped by Tigraine who seized her arm and forced her forward again with a grim expression.

"What manner of madness is this?" I gasped, glad I could hear myself, but none of the heads responded, not even Grosbeak who clearly wanted to, as he opened his mouth only to shut it with a furious grimace. We'd been silenced to each other, caught in our own bubbles of stillness.

Had all sound been removed from the Wittenhame then? But no, glass crunched under my feet, and as we moved around the broken castle to a new part of the garden, the perfect flowers became still, frozen, in time though they whistled and sang as the wind moved through them.

There were small signs hanging over the paths of the garden as it split off into five different paths between the whistling flowers, and to my surprise, Death stopped there and would not go on, crossing his arms over his chest and raising an eyebrow at me.

"This is for me to decide?" I asked, a little huffily.

But there would be no help — not from Death and not from any of my advisors. Annoyed, I read the signs.

Paradise
Hades
Pennstein
Angstbite
Desire

What a truly eclectic list of names. And now I must choose a path with nothing more than the names to go by. I hummed, trying to think, and to my surprise, the glass flowers all shifted with a tinkle and turned toward me. How odd.

Death shifted, and then suddenly faded away.

No! No. No. No. My breath was caught in my throat.

I turned in a circle in a panic, but he was truly gone. There was no one here with me except the silent parade behind me, and my beloved on my back.

Bluebeard? I asked in my mind, reaching for him mind to mind, heart to heart. *Arrow?*

He was not there. I carried nothing but a fading corpse. I was on my own.

I needed to choose a path and walk down it and I needed to hurry before I lost Bluebeard entirely.

Should I follow the path marked Desire? Perhaps I would find what I wished at the end of it. Or perhaps I should journey to paradise to find my lost love. Or hades. Pennstein sounded like my home and tempted me, but it was the name of the fifth path that arrested me.

Angstbite. The name of the marriage sword Bluebeard had given to me.

He'd known all along that we would come to this path, hadn't he?

He had warned me to be silent, he had chosen me as his sixteenth bride and married me in the Wittenbrand way. One of the first things he'd given me was the golden key that opened the door to his other wives — to the blood of nations I would need to rescue him once he had given himself to the grave. Did it not make sense that his very first gift to me — my marriage sword — might contain another clue?

With my heart in my throat, I set down that path, only to have the glass flowers shuffle, tinkling as they moved, and barring my way. I turned, but they had sealed the way behind our parade, too. The big eyes of the wives and advisors met mine, glaring at me, demanding that I do better. And Grosbeak stared at me with slitted eyes like I should know the solution.

Sing for your Sovereign.

Perhaps, I should try that.

I began to sing, a song about a horse and rider but as I sang, the glass flowers pressed in, the nearest one slicing my arm and leaving a red weal. Grosbeak's cheekbone was slashed, too, and when I glanced behind me my fellow brides were also marked.

Wrong song, perhaps?

But what song should I sing?

So I tried singing the song I had grown to loathe, and as the first words fell from my lips,

"Fly with the arrow," the flowers backed up, and by the

second line they cleared a path for us. I was already walking by the third line as — to my shock — the flowers joined in. Tinkling, whistling, shivering, they sang with us in pristine voices as if glass itself had been given a voice. The singing flowers were joined by my followers, and by the fourth line, I heard the entire chorus joining in the song.

Grosbeak's clearly reluctant baritone was quickly joined by Vireo's unwilling tenor and Margaretta's soprano and then we were singing in a powerful chorus and the flowers relented, allowing us through. I could tell by the expressions of those around me that the song was pulled unwillingly from them, as unwanted as the forced silence had been, but there was nothing I could do to ease their frustration. We had to walk this path. All of it.

It felt as though we traveled for hours. My legs grew so tired that I often tripped. My throat was dry and parched and my tongue stumbled over the repeated words, etched so deeply now into my brain that nothing would ever remove them.

And as we walked, the ground beneath us began to melt, to drip like wax from a spent candle, but our feet trod on air as the ground dripped away, leaving nothing but the black broken heavens above with their dissipated sun, and the black void of the missing ground below.

My stomach dropped with them and my hope melted. Surely, I had finally gone insane, lost to this world. Lost to all sanity. I tried to look over my shoulder at my beloved, tried to find solace in his presence but his head lolled lifelessly on my shoulder and his mouth had fallen open, his eyes no longer closed but open in a slit and what I saw of them was insensate. Within me, my heart sunk.

I'd taken too long. I had not made enough haste. My husband's breath no longer shook the earth. He no longer breathed at all.

And then all light winked out and I was left in utter darkness.

CHAPTER SEVENTEEN

When I blinked again, there was Death. And there was light once more from a huge white moon.

We were no longer in the Wittenhame. Or at least, I did not think we were. The smells around me were faint and tepid, the wind did not bite as strongly nor the moon shine as brightly as it did in the Wittenhame, and when I shifted, a coney shot out from the underbrush, running in a wild back-and-forth pattern, and then disappearing into rustling bushes. Since none of them came alive and ate him, or turned to glass and sang, this could only be the mortal world.

I swallowed, nervous now because time passed differently here. That single rabbit escape might have used up the last of my time. And as if to agree with that, my body lurched, the numbness I'd felt in my fingers now running up my arms and legs so that using them felt strange and foreign, as if they were not my limbs at all. My mouth tasted of acid and my belly flared with pain.

I was — most certainly — dying.

It was hard not to panic at the thought. For some reason, memories of my mother and father swam to the surface of my mind as I fought down blind fear. My mother murmuring over me when I was ill as a child. My father's strong hands steadying me on a horse. Had they been fearful when they had died? Had they wondered about me then? Their missing child, snatched away forever by a stranger from another world?

"I hate the stench of mortals," Grosbeak said in a voice that seemed to creak from overuse. "Lead on, Master Death. I have no desire to linger here."

But Death was in no hurry, his eyes flicked from face to face as if counting us, and then he raised a hand.

"Ask your friends to form a circle with us," the head wearing the coronet said gruffly. Her voice also sounded worn and rough.

"Form a circle," I said, and yes, my own voice cut out on some words and burred on others. How long had we sung, that we struggled now to speak?

My fellow brides stumbled into the circle, eyes dull, feet heavy, hands barely holding onto their burdens as they hung at their sides. We were a ghastly group worthy of nightmares. Likely, Death would reap a great harvest if we stumbled into a mortal community. Folk would die of shock and horror at the mere sight of my band of tattered brides and me— at their head — the worst horror of all.

I looked down at my living hand, only to see it was black from the poison and that blackness trailed right up my arm to my elbow. I sucked in a wavering breath and glanced backward at my husband. He hadn't so much as flinched in hours. He was cold as night to the touch. Was I already too late?

"Thirty makes a quorum," Vireo said sourly. "He planned this well. Are you calling on us for our vote, Death?"

At the nod of our spectral guide, Vireo laughed long and bitter.

"He picked *us*?" the mermaid asked, her gaze flicking toward my dead husband.

His ruined hands were blackened, too, I realized. Again, I clung to thoughts of my parents to keep panic at bay. My mother sewing in her chair and laughing over a story she was telling my father as he ate his breakfast.

"What manner of madman picks his enemies to judge in the end?" Vireo asked acidly.

Grosbeak's laugh was familiar. I knew this one. It was the one he used when someone was in deep trouble and he was entertained by their possible grim death.

It was the coronet head that spoke, her voice firm and even. "One who must have been very certain that he would win so thoroughly that even his enemies must judge it so."

They were silent then for a long beat and I was so tired, so very tired. I wanted to sit down and sleep on the ground right here. I did not dare. I was running out of time.

"What's going on?" I murmured to Grosbeak.

He turned his horrific grin toward me, his missing ear seeming to stand out in the mortal moonlight.

"Death has called on a quorum of dead Wittenbrand to vote. And you are lucky enough to have thirty dead Wittenbrand with you — the exact number needed for a vote — minus me, of course."

"Why not you?"

"You can't have friends vote. Conflict of interest."

"Does that make you my friend?" I asked tiredly, but when he wouldn't answer I asked instead, "A vote for what?"

"Can we please get on with it? I grow weary," Vireo interrupted.

Death lifted his other hand as if in response.

"A Vote of Esteem," Grosbeak whispered to me. "If a Quorum passes a Vote of Esteem a mortal may be elevated to the ranks of the Wittenbrand. But this never happens. The requirements are too high. You must have succeeded at an impossible task and be respected for it — oh, and you will die very painfully if you fail to achieve the esteem of the quorum."

"Me?"

"Well, who else would they be voting on."

I looked around at the heads. They were all winking — one eye closed. I did not know what that meant.

"I am already dying," I said grimly. "Indeed, I am nearly dead."

I could no longer feel anything beneath my waist and my heart was slowing, each ka-thump a little more erratic than the last.

Death lowered his arms, his hair and beard dancing in a wind I did not feel.

"Well, I suppose you'll die as an honorary Wittenbrand," Grosbeak said, and was that *pride* in his voice? "The Quorum has spoken. You have risen in Esteem."

"Wait ..." I said as Death began to walk again and I

hurried to keep up. "Esteem. Have I walked the Path of Princes?"

"It would seem so," Grosbeak said, his voice breathless in awe. "To have achieved this, Izolda — even if you die in the next few moments — is an honor that will trail behind you beyond death."

"How lovely," I said dryly. "I can parade about with it when it no longer matters a single whit."

"Don't be crass," the head with the coronet said in a clipped voice. "You've been granted an honor you do not deserve by those unhappy to give it. Take your honor and show some respect."

I swallowed, for she was right. Was this why he collected these heads? Had he foreseen the need for this, too?

Death strode ahead, his hair flowing behind him as if it were weightless, the tiny skulls on his robe clinking. Shadowless, he floated over the mortal grass, but he did not walk up the great hillside ... he walked into it. And with my heart in my throat, I followed, stepping with my eyes closed and my breath held.

"Open your eyes, Izolda," Grosbeak whispered and when I opened them, there was only blackness for a moment and a creeping sensation like I was feeling the earth and worms and roots pressing against my skin, even though I had no feeling anymore in most of my limbs, and then I stepped through, and I was within the hill.

Or maybe I was not.

What I saw on the other side chilled me. There was no moon or sun, though I could see just fine. There was no color. And when I looked to Death, he was white and pale and the brightest thing to be seen. He flicked a hand and then my own living hand in his possession snapped its fingers, and he was gone.

I gasped, startled.

"Where did he go?" I breathed as the brides filled up the space behind me and I looked at what lay before.

"Your bargain is complete," Grosbeak reminded me. "He brought you into the barrow — into his land where the dead are stored until the end of the age."

I stepped lightly down the path, barely willing to take any step at all.

I had to pick my way with great care to stay on the path, for it was overrun and tangled, as were the rolling hills in every direction. What it was tangled with horrified me to such a degree that I dare not step off the path at all.

The ground, in every direction, was littered with the dead, displayed as though they had been brought directly here from their resting place. They were not laid out respectfully, but rather one still figure was curled over herself as if she had retched to death, and another, half tangled over her, had been disemboweled. His foot was thrown haphazardly over a man missing a head and a hand, and he, in turn, was draped over a woman still clutching the snake wrapped 'round her bulging throat.

They were all white as Death as if their passing had leeched all color from them. White and cold and frozen in agony.

I retched, gagged, and retched again, trying with great difficulty to follow the path without stepping on limbs or hands or — sweet mother of mine — someone's eye.

"No one said the path into the barrow would be an easy one," Grosbeak growled.

My lips were numb — whether from horror or the poison killing me — and my voice came out high-pitched with despair, "But how will I find him here?"

Jumbled as the dead were, their state was made worse by infestation. Colorless beetles scuttled between them, cobwebs draped wildly from one to another, as if some mad spider were intent on working a last masterpiece. Pale squirrels chittered and scrambled round and round one leg, and then a face, and then darted into a nest somewhere below. I did not wish to notice the flies, but it could not be helped for the milky infestation of them crawled on everything as if an army seeking to devour the world.

"Death set us on this path," I said and my words were clouded by the thickness of my numb lips. "It must take us there."

Behind me, the other brides murmured or sobbed or hiccuped their distress and in their hands, their heads advised them likewise.

"Stay on the path."

"Do not tarry."

I swallowed and forced myself onward through the hills, which I now realized were uneven heaps of the dead.

"No wonder you prefer an afterlife with me, Grosbeak." My voice was faint even to my own ears. "I half wonder that all of the Wittenbrand do not beg for such a half-life if it would avoid this place."

Grosbeak laughed boorishly. "This is not the afterlife, Izolda. This is merely a waiting place. When the age turns, all these will pass on to what is to come."

"I thought the age turned with the change of the Bramble King and the end of the Game," I said and it was getting hard to speak. My lips and tongue were too numb. I stumbled, not even feeling when my ankle rolled under me until I looked down and saw myself standing on ankle rather than foot.

"It lends credence to your blind hope that you carry the Bramble King with you even now, does it not?" Grosbeak said lightly. "But I fear you will never make it. Already you stumble and trip. And you have all this vast land to search." He made a happy sound in the back of his throat. "Ahh, but I love a fated hero. Doomed to die. Destined to perish. Yet forging forward, writing her own damnation with every decision she makes."

His eyelids fluttered with pleasure.

"Curse you, Grosbeak," I murmured. "Curse you for not helping. Were you not son and husband once to those who will be found somewhere in these heaps?"

He spat, and think if there were colors remaining, he might have been flushed. "How do you know about my wife?"

"It was spoken at your funeral."

"What else was said at that funeral?"

"It was mentioned that you were tall."

"Ha!"

"And that you had a herd of Clay Horses."

He grew silent at that, and we were nearly to the next hill when he finally said, "I had forgotten that. Lend me your fingers, Izolda."

"I do not care what you're planning," I said coldly. "I

absolutely won't agree to *that*. Is it not enough that I have bargained away my hand again and again?"

He scoffed. "No, it's not. Here at the very end, the least you can do is lend me what I ask for. I said *lend* not *give*."

"In exchange for what?"

"You're too Wittenbrand for your own good, fool of an Arrow's wife! In exchange for my help, is that not good enough? Lend me your fingers and I will lend you my help."

Behind me, I heard murmurs of interest from the heads. But I cared not. I had but hours left, if that. Why not take any gift offered me?

"Fine. What do I do with my fingers?"

"Set the pole down. No, not there! Gross! Fine. Yes, that's fine. Right there. Lovely belly you have here, lady corpse, don't mind me while I rest on it a moment. And now, Izolda, if you'll put your first two fingers in my mouth."

"You accused me once of not having the imagination to dream of what you might do with only a head. If this is a part of it, then I beg you not to go on."

He rolled his eyes. "Before you had too little imagination, now you have too much? Just shove them in there and spread them wide."

Grimacing, I acquiesced.

To my surprise, Grosbeak pursed his lips around them and made a piercing whistle that seemed to echo far over the heaps of the dead, reverberating back and back until it returned to us. He repeated his whistle twice and then around my fingers he spoke.

"Et em oww ow."

I took my fingers out.

"I fear that has turned my stomach," he said, looking miserable.

"*Your* stomach?" I repeated as I wiped my sticky fingers on my dress. "You must be joking. I am the one with dead-person spit on me, and I should note it smells of rotted fish."

"You're one to talk. If I had an hourglass I could only watch a fraction of the sand run before I'd have to give a speech at *your* funeral." He paused to pull a long face. "She was wishy-washy as dishwater, never grabbing hold entirely of her opportunities, but never having the good grace to be properly stamped into the ground either, and those who most hoped she would be a practical heroine were most devastated to discover she was human after all."

"If I die in the next few minutes," I said as I heaved myself back up and then his pole with me. "Then I shall die cursing your name for all the gods and angels to hear."

"I would have it no other way."

But before he was finished speaking there was a tremble in the ground like the sound of many horses and as my eyes were still widening, they came thundering over the dead toward us, kicking up cobwebs and insects as they went.

"You had these at your disposal all along?" I asked him in wonder.

"I forgot until you mentioned it, but I think I wouldn't mind a last ride before I die."

"I'm sure you wouldn't," I said absently, watching as the great mass of bodies thundered toward us.

There were maybe fifty of them — great stamping, hearty warhorses. Had I been buying for the king, I would have bought every single one, even knowing they were made of clay and not able to breed more. They held their necks in perfectly formed curves, ears back properly, hooves and limbs still bearing marks as if they'd been cut from premium clay by a fettling knife.

They moved like real horses, not cracking or jointed like a man-made thing, but their expressions changed not one whit, and their eyes were lifeless. With all the furor of a cavalry exhibition, they ran up and wheeled in front of us, stomping and neighing and throwing back heads as they approached.

"These will take us to your husband," Grosbeak said.

"A kingly gift," I said a little breathlessly.

"Not a gift," he objected. "Not at all. You've done tasks for everyone else. You'll do one now for me."

"Don't you see I am running out of time?" I asked, almost wailing in my despair.

"Which is why you must do this first," he insisted, his horrible face screwing up in hostility. "Or else you'll be dead and it will be too late."

"Fine then," I practically spat through my numb lips. "What will it be? Shall I give my other hand? A foot? My still beating heart?"

"Take my pole and strike the nearest horse in the neck."

"You're mad!" I said, furious now, but I did exactly as he said, hitting the horse across the neck as hard as I could. I did not want to look at its feet for fear of what those clay hooves might have done to the bodies sleeping in eternal rest, so I did not see what size of shards the head and neck broke into, but they shattered like struck clay pots, leaving only a jagged stump where once had been a head and neck.

The other horses did not care.

"I think it's best you mount," I told the other brides. "If I survive his task, there will be little time to ride."

"Follow me!" Tigraine said jubilantly as if her whole life had been leading up to the moment she could ride a clay horse over a heap of corpses.

I turned to Grosbeak. "You have what you wished."

"That is only the first part. Now. Jam my pole into the hole in the neck."

Easy enough. In fact, if I were to be rid of him, I may even glory in it.

"Now," he said, his voice still commanding as he swung from the empty neck of the horse. "Use one of the shards to dig the ground. Dig up earth and clay and form for me around this pole, a body."

"Out of dirt?" I asked, incredulous. "It will be terribly inferior."

"Do it, or see no help from me."

And this was the Grosbeak I remembered from life. The furious, demanding Wittenbrand who wanted me dead. And it was he who I was now bargaining with, so with the last of my energy, I dug until my nails were torn and my palms bloody from the edges of the sharp shards. And I built him a patchy thick body, slumping dirt shoulders, and long, lumpy arms.

"There," I spat. "You have your ugly dirt body and I hope it falls to dust in your face."

"Place my head upon it," he demanded and with relish, I jammed his dead, fly-infested head into the earth. "And now, lady of dust, bound to Pensmoore, Ayyadmoore, and

Rouranmoore, give me one last thing. A drop of your blood, if you please."

Easy enough. My hand was already cut and bleeding, though it was a moment before I realized it was red in this black and white world.

"On my cheek, Izolda. Draw your husband's sign. Give me one last taste of his power."

"He's too worn to work magic," I said.

"And yet there's enough power still in his sign alone to grant me this one last wish."

"Just be done with it," I muttered, and I traced the bloody tear trail down Grosbeak's cheek and when I was done I looked down, and then up again, as he rose above me. I gasped, for there was no longer a clay horse and a rotting head before me.

There was, instead, a living, breathing centaur.

"Stop staring and mount up — or if you're too dainty and lily-livered, then just die already. I have no need of you to carry me anymore, and no desire to wait around here," Grosbeak said with a very horsey toss of his head, and to my surprise, I found myself scrambling numbly up his back.

CHAPTER EIGHTEEN

When you are the master of a herd of Clay Horses you can direct them anywhere you wish and Grosbeak did without so much as consulting me.

"Fan out, you fools," he said to the other wives and advisors, grinning like a mad man. "And stop gaping like fresh-caught fish. Your jealousy at my elevation could not be more apparent."

For my part, I did not care that he was going to lead the search. Relieved of his lantern pole, I slid Bluebeard around my body so I could cup him to my chest. He was limp and did not move easily, his head lolling, the wound in his side bleeding so sluggishly, that it seemed not to bleed at all.

I let my tears fall freely over him, washing his face as I moved it to my shoulder and held the back of his head as though he were an infant.

I couldn't feel the hands touching him or even my own cheek when I pressed it against the top of his head.

Here in the depths of the grave, I did not know if it were day or night, and I did not dare trigger the curse still lingering, as if I still hoped there could be salvation even now, so I did not speak aloud to him as I would have liked.

I spoke, instead, inside my mind.

My husband, Lord Arrow of the Riverbarrow, I do not know to what destination you fly now. I fear that — king though you are of all lands both Wittenbrand and mortal — you are a dying king, a passing sovereign. I wish only to say one last word to you. It has been an honor to travel these past seven years as your wife. I would not bargain them away. Not even to spare myself such pain as I have eaten and such bitterness as I have drunk. You chose well when you chose me. For I have married you both in heart and soul and I cling to you yet, here in the lands beyond death.

And as we rode, I spoke back to him our vows, one final time.

As long as rivers run and moon shines, as long as the earth has bones and death has claws, as long as the ages pass and fail – that long shall I be wife to you.

Little had I known the bones of the earth would be his and that Death would sink long claws into both of us.

Flesh of my flesh and bone of my bone you will be.

I would give my own healthy flesh to make him whole — had I any left to give.

Spirit of my spirit, heart of my own heart, fall what may, we shall be one. Your days shall be mine and your happiness my own.

We would spend the last of my days together, shared. Halved. And yet somehow multiplied.

My body I dedicate to none other. The bounty of my wealth is yours. If ever it be otherwise, may I waste away with sickness and may famine eat my strength, and may my enemies overtake me, and siphon from me the blood of my life.

Well. They could get in line.

We were riding up a hill — an actual hill still strewn with the dead in their age-long sleep, not a heap of the dead.

"You will owe me a thousand thanks, Izolda Savataz," Grosbeak said happily. "For look what I have found? Is that not your husband, the Bramble King, seated on his broken throne and dead as dead can be?"

I leaned forward, twisting to see around his clay torso, and gasped for he was right.

At the top of the great tor — so massive in size that it dwarfed all else — was a throne made of a Wittenbrand rib cage half submerged in the earth. The broken-ended ribs grasped upward toward the sky —fifteen of them and one broken off to a bare stump. Fat chains wrapped in brambles ran from each rib to snake around a pale throne and trussed there on the throne — bound so thoroughly that limbs and torso were lost in the jumble of chain on chain — was the form of my husband, his dead eyes open but unseeing, one dead hand reaching out, grasping, the broken rib crown displayed on his head.

I looked back and forth for a moment from the dead man on the throne to the dead man in my arms and back. Two halves of a whole? Two representations of the same man? Or something more? I did not know. This land of Death bent the mind to uncertainty.

I was leaping from Grosbeak's back before he'd stopped moving.

"Sixteen locks with sixteen keys," I murmured,

following each chain back to the rib and seeing on each rib a complicated lock-like shape where a depression had been carved into the ivory rib — a depression just like a seat. "I wonder if it matters how they are arranged."

"I rather think so," Grosbeak said, seeming as absorbed in the puzzle as I was. "He always did seem very precise in how he placed them on those pedestals."

At the base of each rib were two impressions like shelves. For the heads, I realized.

But who could be such a seer as to have seen this coming in every detail? Who could have planned it all and yet trusted that one mortal woman would have gathered up these all ...

"The blood of nations," I murmured. "All the prophecies come true here."

"All what prophecies come true?" Tigraine asked from just behind my shoulder. "Margaretta would you stop petting him? He was a bodiless head just a moment ago!"

"I bid you pay mind to your own business," Grosbeak snarled.

I did not turn. Whatever nonsense he was getting up to was no longer of concern to me. Before me, lay the last puzzle.

Here lay Wittentree's riddle and I said it aloud as my eyes ran over the ribs. They couldn't be *the* ribs, and yet here they were. Perhaps they were a representation of them, just as I carried one husband while watching the other chained there, just as the world could not fit entirely in the chest of my dead husband, Bramble King though he may be.

"What once stood in a line, now missing a brother.

What was taken for wealth and refined by another. What holds life or death in the gap left behind. What holds endless damnation in similar kind."

There was still something missing. I chewed my lip for I could not tell what it was.

"I suppose we find our places in the seats?" Tigraine asked, looking at me.

"Wait." The word ripped from my tense lips. "Wait only a moment."

"Ah, she's remembered then," Grosbeak said, amused. "It won't be endless damnation, then?"

The blood. The blood of nations.

"Each of you come to me here," I said, a little breathlessly. And with a kiss of apology, I slid my husband's dagger from his belt and as each stepped forward I made his mark down her cheek. Bold Tigraine — first of course, right through to trembling Corinnian and Margaretta who was stealing little flirtatious glances at centaur Grosbeak — I wanted to roll my eyes at that, but this was no time for distractions. Last of all, Ki'e'iren received her mark.

"I hope you do not damn us still, last bride," she breathed. "You have little time to get this right."

"Thanks to you," I returned coldly.

"Give me neither your disdain nor your condemnation. They are not my just dessert. Suffering belongs to us in a way that it belongs to none other, for it was given to us as a gift from our husband. I merely deepened yours."

"I do not think he will see it that way."

"Will he see anything again? That, last wife, is the question."

I cleared my throat. I was having trouble bringing

breath into my lungs, my eyes watering constantly now that blinking was an effort.

"Find your places, but do not yet sit," I said thickly and my sister brides arranged themselves as they had been in the Room of Wives, setting the heads they carried in the nooks made for them.

I carried my dead husband across the last steps, heart in my throat, as I brought body to spirit and I had not the time to so much as kiss him goodbye because the moment my fumbling foot connected with the pale frozen man on the throne, the one in my arms vanished and the one wrapped in deep chains flushed with color — color, in this world of white on white on white.

With a dry throat and a thick tongue I spoke the last riddle.

"Sixteen locks with sixteen keys. From grip of death, the vict'ry seize, Silent brides for silent lord, unravel back time's cord. Bought by blood and claimed in oath, only one holds bitter troth. One hand living, one hand dead, she finds the place where hope has fled. Now let her choose what comes last. Freedom now or holding fast."

I swallowed and spoke again.

"I think you sit. And when you do, I think it is goodbye." I looked up and met their eyes one by one. "Either we have succeeded or we are doomed."

"You most certainly are. Your lips are black," Ki'e'iren pointed out."

"Yes, thank you," I said repressively, but then my expression softened as I looked around at them. "Thank you all for achieving this with me."

My throat was thick. I didn't know what else to say.

But it did not matter. Ki'e'iren sat before anyone could say anything and the moment her seat touched the carved slot in the rib, she vanished in a flash along with the heads at her feet, and the chain that led from her to Bluebeard's throne uncurled from around him, and snaked back into the rib on which she had sat.

"I was glad to fight with you," Tigraine said boldly.

And then, as if by mutual accord, the others sat, almost as one, and they vanished in sudden flashes of light and gasps of surprise and little scream from Margaretta and as they sat all the chains retracted with them leaving me alone holding the hand of a dead man — unchained now, but still lifeless.

"Oh," I said aloud. "I thought that would work."

"I think it did work," Grosbeak said, stomping a horsey foot. His tone was hushed. "It's just not complete."

All the chains were gone. My beautiful Arrow lay there still, motionless, color in a world of monochrome, but he spoke neither in my mind nor with his newly freed lips, merely lay there, still sleeping in the barrow, still waiting to be brought back somehow.

I looked to the last rib where it was broken and cracked. And when I looked back at my Bluebeard, Death was there, standing beside him.

"Nrrgh, that one gives me the creeps," Grosbeak said, taking a step forward and flicking his clay tail with a pottery clatter. He sounded delighted as he spoke in hushed wonder. "But of course he's back. Because it's decision time, isn't it Izolda? And how excellent is this? We stand now, on the brink of a new age, the old age and old world are melting away, but who will reign in this new era and how? A mortal will decide. A mortal who we have mocked and made merry with. A mortal stolen from her home. I could never have predicted this."

"What do you mean that it's for me to decide?" I asked, barely managing the words through my thick lips. "I see no choice here. There is simply a broken rib and a king who will not wake."

"The riddle was clear," Grosbeak objected. "Freedom now or holding fast. It speaks to a decision."

"But what is the decision?" I wailed. "Why can these things never be clear? How am I supposed to decide blindly?"

"Where did the brides go?" He pushed.

"Bluebeard said they were meant to go back to their own times and places."

He smiled beatifically, "Then I think that is the freedom you could choose, is it not, Lord Death?"

We both looked to the pasty specter and he inclined his head in assent.

"Or?" I asked.

"Or you die, I think," Grosbeak said. "You hold fast to his damn fool dream and you die here with him just like the song we sing and I think that might be enough magic to repair the rib. If greed broke it, then perhaps generosity will repair it."

"Perhaps? You think?" I asked, aghast.

"Well, I'm hardly the expert here," Grosbeak huffed. "And I don't think Death is going to give us any answers."

The world was spinning. I had to reach out and catch myself on Bluebeard's dead shoulder to keep from collapsing.

"I mean it makes sense with what we know, right?" Grosbeak said. "We know it's a choice of freedom or stubborness. We know the rib needs repairing with something that counters greed. We know that to finish fulfilling the song you'll have to die. So it doesn't seem too big a leap to say that you have about four or five more breaths to pick one or the other and get on with it."

"But I'll be dead!" I objected. "I won't know how the story ends!"

"Well," Grosbeak considered, sounding cold when he finally spoke, "I will, and that's who counts."

I couldn't make out his face anymore. My vision had darkened too much. But I could easily guess he was grinning. He'd wanted to see me die, after all.

"Hop to it, mortal girl. You're just about dead already. Go sit on the seat in the base of that rib and unlock your chance to go back in time and marry that fat horse lord and have his babies and never know a moment of any of this ... or lie down on your dead husband's chest and die with him. But choose quickly, because I see your spirit becoming unmoored, your body quaking. You have not a day left to spare, I fear."

His voice felt like it was coming from far away. But it had never been a choice, had it? Not really. Not from the moment I realized that I loved Bluebeard and that I'd do anything for him.

"Not an hour," Grosbeak's voice came from a long way off.

Well. I was a sensible girl. I could accept death just like everything else. I reached blindly to his side, wounded here just as it was everywhere else, dipped my finger in his blood, and smeared it over my cheek in his sign. The line I drew was nothing more than a smear, my hands no longer worked.

I could only hope it had just enough magic left in it.

"Not a minute."

I tried to lean forward to kiss him one last time, dead though he was, but I had not the control to manage it. I fell, sprawling over his chest, my heartbeat erratic, my breath caught somewhere in my throat.

My lungs would not expand. My poor eyes would not close. I was staring at the blue of my husband's beard.

Blue.

Not white anymore but blue.

"Not a heartbeat."

I felt the last thump and tried to reach for it, but it shivered away.

"Well, I suppose that's her choice then, don't you think? I would have bet on her choosing the other way but I've never been a good judge of what fool mortals might do with their mayfly lives. At least I got to see the end. I do hate it when a story is unfinished."

A white hand pressed over my mouth, my nose, my eyes as Death stole what was left of me, unwilling though I was to leave those I loved. Just as once, long ago, my husband had plucked me from a mortal life, so I was plucked now from a Wittenbrand one. Just one more head of grain harvested by the Great Reaper.

CHAPTER NINETEEN

The Wittentales my mother told were always full of strange magic and stranger magicians and those poor mortals found within those stories were never more than leaves swept by on a current or coins tossed into a fountain. Happy fortunes and living forever after were never theirs to claim. Only the Wittenbrand ever found justice for ills done to them or reward for their great deeds. For mortals, the best that could be hoped for was to be entirely forgotten.

I woke, forgotten.

My eyes blinked awake slowly. A small bird sang in the tree, a simple trill followed by the response — and I did not know why that made my heart ache cruelly, or why I clutched at my chest and shook with silent sobs. I felt as though I had lost something I never knew.

I rose from my bed in my father's house in Northpeak and I readied myself for a day in my third best dress — noting that the stitching needed repair around one of the cuffs. I dressed my hair and then I sat on the edge of my bed and I listened to the bird again.

My room with its simple wood furniture and carved lintel felt odd. Unreal. As if I had not been living within it for the past nineteen years.

I couldn't quite remember ...

I shook my head. I did not know what I had forgotten, only that it was terribly important. The broken memory ripped at me and tore at the seeming tranquility of the morning, as if my heart could hear a trumpet blast of warning that bypassed my ears entirely.

I made my way down to the Common Room, nodding idly to Raisa, one of the maids who I'd known all my life. Seeing her face made me feel surprise, but why would I be surprised when surely I had seen her only yesterday?

In the Common Room, my father spoke quietly but firmly with my brother Rolgrin over something regarding the rotation of grazing land on northern fields. My mother sat with them but her gaze was dreamy as she looked out the window. I paused in the doorway of the room, uncertain why I was blinking back tears or why the mere sight of them caught at my chest.

Svetgin ran in, bumping into me on the way past. It broke the moment. I stepped forward and moved to kiss my mother's brow.

"Izolda, my sweet girl," she said with a smile.

And the pain in my chest moved me around the table to kiss my father's brow, too. He paused long enough to look up at me with a warm smile before returning to his instruction. My brothers, I did not kiss, though Svetgin winked at me from across the table and Rolgrin caught my eye and offered a tight smile of greeting. And then I was breakfasting with my family, smiling as the wash of their conversation calmed me, and the busy mundane seized both time and energy.

I spent my morning moving from task to task, feeling as though I were in a dream, not understanding why the sight of Svetgin red-cheeked and laughing brought to mind a sudden image of a broken, drunken man looking toward me with desperate eyes, or why, in that moment, I felt the urge to glance down at my hand and be sure it had flesh on it.

When I helped Rolgrin bring up supplies of parchment and ink to our father's business chambers, I did not know why, when I saw him, I also saw a grave young man only a little older than me asking me about a battle.

When my father gave me one of his rare embraces, I did not know why it felt as though the dead had come back to life.

And when — every time she passed me in a hall, or brought me a little bit of something to eat or drink — my mother kissed the top of my head or cheek or drew me into a cuddle, it made me shiver and cling back twice as tightly.

"My affectionate girl," she whispered into my hair. "My sweet outdoor girl."

And in the afternoon, when I rode my horse out to the pasture, and down to where the North River was swollen with spring melt, I did not know why I was drawn to the banks of the turbulent water and found myself leaving my mare to graze while I stood and watched the vigor and froth of the mighty river sweeping down from the mountains and swelling powerfully.

I studied the furor of the water and felt the spray upon my face and I felt a loss I could not name and a hollowness in my belly to which I could put no place. I only knew that it gutted me, hollowing me inside so that I could hardly breathe, my thoughts flying frantically within the confines of my mind like trapped birds.

I stared a long time at the raging waters before I returned home for the work and routine of the evening.

I returned to the river the following day to see it had swelled further.

And the following day.

And the next.

Until my father joked that at least we would have warning if there was to be a flood, and my brother joked that perhaps I had grown bored of my maidenhood and wished to be swept down the river to whichever hold had an empty spot for a mistress and was willing to take a half-drowned noblewoman to heart.

And still, I went, as the rains came, pounding the earth and filling the river, until great trees were swept down with blocks of ice and the last of the melt broke out the dams of both ice and beavers, and brought the flotsam of winter down our hills, intent on sweeping out upon the plains.

It was there, as I rode along the deafening banks of the swollen North River, that I saw the water foam up and rise — but rather than crashing back immediately it continued to build and shift until it was a great pawing stallion garlanded in river weeds. Branches that had been washing down the way formed the tail and nose and great legs and water, moving, foaming, rippling water filling out its form and spirit.

The great beast's neigh was loud enough to be heard even over the crash of the river and to my surprise, it looked directly at me and I felt something release deep in my heart — something that somehow had been waiting for this, though I knew not how.

Something that was one with this great river kelpie, that soared with excitement even when the creature snarled and showed not horse teeth at all but massive gleaming spike teeth that were as apt to rip a creature apart as any predator's.

This — this impossible legend, this fanciful nightmare — was what I wanted more than my own life.

I leapt from my horse's back. He tore the turf up in clumps as he fled to safety, but I — I stood before the creature head flung back and arms spread wide, letting the freezing droplets of the river wash over me.

I did not understand myself at all. Never in my memory had I done such a wild, untamed thing. I had not reason to seek death, no motivation to fling myself upon the cold, uncaring draught.

Practicality demanded that I return home to my loving family. Good sense bid me now at least turn and walk away.

And I threw it all away as I offered myself to the rearing, pawing water horse, my heart pounding to nearly bursting in my chest and my lungs heaving with what seemed to be sobs though I couldn't remember why I was crying and I couldn't understand why — when I saw this impossible equine creature formed of magic and likely a good dose of insanity — I felt a surge of loss so great it nearly overwhelmed me.

And then a fractured memory I could not place split

into my head as if someone had stabbed a knife into my mind.

A man with a white face and a tongue like a slug leaning over me.

My vision growing narrow and dim.

And behind that man, another rising like a king from his throne, his bare chest crisscrossed with silver scars, his pale skin growing suddenly flushed with life, his short beard blue — blue like a horse or a dog. A crown was on his head, and as he stood he plucked a rib from the crown, and thrust it into the neck of the pale white man with the beard that flowed like milk over rocks. And the creature choked, spitting blood white and thick as cream, and my vision spun and faded as the man called my name, stepping forward with a look very like panic in his rolling eyes.

"Izolda! Izolda!"

And now, this strange horse made of river and shadow rose up over me and rolled his eyes in just the same way and something in me called back to him.

I gasped, and though I did not know how I knew the name or why it made my whole body tremble, the urge to utter it was overwhelming.

"Riverbarrow."

With water flinging in every direction, the kelpie spun in a sudden circle and as it spun, it grew smaller and smaller, and then, drenched from head to toe, the water washing right down him in sheets, a man stood where the kelpie had been.

I gasped at his beauty for surely no mortal man could look so lovely and so yet terrible. His short hair and beard shed water, darkening his already black hair and the strange blue-grey of his shadowed beard. Despite its color, his face was not old. Nor was it young, though I felt like I once knew it younger than this.

It had an agelessness that could have been thirty or fifty or perhaps five hundred and fifty and his eyes were the eyes of cats. The pupils dilated as they came to rest on me and a thrill of fear shot through me for he was naked to the waist and had the build and crisscrossed scars of a feared warrior.

On his head, the twisted crown looked more like thorns than anything else. In one hand — marked with a ragged hole in the center — he held a rib stained with white and in his side where that rib might have originated was a thick knot of scar and a hole that seemed to be punched straight through his body though it was neither bloody nor gory.

He did not remain still. He was striding from the river to me and to my shock he threw himself to the ground on one bent knee and lowered his glorious head.

"Oh," I gasped, stepping backward in my surprise, "Sir, your obeisance is not warranted."

"Speak to my riddle," he said and the face he turned up to me was twisted as if he mocked me, and yet his eyes shone with a joy so bright and full, that it hurt to watch it. I had to look down and bite my lip for a moment lest I be swept into any machinations he might please, for I was powerless beneath both its intensity and the desire to share in so great a joy. "Speak to my riddle, you stern visage, you startling aspect. Who has walked the Path of Princes? Who has broken the curse of the rib and set free the blood of nations? Who has flown with the Arrow? Who has danced with the Sword? Whose heart lay bleeding in the barrow?

Who now — tell me who, if you can — has died side by side with her Lord in the realms of death, beneath his feet and his dominion."

I swallowed, my mouth and throat suddenly dry. "I know not, my lord."

The twist in his mouth turned to a smile of devastating triumph and he stood, suddenly, catching my hands in his and leaning down in a predatory way that made my mind scream at me to run, and yet, I held fast and met his eyes with my own.

"One last choice remains to you, Izolda, and I must ask this with you blind to the consequences. You have behind you all you once held dear. Mother, father, brothers. Hale and happy they are. Soon enough, your father will ride to the capital and find for you a good husband who breeds lovely horses fit for a king. And soon enough you will give to him fat babies and live out your life in simple satisfaction."

"If you say so, my Lord," I said, blushing at his implications. His hands on mine felt so familiar. As if they were a matching set, a team of horses trained in draft together.

"Or," he let the word hang in the air and I waited, swallowing. "Or, you can leave all that behind and come with me ... one more time." He leaned his forehead against mine in a way far too familiar for a stranger and there was a vulnerability in his eyes and a softness to his voice as he lowered it to speak this last part. "And this time, fire of my eyes, I will not bid you descend with me into the grasp of hell but instead help me birth, into the fresh age, a paradise beyond anything you've ever tasted."

I swallowed. I did not know this man. Or at least, I did not think so.

And then he lifted my hands, bringing the knuckles up to where his lips grazed them lightly as he spoke, his warm breath sending little tingles down my hands and wrists and arms where gooseflesh broke out. My heart began to race again, not out of fear or danger but out of a sudden, overwhelming attraction. I swallowed and without meaning to, I stepped forward, causing his lips to curl slightly as he kissed my knuckles and whispered.

"Heart of my own heart, fall what may. I have bought you by oath and blood, and made you my wife, and though you have been snatched from me by the currents of time and washed up upon this shore, my vows to you remain. Stay here if you wish. Enjoy the life you might have had apart from me. Or come with me now, and take your rightful place at my side, be queen to me and cherished wife, until the sands of time have all run out, and the earth has rotted away like spoiled fruit, and Death himself is so long past that the stars have burned to dust."

"I don't know what any of that means," I said, and yet ... I could feel some tug to him. It was something that went beyond my attraction to this man I'd never met, beyond how he spoke to me with such intimacy. It was something deeper and longer though I could not have guessed what it might be.

He bit his lip looking up at the sky, releasing my hands with a frustrated huff, and then turned to me with his fists on his hips. I worked very hard to keep my eyes up on his face. He cut a very fine figure. Enough to make a girl of nineteen blush.

"Speak to my riddle, wife," he said.

"Wife?"

He made a brushing gesture as if his title for me did not matter. "What is better? To lose without knowing, or find you have gained too much?"

"To lose without knowing," I said firmly. "If I must lose, then I shall bear it, but woe to the man who takes from me without expecting me to notice."

"Ha!" He laughed as if I'd solved a problem and the fretful worry on his face evaporated as he snapped his fingers.

I blinked.

And my memory was restored.

With a gasp, I turned to him and for the first time since the joust, he watched me with uncertainty in his eyes as if he did not know whether I might attack or smile.

"Do you remember, my wife?" he asked hesitantly.

"Everything," I whispered and I did not wait a moment more to claim what was mine. I strode forward with certainty, took his bearded face between my hands, and fed myself on his kisses, taking them with softness at first, and then with greater hunger and deeper intensity. Did he truly think I would choose a life without him given the chance? Did he truly think it was a mercy to leave me bereft of him?

I pulled back from him long enough to gasp, "And I choose you every time, Lord Riverbarrow."

His laugh of triumph made my heart sing.

CHAPTER TWENTY

"I hope you do not set much store in titles, wife," Bluebeard said, pausing to lean once more and take for himself a swift, almost violent, kiss. "For that one is passing away now that I have claimed by blood and life the title of the Bramble King."

As if on cue, his crown rustled and the thorns rearranged themselves even though the material it was made from appeared to be black metal.

"And the curse must be broken, for I can hear your voice speaking to me, though it is day," I said, but though I felt shy to be speaking directly to him, I refused to pull back and break out of our embrace. The long days of him pressed to my back as a corpse had returned to my memory, and I was in awe now of how whole he felt — how warm and alive. I skimmed my palm down his bare chest, reveled in his shudder, and slid a finger — feather-light — around the edge of the wound in his side. His wet clothing soaked right through mine and I cradled my head to his chest and listened for his voice in my mind.

"No hold may bar me now," he said aloud and it echoed in my mind, too. "And though you can hear my voice alight upon your ear, still my heart speaks to you as the moon calls to the sea. I will not give up this rare intimacy, even though we have leave to share in others."

"Share in others?" I asked breathlessly.

I pulled back just enough to see his eyes and his quirking half-smile, and before I could demand that he confirm my suspicions, he had caught my jaw between finger and thumb, angled my face as he pleased, and pressed his lips to mine, sliding his tongue between them to open them, as if it were key to my lock.

"Do you choose to come away with me then, my one true wife?" He asked a little breathlessly when he seemed to be sated for a time. His hand was tangled up in my hair as he spoke and he seemed fascinated with it even though I was rolling my eyes. How did he always manage to untangle my braid any time I wasn't watching?

"I do," I agreed. "And will you tell me, then, how this curse was broken?"

He scooped me up before I could finish speaking and held me to his dripping chest, pausing only long enough to bite his lip as if concentrating, and then lean in to nip my cheek so that it bled his sign.

"The first Bramble King, when his rib was stolen —"

"I thought it was the creator's rib who was stolen," I objected, still a little breathless from the sting of his bite. My husband always made my head swirl with his unpredictability. Who would have expected a bite rather than a kiss? Not me.

"One and the same," he assured me with a boyish grin.

"He placed a curse on men and Wittenbrand alike to fall upon them in the last age — this age — unless one soul dared step up to take on the challenge of the curse. If he did, then the curse would fall on only him, but that man must risk all for the rest."

"And you risked it," I said, certain I was right.

"And I won," he says, his grin turning cat-like.

"So you did. And will you answer all my questions now?"

"If I have a mind to do so."

"Will you answer at least a few, my husband?"

"Say that name again, Izolda Savataz, Mad Princess of Pensmoore, wife of the Arrow, Lady Riverbarrow, darling Queen of our current Bramble King."

And I did not need to guess what he wanted, not when I could turn my lips to the curve of his neck and whisper it so my lips brushed his skin and let me taste his shiver.

"Husband," I whispered.

"My true wife," he agreed burying his face into my hair, and then he spun quickly away.

Before I could catch my breath, he was once again the stomping water horse of the river, and he surged forward under me, catching me up upon his back. My fists sank into seaweed and froth when I tried to hold on, but he did not drop me as he reared, came down hard, and ducked into the river, dragging me behind him like an anchor.

It seemed I did not need to breathe as I usually did, or at least I did not need to breathe when I was with him, for I sank beneath the water and into the cold, clammy depths and I smelled the fecundity of creeks in spring, and the sharp tang of a river in autumn, the scalding ice of winter flows and the warm caress of summer streams, all at once without having to take a breath of air.

And when we emerged, it was not the mortal world we emerged into, but the sparkling, flashing, dance of the river that flowed through Riverbarrow.

I gasped.

"Am I not to be made mad then?" I asked him, as I plunged my fingers deeper into his watery mane and his fluid muscles bunched beneath me and sprang us across the width of the river to where the white pavilion formed of growing stone roots spread wide in welcome.

"Not when you are with me," he spoke into my mind.

"And what of when we are apart?" I asked, probing, for though he was here with me now, I felt very uncertain.

"Forfend that it ever be so," he spoke into my mind, and then he whirled again, scattering water in every direction and leaving me too dizzy to properly see the transformation from watery horse to half-naked, dripping man, though the one carried me on his back and the other in his arms. He ducked his wet head in close to me and when the tips of our noses touched, he drew in a long breath as if he were drinking me in and he whispered, "I journeyed through the folds of time and climbed across the tides of space to find you and pluck you out of your life and home and gather you up into my arms. What manner of thing could exist that would ever tempt me to leave you, love of my love, heart of my heart? Speak a new riddle and tell me of what villain could separate we two now, or what terror could part us. Tell me of what wonder or charm might steal your heart from mine, or what cataclysm rob from my grasp what

has been bought by blood and bone, by sweat and cold death?"

"None," I gasped and his lower lip trembled for a moment before his lips parted lightly, his eyes closed, and he tilted his face just enough to catch my lips in his and drink deeply of me.

I could never tell what had bought me such fortune as to be chosen by one like this, to be swept away into madness and sanity by so precious and powerful a ... man? A king? A champion.

I did not know what to call him, but I had been given this tiny chance to leap from mortality and into his arms, and I dared not lose it, so I leapt with him not knowing where I might fall, only that it would be with the husband I had married thrice: once by law, once by vow, and once more by choice made in death.

To my startled surprise, he leaned me against the pillar of the pavilion and took his time unraveling my hair from the rest of its braid as if *that* were the main concern rather than that it was cool and he was soaking wet and mostly unclothed. But he did not look cold as he combed his fingers through my hair and then asked me, "Would you wear my token in your hair, wife of mine?"

"I'll wear whatever you like, my Bluebeard," I said, scraping his rough beard with my fingernails boldly.

"I crave your touch, wife. Do you require further invitation?"

"I rather think I do," I said shyly, watching his eyes as they warmed to me and the lines of his face as they tightened in a half-smile.

"Did I not vow to you the dedication of my body?" His

eyes darkened as he watched me and his throat bobbed with a swallow. Was he — somehow — nervous, too? Though he was Bramble King now and resurrected from death?

"But was that you as a man, or you as a king, or you as a river, or you as a kelpie?" I asked. "And how many husbands am I to have, precisely?"

"Sixteen wives were required of me, and only one of my own desire," he said, his expression turning sober, though I shivered when he said the word desire and licked his lower lip in emphasis. "Who are you to demand that you will be gifted fewer husbands?" He paused and made a sound like a growl before finishing his thought. "But know this, Izolda my wife, all of them will be me."

"And what will these husbands do with me?" I asked boldly.

His grin was like lightning. It lit his face fast and violent. "Whatever I wish."

And this time when he kissed my neck, he nipped me with his sharp teeth, and when I gasped he shifted so suddenly that his movement was more like a striking snake than a mortal man, and he caught the gasp of my lips in his, and laughed as he kissed me long and deep, trapping me against the pillar so that I must submit to his kisses and the strength of his steaming body against mine.

I was happy enough to allow him this, and to add to it my own embrace and another boldness as I ran my fingers lightly over his cheeks and up to the tips of his ears and then threaded them through his hair and when he gasped and shuddered and his eyes lit with delight, I caught his gasp and stole it back and looked him in the eye, as I demanded more kisses with urgent lips and drew him closer still into my embrace.

"I have waited long centuries for this, bound to one path and one passion," he gasped when I finally allowed him to pull free, "and like my victory in all else, I have made plans to savor this, every moment, and every touch. So we must wait a little while longer, for many things require my sovereignty to set them right once more."

"I thought you were master of time herself," I gasped, lifting a leg to catch his hip and pull him back to me.

He laughed low and deep and bit his lip, "And so I am, wife of mine, but have you ever feasted a week long and learned to pace yourself a bite at a time? One small morsel of each delicacy?"

"I fear I have not," I said wryly. "My life in the mortal world was far more frugal and your world has fed me only on pain and fear."

"Then I shall teach you," he said with a decadent smile that told of pleasures to come. "And you shall attend well and learn from me how to savor each taste to its full extent."

I swallowed as he stepped back and the sight of him from head to toe made my cheeks hot. "I'm savoring now, I think."

"But only for a moment, for I fear we both present poor rulers as we stand and must clothe ourselves more ably for what is next," he said but he did not look ashamed of his current mode of dress as he strolled out across the pavilion and up the steps to the great rooted tower that presided over the waterfall. I followed him, admiring him as he walked and climbed, and worrying that perhaps I did not have his ability to savor a meal over many days for my own thoughts were hot and sharp and fast and very unbefitting of a virgin bride — if I could be such a thing now that I was seven years and one death married.

The tower was sparsely appointed, but he led me to the uppermost room and there we found three things. A pool, his mirror — which I had thought was gone forever — and a long empty bed with a ring set on it.

Bluebeard gestured to the pool and when I balked he said, "Surely, it will be more embarrassing to walk around smelling mortal than to bathe before your husband."

I had no idea what it meant to smell mortal.

"Orderly thing of designations and logic, this must appeal to you," he said lightly but he turned his back and bowed to his mirror. "We'll be needing fitting accouterments, mirror."

I stripped out of my homespun woolen dress and underthings as quickly as I could, taking advantage of his turned back. I was already briskly bathing myself in the warm pool when he began to dress, and I could not help it, my eyes roamed over him, admiring him as he outfitted himself in strange clothing — no underthings at all, because I supposed a king required no modesty, breeches made of something that seemed to be dragonfly wings woven into cloth. They fitted like fine silk and had he been less of a man or lower than a king he would reasonably feel shame in such strange attire.

The jerkin to follow was spiderweb and both it and the more scandalous portions of his breeches were masked by a crisscross of hand-thick belts that both accentuated his lithe figure and were used to sling various swords and knives and even a pair of curved sickles, about his person. His doublet — when it was produced — was lined with rabbit and sewn all over with what appeared to me to be the moment he was placed in the land of death, his wives surrounding him in the embrace of the jutting ribs. There was even a small Grosbeak picked out as a centaur and the brooding figure of Death.

I gasped at it and could not tear my eyes from it even as he cloaked it with a short cape made entirely of living moss, and then took out a sickle no larger than my finger and set to work trimming his beard until it was nearly clean shaven, revealing only enough of itself to remind us it had been there until moments ago. I was still staring when he turned his boyish grin to me and let his eyes light at the sight of me.

So enamored was I by the light in his eyes, that I forgot what he was seeing for a full breath before sense came over me and I felt the heat of my blush fill my face and climb up my ears.

"Shall I be dressed so gorgeously?" I asked, trying desperately to stay cool under his careful scrutiny.

"I care not," he said, flicking an idle hand as if to dismiss what I might wear. "But I'll not deny that it will delight me to know you wear this flesh beneath your garment, for I missed it when you wore the flesh of another."

"The hand, especially," I said dryly, flexing my flesh hand that once was a skeleton and stepping out from the pool to see what the mirror had spat out for me.

"On the contrary, the hand is the only part that pains me to lose."

"Not the perfect hourglass figure or the heart-shaped face?"

"Indeed no, for you wear this sober visage much more fittingly. "The hand, however, set you off most magnificently, and I shall think long on whether to restore it to you."

"I rather think that should be my decision."

He made a moue that was almost a pout, but inclined his head in agreement. "If you say so. Though you did dedicate your flesh to me in our wedding vows."

"I imagined you using it differently."

That pleased him. He smiled broadly. "And you shall tell me of all these imaginings. Later."

And then he leaned against a post of the bed, clearly intent on watching me as I dressed.

I did not think it was possible for my face to grow hotter. I was wrong. But I swept up the offerings of the mirror and dressed with my chin held high, bold as you please. I had nothing to be ashamed of and I refused to hide girlishly from the only gaze I sought.

Fortunately, the ban on underthings did not seem to extend to me. I dressed in a filmy silk shift first — real silk, not spiderweb, though I supposed there was little difference — and then carefully fitted on the dress offered by the mirror.

It was backless, of course.

"I left the scars. I hope you don't mind," Bluebeard said quietly, referring to my back with a gesture. I paused.

"*You* left the scars?" I felt a little breathless at that admission.

"When I brought you back from the lands of death and

restored you to your place in time. I gave you back the hand, and healed your wounds, but I left the scars. They are dear to me. You took them for my sake."

"Very sensible," I said, though it was not at all sensible. It was sentimental and something about it made my heart burn so hard that I wanted to ignite his, too.

The dress was fitted around the bodice and boned for shape and support, with soft draping white fabric emphasizing the faint curve of my breast. No one would notice the top of the dress, for the skirt was in a style where the ivory outer skirt swept up to show a layer of filmy petticoats underneath, but from the arch of the brocade outskirt hung a great plentitude of swords and knives and daggers of sizes as long as my femur, to as small as my littlest finger hanging down from silver and gold chains decorated with thick brambles. They ought to have been ridiculously heavy and yet by dint of magic — most likely — were no heavier than brocade. And rather than the clatter they ought to produce when I moved, they made a sound like faint wind chimes and swirled gracefully with my every movement. They were woven in and out with more silver and gold chains all fitted to drape from a woven belt of brambles as wide as my hand that clasped around my waist.

"This is rather much," I said calmly as I beheld myself in the glass but I did not think my husband agreed for his face was lit with pride. He bit his bottom lip as if he were holding back a laugh or perhaps a snarl, and he moved to stand behind me and look in the mirror at the pair of us.

I shivered under his scrutiny and then barely kept myself from melting when his head tilted, and he put his hands in my hair. With a look of concentration, he teased and tangled it until it looked as wild as he was, and only when I appeared as if I were a warrior queen out of a Wittentale, did he finally stop.

"Perfect," he declared with a smile. "My fearsome bride, ready to work her will across the face of the earth."

I did not think it suited me any more than all these impractical Wittenhame creations did, but I did look more fit for a Wittenhame court than I did in my threadbare wool dress, so I smiled my agreement.

"And now," Bluebeard said, turning to the bed. "We deal with something long overdue."

CHAPTER TWENTY-ONE

I swallowed nervously but found myself blinking when he said, "Sparrow. She who was faithful until the end is owed what she was promised."

And before I could say one word or another, he picked up the ring from the bed and I realized it was a small silver one in the shape of a Sparrow.

"She bid me hide her token here and it is well I did," he told me, smiling as if sharing a secret with me, but I did not know what he meant by that until he led me out of the room and down the steps and back out to the pavilion. I was nearly out of breath when we reached the spot overlooking the river and misted by the waterfall but his boyish grin told me he was about to do something amazing. "Ready?"

I nodded, though I did not know what I was agreeing to.

And then he lifted a hand, easily, as if he was waving to a friend, and there was a ripple in the water. Then out of the river, good as new, Sparrow walked out, dripping wet.

She was perfectly whole, no longer a severed head and missing body, and the smile she gave my husband made me feel both nervous and jealous. After all, had she not died with me unable to prevent it — twice? Would she bring a complaint to my husband?

"My captain," Bluebeard said smiling with a powerful pride as he looked at her. Unlike her master, she had the decency to exit the river fully clothed. "Come to your due."

And she was smiling, too, as she walked up to the pavilion, mounted the steps, and then knelt gracefully to him as he offered her the ring.

"I give back to you both your ring and your life, dedicated in my service and lost for a time. My gratitude you had already, my respect you have now earned."

As he spoke there was a flutter of wings as songbirds came drifting in from the open sky, landing on his head and shoulders. He looked over his shoulder at me and his eyes softened.

"And I believe you have a gift for her, fire of my eyes?"

I felt my brow furrow and I tried to think, but no answer came to me. What gift would I have to offer? I looked down at myself, thinking perhaps one of the daggers might suffice.

"It is gift enough that she is no longer dogged by that grim pet of hers," Sparrow said lightly, but she was watching me, too, not yet standing as she awaited my gift.

"A name, I think, that you no longer require now that you find yourself to be wife of the Bramble King," Bluebeard prompted me and I gasped.

"Lady Riverbarrow," I realized as I said it. He was giving her his landhold, wasn't he? Bequeathing it to her as if he had died, which of course he had, but he was alive again now. Alive and king. And that meant he must relinquish direct reign over his former landhold.

I met Bluebeard's eyes and saw the sadness there, lingering, like watching your former home from decades past. And then he reached into his shirt and drew out a pendant — the very one I had worn with the pearl of Riverbarrow strung on it — and he passed it to me and I offered it to Sparrow.

She took the pendant, smiling. "I knew that in the end, you would conquer all your foes, Lord Arrow."

"Of course you did," Bluebeard said lightly. "How could I not?"

And I barely managed to hold back a laugh at how light his tone was over such a very narrow miss.

"And as you took on the risk of my defeat and with it lost your immortality, so I give now to you, your portion of the reward. Your Wittenbrand life is returned to you, and with it my lands, the lordship over Riverbarrow from the boundary of the northern snows to the southern heat, from the western mountains to the eastern sea. I offer to you the care of my people and disposition of the wealth and power inherent in this place. Along with all of it, I bequeath to you the name Arrow. Fly from my bow, Lady Arrow, and accomplish for me all the things that must be made so from beginning to end."

He took her hand and drew her up on her feet, and I couldn't help my pang of jealousy as he put his hand on her shoulder and escorted her out of the pavilion and then stepped to the edge of it, drew from the waves a great horn, and blew it soundly.

As if they had been waiting for this exact moment, his people appeared. Small and strange, great and shambling, they came. Toads in top hats and mice in waistcoats, strange branch-and-root creatures that shuffled across the ground, a massive creature large as a tower made entirely of rock and her two sons also made of rock, a pair of dragonflies, and an elderly beaver carrying a spear, and more besides, each odder and wilder and further from the mortal world than the last.

And when all had assembled, Bluebeard stood before them and simply breathed, in and out. They waited for him, seeming to hold their breaths, but with every breath he took, I realized things were changing. The creatures grew larger and stronger and brighter, backs straightening, bodies healing from wounds I had not noticed, eyes brightening. And with each breath, the world around them greened and flourished, and they began to dance and sing as more and more of them came, being healed and made whole.

This, then, was what they had been pleading for when they had come to him in his home. One who looked like a tree winked at me as he passed by and all placed a kiss — or something like a kiss — on Sparrow's hand and she looked both eager and shy all at once as they processed past her, making their obeisances. This was the healing they'd asked for. This was the restoration.

Each time I glanced around me, Riverbarrow was brighter and more flourishing, the river swelling, the trees growing before my eyes, flowers bursting from the ground and fruiting, pink returning to the cheeks of children, and a bounce coming back to their elders' steps.

It was like watching Spring come to the world in a single hour instead of months, and my heart swelled to it. I felt the warmth of pride when I looked to my husband who was fulfilling all his promises to his land and people. They would be well now. And they would be happy.

"My folk," Bluebeard said gravely when they seemed to be all assembled and they crowded around him with a familiarity I envied, some going so far as to sit on his shoulders and head, as he spoke and others crowding right up against his legs, one large furry horse with her head bumping against his shoulder so often that he had to fight to keep his balance. "You pled with me for mercy and it is yours. You asked for prosperity, I have given it to you four times over. My heart would have been very glad to go on being your lord, to lead you through this dawning age of delight and prosperity, but my place is with all of the Wittenhame now, and thus it is not to be. And so I offer to you Sparrow, once my captain of war, now my captain of peace, first a member of my Court of Fools, then a counselor of the wise when my wife sought aid, now pledged to me and to you as the Arrow, the shot of the Bramble King out into the world. May she strike true and strike down your fears and worries."

There was a cheer — a strange one as it came from the lips of both men and beasts — and it rippled out from among them and Bluebeard lifted his voice and said, "The Lady Riverbarrow has taken my place as Lord and as your river. May her reign over you be blessed and may I offer both her and you this one last gift."

And then he closed his eyes and opened his hands and flowers burst up from every plant and tree and ripened and exploded into fruit — all kinds, all at once — raspberries and strawberries, peaches and apples, watermelon, and honeydew, and grapes and I was still in awe when he whispered loudly to Sparrow.

"They all have wine at the core. Your festivities tonight will be the envy of every landhold in the Wittenhame."

And to my surprise, I realized she was crying. At first, I thought it was from gratitude, but after a heartbeat, I realized he was crying too, and he leaned over suddenly and wrapped an arm around me, gently displacing the creatures who had been resting on him, and it was only when he spoke that I understood.

"I will not see you again, my people. This place is hidden from all but those of Riverbarrow, and though my life and strength will sustain you, this is no longer solely my realm. I will visit you here only as Bramble King. But I wish for you untold blessings, for by your faithfulness and steadfastness you have remained mine through ash and dust, and so now you must reap fruit, wine, and happiness with the guardian I have set up for you."

And he nodded once to Sparrow — the new Arrow and Lady Riverbarrow — a brisk nod of finality.

And then a cloud of songbirds poured in from every direction and swept us up and away, and I was not at all surprised when my husband's arms wrapped tight around me and turned me so he could bury his face in my belly, ignoring the sharp blades of my skirt or how the chains tried to catch on his crown of brambles as he shook with what I thought might be the tearing pain of walking away from a place that had anchored him from a time before Pensmoore was even an inkling in the mind of King Pen.

I knew this feeling. I'd felt it myself, not just once, but twice when I was ripped from the family I loved into the arms of the unknown. I felt my own eyes smarting as I felt the echo of his pain through his mental voice and I leaned into it, caressing his silken hair and whispered into his ear.

"All things pass, but some things remain."

"Remain with me then, wife," he whispered into my ribs and I let my hands drift to his sides and hitch him a little closer to show that I agreed. And though I was comforting him, I had never felt so comforted myself as his lightly furred arms — stronger than tree roots and just as hard where they wrapped around me — gave me the feeling of being encircled and guarded all around. His tears, though they soaked my white dress, felt like spring rains. They brought with them the certainty that something old was passing and something new was yet to be discovered.

"I will remain with you all the days of our lives, my Bluebeard."

"Do not forget that name, fire of my eyes," he whispered and I felt the move and pull of his lips through the cloth of my dress against my sensitive ribs. "For I am quickly losing every name and title ever bequeathed to me except this last one, and though I must become the Bramble King, it pains me to lose what I once was."

"I will not forget," I whispered, leaning my head down so that I might let my own lips brush the shell of his ear, and let one of my hands fist in his hair as I held him even closer. "Though places and ages pass, never will I forget you."

CHAPTER TWENTY-TWO

I did not know how far we flew like that or where we went, not even whether it was in this time or the next but when the birds let us down it was in a forest on the edge of a river. The water of the river was pewter and the forest shades of grey and white of mist. The mortal world, then, for nowhere in the Wittenhame could be so plain.

"Will you bring restoration to every place then, husband?" I whispered as his arms unraveled from me and we found our feet. "To all who served you? Will they dance for ten years like in the story of the Wittenbrand?"

In answer, he drew out a key from around his neck — my golden key. My hand flew to my chest where it had been before.

"Shall we look at this room one last time before I close it forever?" he asked as if that would answer my question.

I did not want to go back into that room and watch my days disappear, but I nodded gravely to him.

"How was it, husband, that you triumphed over Death

in the end?" I whispered as he set the key in my hand and he leaned in to where he could speak over my shoulder as he replied.

"He could not forbid me rise. Not when I had brought all things to a close. Not when my blood had graced the Wittenbrand and bought a new age. He did indeed try to hold me down, and I fought him for what felt like an age and half an age but in the end, the Bramble King wins, and all those who set themselves up as his enemies must fall — even Death himself."

I made a sound of agreement in the back of my throat. Had I not once been his enemy? I found that I much preferred a world where Bluebeard was Bramble King, for while I could not predict all that would mean, I knew it would be a world much better than the alternative.

"Do not hesitate too long, wife," he whispered in my ear. "For our enemies still roam across this earth tearing apart its sinews and nesting in its bones. I feel them as if they were an itch within my own body. I own a violent urge to drive them out and drink their despair as a tonic."

"Don't let me slow you, then," I said dryly and I turned the key in the air and strode into the room before I'd taken in what I was seeing.

The moment I did, I froze.

The hourglass at the end of the room was shattered, not a garnet was in sight, and there was broken glass and bent, molten metal on the floor where once it had been.

"My days," I gasped.

"Gone now," my husband whispered to me and when I looked at him he licked his lips nervously, pitched his voice low, and met my gaze with a burning look in his. "I fear, true wife, that you are burdened with me for many centuries to come for while I shared in your days and spent them like water while you still lived and I had perished, now you spend my days for yours have all run out. We drank too deeply of them and found their end just as the poison sapped your strength."

I swallowed, feeling slightly ill. "And how great is the store of your days, Bramble King, can you spare even one for me?"

But his laugh was the type that restored strength to the bones like a hearty broth. It rang out full and deep and echoed through the chamber and he smiled so widely at me that I found myself beginning to smile too, when at last he was able to answer me.

"Speak to my riddle, Mad Princess. How deep is the ocean, how many are the stars, what number will you give to the insects that crawl upon the mortal earth? Know you that my days number more than all these."

"Oh," I said, feeling too stunned to say more.

"And now, bid your sisters goodbye for you'll not see them again," he said firmly, and I looked around at the crumbling walls, the ceiling that had fallen in revealing a blank sky, and the pillars crumbled to dust. Nothing at all remained of the room except for the books the others had kept.

I walked to the nearest one and opened it. I was Margaretta's. And when I opened it, I saw a pretty girl of about nineteen dancing at a ball in the court of Pensmoore and there was the king I had known, only he was a child, and she danced and danced with a mortal man. I flipped the page and she held a baby as soft and golden as she, flipped another, and she ran with him as a toddler, and with every page I flipped I saw her life as if it were a story spooling out into children and grandchildren and the bounty of life and when the story was over the book faded from my hand.

"She lived the life she was meant for, her days returned to her with interest," Bluebeard said, leaning casually against a crumbling wall and kicking at a piece of mortar. "Will you read the others?"

"I think I ought to," I said, swallowing. "Someone should remember them."

"I remember," he said firmly.

"And do you miss them?" I asked, raising a single eyebrow. He cocked his head in confusion.

"I honor their sacrifice, though in the end, it was no loss to them, as I did try to tell each of them when I stole her as a bride."

"But it might not have gone that way," I reminded him, sensibly. "And you were never very clear on what you meant."

He waved a hand. "Success was never in question."

"I rather think it was," I said acidly, because it was all very well and good to be glad of a victory but rather silly to pretend it had been a sure thing when it had been anything but that.

I read through the books and he watched me read, and I was pleased to see his foxy first wife find a brutish-looking husband who treated her kindly and gave her fifteen sons. Happier still to watch Tigraine become a mighty warrior queen. She did not marry at all, but ruled until she died in battle when her hair was white and her strength faded.

Each wife lived a life full and long — even Ki'e'iren whose life I did not wish to honor seemed settled in a palace and if she looked somewhat distracted and seemed to peer into shadows that were not there, that might only be her suspicious temperament at work. When the last book was shut and winked out, I looked at my smug husband.

"And so you kept these promises, too. For all sixteen of your wives."

He held up a single finger.

"Speak to this riddle wife. If a man has sixteen coins but has never had fifteen of them, how many does he have."

I rolled my eyes. "You can hardly pretend you were not married to all these other women."

He shook his single finger at me, a look of repressed mirth in his eyes. "Have you no answer to the riddle, then?"

"One," I said dryly. "He has one coin."

"And I have one wife," Bluebeard said, grinning in triumph, and then to my shock he sprang forward and flung me over his shoulder, laughing as he bounded from the room in one leap and tossed the key over his shoulder.

The room closed behind us, and it took its secrets with it. Though I lived a very long time — forever by the reckoning of mortals — I never again saw the room nor the wives who had helped me fight for the life of our husband, but that did not stop me from teasing the man relentlessly about them for what else was there to do?

CHAPTER TWENTY-THREE

He brought me out to the misty clearing between the dark trees and I revised my opinion of this place. It might not be the mortal world at all. I stood in one place and turned, frowning, as he lounged against a tree. He was letting a small bird dress his hair for him as he studied his fingernails.

Around us, pollen thick as snow drifted through the faint breeze. As the mists lifted, the pollen grew thicker and I felt some grand shift in the land — the passing of one into the other. Night was falling, soft, orchid-toned, and billowy.

I yawned and Bluebeard made a rumbling sound much like a growl.

"Where are we now, Bramble King?" I asked him, feeling a little wistful. I was a queen without a castle or so much as a loft to call my own, and I was very tired.

"The Wittenhame burned and melted and collapsed into the mortal world," Bluebeard said, lifting his chin and preening a little as the small nuthatch put finishing touches on his grooming. "This spot is one of those where they melted together."

"So it is both mortal and Wittenhame," I said, studying it. The tiny clearing was hardly bigger than a space where a pair of deer might bed down, but it was soft with moss and drifts of pollen. I could not see the Wittenhame here at all.

"A fitting place to spend our first night after we have walked death's land, don't you think?" he asked me with a slight smile and his own wistful look in his eye.

"A bed and a warm fire would not go amiss," I suggested a little daunted by the idea of camping in this glen with no tinderbox or blanket, wearing a cold hard dress of knives. And how would he stay warm clothed in spiderweb and insect wings?

He swallowed in a way that suggested to me that pollen and nuthatches were all he had to offer me tonight.

"I shall keep you warm and pillow your head on my chest — if you will consent to spend this night here with me."

His eyes were shadowed as he spoke and they seemed to darken with his words, catching my breath a little as if it were fabric sliding along a rough fence post. I had to swallow to find my voice.

"If this is your home, then it is mine, lord of the Wittenhame," I said, a little breathless.

He made no move toward me, regarding me from his place against the tree. The little nuthatch leapt from his shoulder and away and he pulled the crown of brambles from his head like a girl might drag down a drooping daisy chain. He toyed with it in his hands as it rustled and shifted and then he looked up at me with blazing eyes, and behind them, I saw not a great king of power who had defeated death but a nervous bridegroom approaching his new bride. He bit his lip, catching it between his teeth, and drew in a long breath.

I waited. His thoughts were opaque to me.

"Something troubles you, husband?" I said carefully. "You, who have flown on the backs of birds and broken the neck of Death?"

His chuckle was grim. "Here I stand before you and I find I must clutch at courage to take another step." He paused and swallowed, hanging his crown on a broken stub of a branch sticking out from one of the trees encircling our hollow. "Can you accept me as bridegroom, Izolda? Can you embrace me knowing I am this man but also this hollow in which we stand? That I am the river you hear bubbling, and the moon that rises to limn your lovely skin, and the nuthatch who flew away just now?"

"You are all that?" I asked, teasingly. "How shall it all fit in this hollow, then?"

But he was not wrong to ask, for how could a mortal mind accept all that and also bring him into her bed?

"Tell me true, wife," he said, still keeping himself across the hollow from me.

I spread my hands wide and spoke my heart. "If I cannot accept that, my Bluebeard, then where shall I go? For you are not only everywhere by right of Bramble King, you are also everywhere to me by right of heart and vow. When I look at the moon I will see you, whether you are moon or mortal. When I hear the bird sing, it will be your voice echoing in my mind whether you are bird or memory. Such is the way of a heart anchored deep in love."

A faint smile appeared on his lips, but still, he hung back. I was not much of one with words — not like him. Perhaps mine were not enough to assure him.

"All these must be our children," he said, gesturing to the singing frogs along the river and the birds in the trees nearby, bedding down for the night. "For as Bramble King, I cannot give you natural-born little ones."

I swallowed. "Are you saying you cannot make love to me as a man to a woman?"

For some reason, this question left me feeling raw inside in a way I had not expected.

His eyes darkened further and this time he took a sudden step to shorten the gap between us. He looked surprised at that, as if he had not meant to move.

"That is not what I am saying at all. I shall feed you on love until you are overflowing. I shall drink of you long and deep as a thirsty man who finds water. I shall pour into you all the wild passions of my untamed soul and find in you the rest I have long sought and never acquired. You are order to my chaos, stillness to my energy, feather to my flint, and I shall love you as no mortal had ever loved, as no Wittenbrand has ever dreamed of, and you shall never lack but I fill it, never want but I sate you, never tire of my endless offerings at the altar of your heart."

I swallowed, somewhat overwhelmed, and this time it was I who took a slow step forward and I gestured to the land around us, "Then I shall take all these to my heart, my husband. And I shall take you deeper into it, too. Together we will tend your land and people as though they were children to us."

He made a humming sound in the back of his throat. I

thought that perhaps he was pleased. But I had worries of my own as we stood here, finding our places as man and wife.

"But what of my life, Bramble King? For I am dust and ashes. I will fade and die in what will feel to you but a moment."

"Ah," he said and now he was smiling as he took the last step between us and cupped my cheek with his hand. The look in his eye was triumph as if he had won yet another battle. "But I am now and I am later, I am this moment and I am what is to come. And as you are one with me as my wife, so are you the same."

I turned my face and kissed his palm and he let me, his lips parting slightly as if he were enjoying the gesture. I certainly was.

"Tell me then," I whispered into his palm, still confused. "How are you one with time and the land?"

"Each life and moment is sustained by me."

"And me?"

He leaned forward and put his forehead to mine.

"I sustain you, too. More than any of these, since our days — both in number and substance — are shared." He leaned down and kissed me softly. "I could never stop breathing this life into you. How could I? I have made you my very heart. Given to the barrow. Taken back by my own hand. I refuse to surrender you to another. All challengers must hear and tremble, or find themselves lost without land or time to succor them."

"Well," I said between his kisses, a little breathless as they turned fervent and wordless. "I suppose that settles it then."

And my own kisses joined his and for a time our language was the language of affection and reverence and there was no room for words or rational thoughts. I did not miss them. This new speech filled my mouth and heart and hands and left room for little else.

He was right, it turned out. The hollow was warm enough and his chest made an excellent pillow and the sword dress was not an issue at all. It hung in the tree next to the crown and sang pretty wind chime songs as the moon rose high and watched us. But it was not spying for it was not only the moon but also the lover I held in my arms, just as the hollow held me while the man kissed and adored. Had I never tasted the Wittenhame, I might find such contradictions impossible, but I had walked the Path of Princes and found now that I did not care if my world was comprehensible so long as it was full of my Bluebeard.

CHAPTER TWENTY-FOUR

I woke with my head on my husband's warm chest and his breath in my hair. His arms came around me, warm and secure, a gentle weight on my skin.

"I dreamed all the world blossomed for you and you sang to me of the stars," he whispered into my hair and I pressed my cheek to his chest and pushed up so I could meet his cat's eyes gaze with my own and our shared smile shot through me with warmth and security.

"I slept like the dead," I said. "And I would know exactly how they sleep for I have seen their grim repose." I paused there for a breath. "But I woke in your arms this morning, just as I woke to life from death by your word."

"So you have," he agreed, and his smile was so full of burgeoning joy that it was almost painful to watch. It washed over me with the rise of the bright sun, its beams just as warm and golden.

The kiss, when our lips met, sent thrills of joy straight through me and I thought that perhaps he felt the same, for he lingered there a while with me, inhaling deeply as if to memorize my scent, and offering gifts of small kisses to grace my skin. I offered the same, for while my affections might be lesser than what he could give, they held within them all the yearnings of my soul.

"Would that we might linger here, wife, in the heart of the forest, but you and I have work to do this day."

"I am no shirker," I teased, offering one last kiss before I found my feet.

His smile and the twinkle in his eye made my heart flip over and my breath catch.

"Will you let me dress you?" His voice was low and tinged with what I knew now to be desire.

I nodded, mutely, and with a wink, he snapped his fingers, and we were both fully dressed — not what I had imagined, but with him things never were.

My garments were rough and painful and when I looked toward him with a question in my eye. I saw his were the same.

"We go to do grim work today, fire of my eyes. I thought it fitting that we dress for the occasion."

I nodded, taking in his clothing — breeches of woven nettle and bramble belts that wound 'round his hips. Boots of the same. A garland of thistles hanging loose like a baldric across his naked, scarred chest, showing very plainly where his rib had been ripped from his side. A small half-jacket of living brambles that came down to the middle of his rib cage but rose up in a tall collar around his neck and ears. In the brambles, small creatures climbed — beetles, luna moths, and even — I thought — a small saw-whet owl. He reached for the Bramble Crown and set it upon his head, and when it met his brow, the sun itself seemed to grow warmer and more golden as if it, too, were pleased to see its king crowned.

He arranged my hair himself, to my blushes, combing his fingers through the tangles and weaving it across one side and then down to the other. My boots, belt, and short jacket matched his — though, thankfully, the living brambles were not inhabited — and my dress was of woven thistle.

When he had finished my hair, he wove for me a crown of thistles and with red, painful-looking hands, he set it upon my brow and his smile lit my heart and flooded me with warmth and contentment enough that I did not care that my skin was aflame from our garments.

"Grant me a request, my wife," he whispered.

"Ask it," I whispered back, and he lowered his head until his lips were a breath away from mine and then ran his reddened knuckles down my jaw with gentle appreciation.

"Let me take your flesh hand for the breadth of a day."

I gasped, surprised by his request, but what could he ever ask for that I would not give?

"Take it, then," I said and he snapped his fingers and my left hand was bone once more.

"And now we go to the land of mortals and dispense the pain and discomfort we share," he said, smiling as he took my skeletal hand in his and led me through the swirling pollen and out of our hollow.

I expected us to step into a forest, but I was not surprised when we did not. I had lived too long with my husband to be surprised anymore by sudden changes of place and time. I was, however, startled and somewhat horrified by what I saw.

We stood before the palace in Pensmoore, the city fanning out behind us. If I had not been with him, the swirling clouds of pollen and the way every plant in sight was in bloom — from the vines that crawled up shop walls to the grasses growing between cobblestones — might have stunned me. But I was not stunned right now.

"Pensmoore seems very fecund," I murmured.

"My presence has that effect now," he murmured back, shooting me a wicked look that made my cheeks blush hot, and before I could say anything else he led me straight through the gates and directly to the guards standing before us.

They wore blue. They were not mortal.

"Where is the Pensmoore green?" I asked, my voice hard with my worry.

"An apt question, wife," Bluebeard drawled but I knew by the sharp look in his eye that his casual tone was a ruse. "Care to explain, guard?"

"We do not answer to outsiders," the Wittenbrand said. He was a great hulking creature with a massive polearm held in one hand. I said "was" because he quickly became so when Bluebeard snapped his fingers and with a shivery tinkle as if gemstones were being shaken out of a bag, little sparks of green leapt from his heart to Bluebeard's hand and then he collapsed, so dead that he already stank before he hit the floor.

"Who else would call his king an outsider?" Bluebeard asked, eyeing the other Wittenbrand who had stood with the first.

When none spoke, he strode past the stunned guards, mounting the steps to the palace. They trailed behind him like lost puppies.

After so long away, the palace seemed small and dull to me.

A Wittenbrand who was dressed like he thought he was something hurried toward us. His short cape swept behind him, sewn all over with what I thought might be human ears and his doublet was stitched with finger-bone beads as decoration. His face had the faint greenish cast that Bluffroll shared, and I smirked at the concern on his face.

"Lord Bluffroll is not seeing guests in the court at the moment," he said, his voice coming out choked. He must have already heard about the guard Bluebeard had killed.

Bluebeard made a brushing away motion and kept walking and I strode at his side, just as cold-faced and dead-eyed as he was.

It was not a show for me. While Bluebeard had all the attention of the yipping Wittenbrand, my eyes had been searching for mortals, and what I saw deeply troubled me. The staff was not right. There were servants, most certainly. But they scuttled around with heads down and walked with limps or faces hidden. Some bore terrible scars across their faces. Others were missing fingers or even hands. I felt ill at the sight. My family ruled this land and it was bound to me. Why had my people been so mistreated and who would set it right?

"Save it up, my grim monstrosity," Bluebeard murmured to me. "Save it for the ones responsible."

The Wittenbrand following us was still trying to protest when Bluebeard reached the throne room and flicked a finger. There had been two rows of Wittenbrand guards in full regalia there. There were none standing now. They lay on the ground stone dead and already rotting. I swallowed down bile as I stole a glimpse at my husband's face.

"Think you their punishment too great? I do not think you will judge so for long."

He was right. When — at a flick of his wrist — the doors to the throne room opened wide, I certainly did not think his judgment was too harsh. If anything, he had been too merciful.

This was not the throne room as it had been in my brother's day nor even as it had been in the old king's day when first I had broken the Law of Greeting and won for myself a husband. This was entirely different.

Just inside the door, a statue had been erected in bronze and I grimaced at what I depicted. Someone had cast a very recognizable depiction of me — my one hand skeletal and the scars on my back through my open dress were dead giveaways — but they had cast me on all fours, crawling on a slab of rough-hewn rock that I thought was meant to be mud. A leash in a ribbon of silver ran to my captor's hand and one of his feet was positioned between my shoulder blades. The Wittenbrand depicted in this role looked a lot like Bluffroll — but larger, broader, and more handsome. The sculptor had spent time lovingly adding detail upon detail to his bare muscled torso and there were even small details brought to life like the exact angle of his lower incisors sticking out of his lips and the precise curl of his long hair.

I shuddered at my first sight of it, and my husband stiffened enough that I felt it through our clasped hands. I was so shaken by the casting that it took me a moment before my eyes moved onto the rest and when they did I was horrified.

The only mortals in the room were mounted on the walls — not dead as one might expect, but fully alive, just hung up and nailed to the walls through the spot where the chest met the shoulders. They were dressed in blue — forbidden in Pensmoore — and I wished that was the worst shock of what had been done to them. They stared at me through a glaze of pain and hopelessness. And to my horror, each of them was missing their left hand, severed at the wrist.

Well then. This must be why my husband had bid me show my skeletal hand.

On either side of the throne were a man and woman I assumed were king and queen. Her, I did not recognize, though she had the look of Rouranmoore about her. He, however, was my nephew Rolgrin, and on his head was his crown, melted in such a way that it looked as if it had been jammed onto his skull while still hot.

I swallowed down bile and managed to voice my question aloud.

"Why are they dressed in blue?"

The Wittenbrand assembled in the court took this to mean they could laugh, which I rather thought was a foolish response, for if my husband had stiffened at the sight of the degrading statue of me, then he flinched at the sound of their laughter and it was not a flinch of pain or fear or even embarrassment.

Fury radiated off of him like heat and he tilted his head

slightly to the side as he looked past the rows of opulently dressed Wittenbrand dressed in the garb of mortals — perhaps dresses made of living squirrels or flowing waterfalls were too hard to maintain in the mortal world — to the throne where Bluffroll lounged with a shining golden crown on his head and a wide smile on his lips.

"Is this how the Bramble King is to be greeted?" Bluebeard asked quietly. "With laughter? His wife degraded, his people maimed, his court reduced to rubbish?"

"Wear all the brambles you want, it doesn't make you Bramble King," Bluffroll's voice boomed out from across the room, but he straightened on the throne as if he were suddenly less comfortable in the seat. "This place was gifted to me by the true Bramble King who was once Lord Coppertomb, he whose Coronation Ball looms close. It is mine to do as I please. And did I not please well?" He gestured now, coyly, at the statue. "There was a bronze casting of the Mad Princess, Savior of Pensmoore, when I arrived here. She held a sword aloft and was missing a hand. Apparently, she guided their king to victory and prosperity and united this land with Rouranmoore, and on and on. I showed these people who they ought to worship. There will be no savior for them from Bluffroll. And I have put an everlasting reminder in their flesh and in their throne room to keep that ever in their minds."

The green banners in the throne room that once depicted the white horse of Pensmoore had all been replaced by blue, as well. I was too horrified to ask all the other questions I wanted to ask. Instead, I tried a variation of my first question.

"Why blue?"

"Bluffroll takes liberties with my wife's people," Bluebeard said quietly.

And that was when Bluffroll laughed, his booming roar filling the throne room and echoing in the voices of his enthralled court.

"The mortals believe blue is bad luck. They wouldn't wear it. And I agree. It's terrible luck to wear blue. Look what happened to them when I dressed them in it and made them cook their own hands for my dinner."

I swayed, so filled with horror that I could not focus. I had brought this upon my people by coming here and guiding them for the battle. I had brought it on them by being Bluebeard's true wife and defying Coppertomb and all of his folk.

My eyes sought Bluebeard's but his were riveted on the casting.

"Marvelous, don't you think, Arrow?" Bluffroll taunted him. "Surely a man who has clawed his way back from the grave can appreciate a good reversal."

The court laughed with appreciation.

"Your filthy fantasies about my wife ..." Bluebeard said, letting his words hang in the air until the court quieted. "...annoy me."

And perhaps they did not know him as I did, because they laughed at that, even as I tried to draw in a shuddering breath, for fear had gripped me hard and held my heart. Not fear of these monsters, but fear of what devastation my husband might unleash now that I would witness.

"And what will you do, Arrow? You cannot kill a competitor," Bluffroll said smugly. He reached for a chalice of wine and drank it down, leaning forward as if he were anticipating some pleasure. "You can only run away with your tail between your legs while I take new delight in stripping your pride away with every torment I inflict upon the people who saw you as their patron saint."

"I compete for nothing now," Bluebeard said, and his voice was so quiet that I saw the court straining to hear it. "But you will, Bluffroll. You will compete and so will your court. Let us see who will be first to be eaten by worms and forgotten by history."

And then, without any warning at all, he released my hand and spread his hands wide and there was a clinking rush as sparks of every color flew from the Wittenbrand assembled there into his hands, and then they fell like scarecrows when the stick is removed. He marched across their limp bodies as they stared at him, powerless to move as his boots crushed hands and legs and faces. I could hear the crunch of their bones from where I stood. I watched him move with a mix of horror, awe, and a sense that perhaps — finally — there might be someone to right wrongs and turn tables and bring all the violence inflicted upon my people to a sharp end.

Even now, as Bluebeard walked through the throne room, puffs of pollen swirled out from him, settling on his foes and coating the ground.

I picked my way more carefully through the mass, remembering all too well what the land within the barrow had been like.

"There's no need for such dramatics, Arrow," Bluffroll said, looking nervous at the approach of my husband. "The game was won by Coppertomb."

"Speak to my riddle, Bluffroll," Bluebeard said, taking

his time as he strolled over the breaking bodies of his enemies.

He paused to examine one and scoff before moving closer. Bluffroll, for his part, stood, seeming to realize that on the throne he was at a disadvantage now that he had no guards to defend him.

"Who spits in the eye of the hurricane and survives? Who pokes the unicorn and is not gored? Who dances with Death and does not descend to the barrow?"

"Is it you? Is that what you're telling me?" Bluffroll said, trying to keep his tone light, but it shook with the fear he had not managed to leash. He leaned down and plucked a massive two-handed sword from the grip of one of his fallen guards.

As Bluebeard grew closer, their disparity in height was highlighted. My husband was not a short man, but Bluffroll was nearly a head taller.

"Well," Bluebeard said, smiling slightly and then flicking his wrists and like magic — or maybe by magic? — a pair of curving swords appeared in his hands. "It certainly is not you."

I saw Bluffroll swallow from where I stood. And out of the corner of my eye, I saw Rolgrin twitch from on the wall. His eyes were following the pair. When I looked around to check, I saw that every set of eyes in the whole room was following them.

Bluebeard spun his swords and then tossed one and caught it with a laugh.

"I could snap my fingers and take your days, Bluffroll."

"You can't," Bluffroll growled, but he didn't sound entirely convinced.

Bluebeard's laugh this time was rich and full as if he were deeply enjoying himself. He danced in a swirling pattern, tossing and catching swords as if this were a show and he the principle showman, not a confrontation between what had been equals.

"I don't wear nettle and bramble and thistle for the joy of their sting," my husband said conspiratorially. "I am your true king."

"Coppertomb," Bluffroll tried to say.

"Is a weak imposter. Or did you not consider that no true Bramble King would watch the Wittenhame melt and do nothing to stop it?"

"It was the old Bramble King. It melted with him," Bluffroll said, clinging to the lie as he circled the throne, trying to keep my dancing husband in front of him. "And who cares? This mortal world is fun. I have inflicted cruelties upon this place ... this Pensmoore ... that would make the bravest Wittenbrand tremble."

"I don't doubt it," Bluebeard said and I thought that perhaps Bluffroll took his smile as approval, but I knew that smile. Every time I saw it before was right before he took a head. As if thinking the same thing, he said, "It's a shame I don't collect heads anymore. I have no proper use for them now."

Bluffroll laughed. This is all a big game, is what his posture said. We're joking, we two, is what his laugh said. It was all a bluff, just like his name, and I knew it.

"I had planned to let you live, you know," Bluebeard said. "Better the devil you know than the devil you don't, and of the remaining Lords and Ladies the only other one I know well is Sparrow."

"Your lieutenant?" Bluffroll scoffed. "Tanglecott ate her for breakfast, I heard. Better than roasted boar."

"I'd suggest you try to tell that to the new Lady Riverbarrow, but I'm afraid that I don't plan to let you live long enough to try it," Bluebeard said, feinting lightly now and forcing Blufroll to extend an arm to parry. It felt like someone trying something out to see what might happen. My breath caught a little in my chest.

Bluffroll's eyes flicked to me. "Is that not the Lady Riverbarrow?"

"Keep up," Bluebeard barked as his blade slapped Bluffroll's, forcing him to change his footing and lunge at Bluebeard. My husband was somewhere else when the heavy blade landed, the flat of his curved sword slapped Bluffroll's rear. "That's the Bramble Queen, second only to me in the rule of the Wittenhame and your sovereign."

"That's not how it works," Bluffroll said, his breath growing heavy as he tried to match Bluebeard's frenetic pace. I could barely see their blades in the air, but I could see the sweat forming on Bluffroll's brow.

"Speak to this riddle, then, Bluffroll, last of your name."

"Last of my name? You can't declare that!" He sounded panicky now.

"Who speaks and it is so? Who holds the world in his breast and the fates of men and beasts between his fingertips."

Bluffroll was much quicker this time. "You do."

Bluebeard paused in his swordplay and leaned in to wink at him. "Yes."

And then he was rolling away again, spinning, blades

dancing in the air as if to unheard music. "And Izolda Savataz of House Northpeak, of Pensmoore, of the Mortal Lands, known heretofore as the Mad Princess, is my true bride and the Queen of Brambles and she will have your honor."

Bluffroll shot a wild glance at me and then at the statue he had cast in bronze and his mouth opened and then shut and then his face turned hard.

"I regret nothing," he growled. "And were I to do all this again, I would do it in exactly the same fashion."

Bluebeard shrugged. "It seems you wish to hurry your meeting with Death. Do be my most honored guest."

He flung his swords outward and to my surprise, they flew right past Bluffroll and stuck in his gilded throne, and before I could even gasp, Bluebeard had lunged forward, picked up Bluffroll in his powerful grip, and thrown him against the wall behind the throne.

He landed with a smack right between my nephew and his queen, and Bluffroll did not slide down the wall, because brambles erupted through the stone, winding quickly around him. Another branch of them grew — as if by decades, but all done in a heartbeat — right out his open screaming mouth, and two more curled and tangled out his eyes.

I sucked in a gasp as Death erupted from the ground, white and swirling. He bowed once to Bluebeard, and then his slug tongue shot out and sucked something pale from Bluffroll's body. Before I could blink, Death burst apart like smoke in a high wind and was gone and nothing remained of Bluffroll but his grasping rictus of a skeleton caught within the brambles.

"I do hope you'll leave that up on your wall," Bluebeard said, seeming to address my nephew from where he hung beside Bluffroll's desiccated remains. "It's a far better tribute to my beloved wife than that monstrosity. I'd stand on the throne if I were you, wife."

I knew a command when I heard one, gentle or not, so I scrambled up on the throne as Bluebeard raised a single eyebrow and the bronze statue melted, collapsing like water falling from a bucket and eating through the mass of Wittenbrand on the floor, burning them to nothing and bronzing the entire throne room floor in the time it took for me to accidentally let out a little cry.

I recovered myself enough to straighten and draw in a breath. "I prefer your choice of decor, my husband."

"Indeed," he said, smiling cruelly and then stepping up to join me on the floor. "And now, shall we go find Coppertomb and ruin the fun of his Coronation Ball?"

I smiled, but just like his smile, mine did not touch my eyes. "As much as I would love to hurry to his destruction, I think you're forgetting something."

"I forget nothing," he said, waving a hand.

The spikes popped out of the shoulders of the mortals hanging on the walls. And with their removal, some spell was broken and I heard their cries of pain and sorrow and relief as they scrambled to one another, heard my nephew cry, "beloved" and fling himself into his wife's arms. I thought, from what I saw, that he had healed their wounds, though their left hands were still missing.

"All restoration costs something," Bluebeard breathed into my hair. "Days or pain or something else. Their freedom cost the lives of those I melted away under the shame of that terrible rendering."

"Of course," I agreed in a whisper. But though we spoke quietly, I could see the terrified mortals around us watching the strange pair standing together on their king's throne.

"Will you pay a price now? One to restore them?"

I swallowed. "Name the price, husband of mine."

He made a happy murmur in the back of his throat and lifted my skeletal hand, touching the end of each finger with his flesh fingers. "Give up your flesh hand forever and I will restore all of theirs."

"Could you not restore them without such a sacrifice?" I asked, my voice trembling a little. I had liked having my flesh hand back. I did not want to give it up again.

He lifted an eyebrow. "Who values what is not bought at great price? Who treasures what is given for nothing?"

"I do," I said firmly.

"I leave the choice in your excellent hands," he said and I looked from his mercurial expression to the huddled people — maybe a hundred of them — who had just been set free of the curse that pinned them to the walls and I swallowed. He was not going to restore them on his own. That much was clear.

He loved me. I knew it.

And yet he could only be who he was. Incomprehensible as it sometimes was to me.

"I agree to your bargain," I said calmly, though my voice shook a little. "My hand for theirs."

He huffed out a breath as if in relief and leaned in close to breathe me in.

"Well chosen, wife of mine," he said and then he kissed me so thoroughly that the sweetness of his lips dulled the sadness that welled up in me at my loss and when I opened my eyes it was to the sound of mortal awe.

"Remove the blue from this place," Bluebeard said curtly. "And when next I attend these courts, I expect a more fitting tribute will be erected for my queen."

Rolgrin bowed to him, spreading arms wide in agreement and his court and queen were quick to follow.

"And now we ride," Bluebeard said.

"Wait," I interrupted. "I should be sure my folk are safe."

"Is that not what I just accomplished?" He seemed confused by the request.

"I should ascertain that my kinsman is in good enough health to reign."

"He stands, does he not?" Bluebeard gestured at Rolgrin.

"Aunt," Rolgrin said from where he stood, and his throat was dry. "I thank you for your concern. And I assure you all will be well. Only ... please ... we are but mortal. Please withdraw your glory from us."

My mouth fell open and I had to shut it with a click at the look of fear and admiration directed at me from my nephew. None of the others even looked at me. Their heads were bowed in what I now realized was fear.

"If you wish it," I said faintly.

"Please," my kin begged and Bluebeard took my upper arm in his grip and turned me to meet his lifted eyebrow.

"Now we ride," I agreed and he smiled, blinked, and we were no longer in Pensmoore.

CHAPTER TWENTY-FIVE

In the Wittentales that my mother told, the prince would come — or the woodsman, or the firebird, or the deadly Wittenbrand prince — and the fair maiden would be swept away with him after many trials and difficulties and they would kiss and then my mother would say, "And they lived happily ever after."

And I, fool that I was, never asked, "What was that like? Did they have a nice bed and regular meals? Did they have comfortable clothing and make fat babies?"

If I had asked, I suspect she would have given me a mysterious wink, for what other option would she have had? Mortals have no ken of what the Wittenbrand do, or of how their ever afters might be, and the firebird is as like to consume a maiden as live with her, the woodsman is sure to have many days of poverty and grinding exhaustion, and the human prince might have his entire court forced to cook their own hands.

And so, if I had turned my sensible mind to the matter, I might have realized that there would be no such life of luxury for us. My choice of the Bramble King — the mystery prince who had, through boldness and cunning, defeated death and ushered in a new age — was the choice of a man who did not toil nor spin, nor did he worry about human concerns. There was no feast of delicacies or comfortable fire that he brought me to when we finished restoring Pensmoore. Rather, we emerged in the heat of a summer day on the banks of a river that was certainly in the Wittenhame, for no mortal water sparkled so, nor was any human place so heavy with the sweltering doldrums of the ripest summer. Pollen swirled so heavily, clouding all else so that at first I saw nothing but thick puffs of white pollen and the water my feet stood in up to the ankle.

The river ran with bubbling charm up and over my ankles but beneath my feet was firm black stone.

"Let us shed these robes of justice, fire of my eyes," Bluebeard said and I nodded, fighting back a sudden burst of fear.

The judgment we had just rendered was fitting and right. I was not sorry for it. But it had highlighted what I already knew — that I could not return to the mortal world. That there was no place there for me.

"Something troubles you beyond the prickles of the nettles and thorns you wear," my husband said, gently beginning to undress me from my painful garb.

"I fear I have no place now, Bramble King," I said quietly. "I am no princess of Pensmoore any longer, nor am I a daughter of Savataz. I have not a home nor a place."

He was quiet for a long while as he rent my garments and removed them one after another. As he worked, the pollen swirled back, revealing that we stood on a rock shelf and the water ran behind and before us, washing over short waterfalls only as high as my waist or my knees. Cool water flowed from one level to the next, only as deep as ankle or knee.

"Sit and wash yourself of the pain of what we have just done," my husband said but his face was considering as he removed his own ruined clothing and sat with me in the river.

The cold water did, indeed, ease the pain, but I lifted my hand and looked at my skeletal fingers and I sighed.

"Do you regret giving yourself for others?"

"I merely find the consequence grim," I said, blushing a little as I said, "I had hoped for a happy ending."

"And is your ending not happy with me?" he asked, and I realized he was close enough to murmur in my ear. I turned to see him beside me, his face very serious and eyes grave.

And I did not know what seized me for it was not the reasonable, sensible thing to do, but instead of airing my woes to him or asking clearly for a place to call my own, instead, I turned to him and embraced him, body to body, and brought my skeletal hand up to cradle his cheek. I could not feel it, but I could gasp with the pleasure of watching him close his eyes and turn his cheek into my broken embrace.

"I consider your sacrifice a treasure," he whispered as he let his eyes open enough to meet mine and then leaned in very slowly to steal a kiss from my lips. "For it mirrors my own and in all this world, who else will know what it is to be me except you, or what it is to be you except for me? Please, wife of mine, do not give your heart to another."

"I will not," I gasped as his warm flesh arms wrapped themselves around me, reminding me that he remained broken, too, with holes in his palms and his side that would never be whole again. My mind was dazed at his touch and his warmth, and any discomfort the nettles and thorns had left behind was thoroughly gone at the brush of his fingers.

"Do not give it then to comfort, for he is not me," Bluebeard whispered. "Nor to prestige for he is no Bramble King, nor to riches for they are not my affectionate touch."

"I will not." I sounded breathless now, my heart stolen away by his plea. He asked me for so little — only my heart.

"Let me feed you, and clothe you, and show to you what our life together might be."

"Will it be bathing in these falls with all our clothing drifting away?" I asked as my thistle crown fell to cover one of my eyes.

He laughed, catching it between his teeth and then tossing his head to send it into the falls and then he kissed me again.

"If it is those things, are you sorry?" he asked me gently.

"I am not," I gasped, leaning my forehead shyly against his strong shoulder.

"And if I tell you I am slowly making this world new again and that I require your input on some of the most intimate parts of it?"

"Then I will bid you take me to those parts and show to me all your secrets," I said shyly, peering up at him through my lashes.

"And if it will mean deprivation and the loss of many things?" A ghost of his smile has returned.

"Then I will give them," I said, kissing his bare shoulder.

"And if it will mean that I gift you with one good thing after another?"

"Then I will consider all those gifts small beside the gift of your heart," I breathed and to my surprise, he did not answer but instead he ducked down and caught my mouth in a kiss and he was laughing through the kiss and he did not stop kissing me even as he slowly drew me to my feet.

He pulled back only long enough to pounce again. Drew back a second time, his fingers threading through my hair, only to nip at my bottom lip. But the third time he held my gaze with his intent one, and leaned in to press the softest of kisses along my jaw, and when I was drunk with them, eyes half-lidded with the drug of pleasure, he finally stepped back.

When I looked down, I found myself dressed in a gown of soft white with sprays of lace decorating the edge of the deep v-neck in little patches as if it were frost. The full skirts opened to become three great grey owls who fluttered and snapped and hooted with deathly glares at both me and my king.

I was still staring at them in wonder when a movement made me look up and I found my Bluebeard clad similarly. He wore breeches woven of witches' hair today, his feet bare beneath them and his doublet was formed entirely of living hummingbirds which sometimes hovered close to his body and sometimes took flight, flew laps around him, and then returned to their posts and while he wore his bramble crown, the thorns had grown longer and sharper and bore white roses. He smiled and produced for me a crown that was the same and set it upon my hair, before lifting my hands to kiss the backs of my knuckles.

"I'm making all things new," he said sweetly, kissing each knuckle individually. "And your time of waiting and torment is over, wife. Never again will you go hungry. Never again will you be cold. Your place is at my side and here you are Queen of the Wittenhame. Need you a home beyond this?"

I looked around where he was pointing and I realized that as we had talked together the pollen had retreated further and further leaving our shallow waterfall at the top of a great vista that was spread before us, filled with sweeping hills and roaring rivers, green lakes and moss-encrusted bogs, white beaches, dusky forests, and purple mountains. The pollen continued to spread far past what I could see, stretching out across the land.

"When you say you are making all things new ..."

My words trailed away.

"I meant I was rebuilding the Wittenhame for my people. They must not live with mortals on their plane. They must enter this age fresh and new."

"You made all this?" I said, stunned, pushing my flower crown up.

And when I looked back he was grinning with mischief in his eyes. "And I have more yet to make. Will you weave it with me and bring to this some of the order of your practical soul? Be the straight line to all my twists and curves, the sharp edge to my soft billows?"

I smiled. "So long as rivers run and moon shines, so long will I be wife to you."

"Then I shall see that they continue in their courses age

upon age," he said and then he turned from me, took on a look of concentration, and then snatched at the water brimming over the closest step-fall and when his hand came out he had a sleek rainbow trout in his grip. "But first, I will cook you breakfast."

And perhaps happily ever after meant eating fresh-cooked fish beside a fire burning with white and purple flames while your husband created pink and gold clouds in the sky.

Or perhaps it didn't, but it did for me that day.

Maybe the next day it would mean something else. Maybe with Bluebeard, I would never know what it would mean.

"And what will I do in this world you're making?" I asked him between bites. "I feel like a rake in a world without gardens. Like a sword in a world with no enemies."

"Do not fool yourself, once-mortal wife," he said and there was a dangerous glint in his eye. "For I am tied to you as you are tied to me. There will be no blossoms if you fade, no sunshine if your smile ceases, no warmth if your love for me runs cold. All this I have created, but it was made for you, and each day you will bring newness to it."

"And will I have an occupation beyond this marvelous existence I seem to have inspired?" I teased, but I was truly worried. I was not one to sit idle.

"I fear you may have the hardest occupation of all," he said gravely, taking a bite of the fish.

"Loving you?"

"That is easy enough. But someone must keep me from

growing bored or I may forget to bother with setting the seasons in turn, one after another."

"But you have to or everyone will die of starvation," I said, aghast.

His eyes twinkled. "See? You are at it already. If I do not feel challenged enough, I may forget to order the sun to rise."

"You wouldn't," I said with huge eyes.

"I might," he teased, making his eyes grow big and biting his lip as he drew in close to me. "I might forget."

"You can't," I choked.

"Help me," he said, hands spread wide and eyes also wide with feigned innocence.

"For how long?" I asked, giving him a wry smile.

"As long as rivers need to run and the moon needs to shine," he said, putting on a sorrowful expression. "I fear that you will be stuck with me for exactly that long, for who else would remind me of the necessity."

"That will be forever," I warned.

"So it will." And his smile was beatific again. "And will you take the occupation?"

"I fear that if I do not, the world will fall to chaos," I said grimly.

"Your fears are well-founded."

"Then, I will take this occupation," I agreed and his laugh was deep and rich and told me he had tricked me into being his compatriot in the very best of ways because he dropped his teasing and the rest of his fish and swept me up in his arms and we were busy for a long while like that until our fire went out and he had to remake our crushed flower crowns.

"Can we stay like this forever?" I gasped.

"Soon," he whispered. "But first, we have one last snake in our garden and I fear we must root him out ourselves. Let us hie us to Coppertomb's Coronation Ball for a Battle of the Kings."

CHAPTER TWENTY-SIX

I EXPECTED HIM TO SNAP HIS FINGERS AND TAKE us there like he had so many times before, but to my surprise, my husband took my hand instead and knocked on the rock we'd been standing on. It began to shake, rumbling and rising. I had to grip his hands in mine as tree roots shook loose and soil and river all tumbled off the rock. And then a seam opened up, and out of the seam, a fire flared up hot and rich.

"My fire," Bluebeard said happily. His smile was the kind of smile that could melt the rock itself, holding the light of a lantern in the darkness, the warmth of a welcoming hearth, a kind of glowing, pulsing satisfaction.

"My King," the fire rumbled, hissing and popping.

"I require your service."

"I am honored to serve," said the fire.

"Is there a fire at my adversary's Coronation Ball?" my husband asked.

"Of course," said the fire.

"Then you shall deposit your King and Queen there,

my fire, and await my orders." Bluebeard turned and looked at me and there was a teasing smile in his eyes that turned fierce as he said, "Are you ready to turn tables and upend designs, Queen of my Heart?"

"I am," I said firmly.

"Are you ready to untangle tangles and unravel ravelings?" He leaned in, his half-smile teasing in a way that made me melt a little.

"I'm also ready to tear down what has been built and unmake what was made," I said dryly.

"Ah, excellent. Then we are of an accord." He bent in to steal a sizzling kiss, his fingers trailing lightly over my waist. And then, before I had time to so much as take a breath he whirled me as if we were dancing, right through the air and into the fire.

The fire grew, burning bright and hot, though I was not scalded by it, and when it cleared enough to see out through the flames, there was a great statue that looked as if it were a depiction of Death himself, for it accurately showed his beard and fluttering cloak and it held in its hand a severed hand — my hand, I thought. But the statue was old and beaten by winds and weather to the point where the glazed-over eyes and slug tongue were worn to nubs and the face was unrecognizable.

"Where are we?" I gasped from within the fire.

"The Plains of Myygddo," my husband whispered in my ear, leaning around me so we could both peer up at the statue. "Recall how I required you lead the armies of mortals to fight here on these very Plains? Recall also how Coppertomb thought he had won the day before the fight occurred. He called me 'ancient' even among my own kind.

What he never guessed was that ancient people hatch ancient plans. This statue, I had placed here over a thousand years before."

"This statue?" I asked with a cocked brow. "This one that holds my severed hand? How could that be?"

"Some things must be, one way or another," he murmured.

"So you ... what? Crafted it out of magic?"

"Not at all," he said and his eyes were far away as if in memory. "There was a mortal with clever hands, Halifast, I think his name was. And to him, I granted riches and power and showed him the face of Death that he might set the depiction in stone."

"I don't remember seeing this when I was on the edge of the Plains with Rolgrin," I said frowning. "I would certainly have remembered."

"Indeed," my husband breathed, "but the Plains are vast and this image is often obscured by the rising mists and the sun baking the nearby ground and disturbing the vision of mortals."

I nodded. "Well enough, but why place it here at all?"

"When it was complete, I set it under a geas, that if one who shared my days and wore my token led an army to this Plain, then the magic stored within would pour out and lend aid to her armies. None who fought under my standard could be so much as touched while fighting in the shadow of this statue, nor afflicted by deadly thirst, nor poisoned by draught. You may recall that my adversary was very sure of himself. He'd had the local water sources laced with poison."

"But did anyone know there was protection here?" I

asked, my brow wrinkling as I turned to him. It was so Wittenbrand to offer a way to win and be safe without ever telling anyone what it was.

"I was not there when King Rolgrin fought," Bluebeard said, scratching his beard as if thinking. "But I know much more as Bramble King than I knew as a mortal, and I can see that battle in my mind's eye. The fight was grim and tight. A near thing, indeed. But when your people rallied at the base of the statue, sheltered in the cool shade, they fought like lions, and were untouched by blade or arrow until their enemies lay scattered at their feet."

"But what if I'd failed?" I asked, aghast. "Or what if I left before I brought them to the edge of the Plain? None of that was a certain thing!"

"Did I not instruct you to bring them to the Plains? Did I not bid you succeed?"

"You did," I said. I could so easily have failed, for he had not told me of the importance. How many other things like this had been very close with me utterly blind to their importance?

"I had every confidence in your fidelity," he said with a kiss pressed to my cheek.

"I hardly dare imagine what would have happened had I not followed your commands precisely." I was still having trouble drawing in a full breath with this new knowledge hovering over me.

"I did not need imagine it. I know you too well, my sober monstrosity. You would not have drawn up short. Not then or ever."

"Your confidence in me is too great," I said grimly.

"It was not then, and is not now," he said with a last

soft kiss to my cheek. "But come now. Explanations grow dull. Let us go and act instead."

He spun me, still in the flames of the fire, and we emerged from a new fire. This fire was set in the very middle of what was most certainly the Wittenbrand Court in Exile.

Around the fire was the grandest display I'd ever seen. Dancers by the hundred rushed around the fire and then closed in toward it, only to back slowly away with dragging steps, huge fans like the tails of birds were in each hand and they used the fans to mask their forms or accentuate their beauty, to tantalize with revealing, and then disguising, their loveliness.

Mortals had been set to play the music, their eyes dreamy and far away, as if they were drunk on wine or the seeds of the poppy. I rather thought this was a Wittenbrand trick done to them. A stealing of their wills, and perhaps even their memories.

They were not alone, other mortals served food from silver platters with glazed expressions and slow movements. I frowned at those chosen to serve. They were of every race and mode of dress known to me, but without exception, each stolen to serve was of great beauty and lithe in form. Curse the Wittenbrand and their obsession with taking everything beautiful for themselves.

"I took you, my beautiful one," Bluebeard whispered in my ear as if he could hear my thoughts.

"Then you failed in your task, for I am not beautiful," I whispered back.

He lifted my skeletal hand in his so that they hovered at

shoulder height and he escorted me forward as if we were partners in a dance of our own.

"I see none other with so singular a hand."

"A hand you demanded of me," I challenged.

"But did I?" His eyes met mine, blazing with intensity. "I think rather that you chose this. For you are my match, rib for rib, hand for hand, ambition for ambition, and who better to remake the whole world than the two who wish to drink it all up whole?"

And what could I say to that? For I knew myself entirely from our time apart, and I knew I was not content with the mortal world or with mortal power. I had been willing to shipwreck my very self on the rocks of the Wittenhame if only I could seize hold of his soul once more, and I knew to my very bones that I would do it all again exactly as I had before if I were given the chance.

He knew me too well. I withdrew from the thought, lest I be distracted from our task, and focused instead on our surroundings.

I did not know where we were as we emerged from the fire, only that it seemed to be a series of isles with a low river trickling between them. The water was no higher than my ankle and limned by the light of the huge, golden hunter's moon.

On each island the trees were in full blossom, the moonlight making pale the soft pinks of the petals that fluttered down in little rains and showers. Between the trees, white stones stood out like sharp teeth and claws, and they had been commandeered into tables and chairs. Adding to them, human chairs and tables were set and heaped with delicacies. And these were not plain chairs or tables, but those from royal courts, carved and inlaid, upholstered, tufted, and brocaded. As if all the wealth of the mortal world had been scattered here, and indeed, did I not see a brightly colored woven rug spread out under one tree, a wine barrel overflowing with gold jewelry under another, and an open chest spilling out pearls under a third?

The island where we emerged was treeless, the fire being the central feature. It had been the focal point of the dancers, but rising before it was a greater island still, set back across the gleaming water a little. Upon that isle, someone had carved a great statue to rival the statue of Death — and the sharpness of the features and rough edges of the work suggested it had been erected in great haste. It was a true likeness of Coppertomb with the rib crown on his head and the Wittenbrand arrow in his hand as a scepter and his lifeless stone eyes faced outward with unflinching calm.

And at the foot of that statue, a throne had been set on a narrow dais, and on that throne sat Coppertomb himself, looking down on us.

Before the dais, a smooth granite dance floor had been carved out of the stone and polished to perfection, ringed in tiny lights and garlanded at intervals with more pink flowers. Drifting petals washed across the slick surface and piled on the edges and I could not help but notice that there were smears of blood hastily wiped from the very edges of that dance floor.

It was the blood smears that made me look more closely at the scene and oh, when I did, I wished I had not.

The dancers were not Wittenbrand. That was my first

observation, and whatever magic made them dance had made their feet bloody and broken, and indeed, some had bone sticking through the flesh or were so ragged that every footstep was awash in blood. I was still gagging at the sight when I turned my eyes to the musicians to see their hands were similarly worn from ill-use by those who thought them playthings and not playmates.

And hanging in the blossom-laden trees were broken mortals, ruined by the Wittenbrand and tossed aside like used handkerchiefs. How they had been used was graven on their broken bodies and rent flesh and I fought hard to remain upright as I took in the hidden horrors done to my people under this veneer of ethereal beauty.

I turned to look away from one woman whose huge staring eyes would never see life again, only to set my eyes on an enchanted server offering a platter of fruit to a horned Wittenbrand. He took an apple from her platter, bit it, and then, quick as you please, bit into her flesh and tore a bite from it, too, and all the while she stood motionless, eyes glassy as she was so used.

My heart sped. This could not be allowed to continue. This must end. Immediately.

"A weak display for a weak king," Bluebeard said in an undertone. "Already their magic fades and their pomp is but the crowning riches of mortals. Dust and ashes and fixed forever within the bounds of time."

I hummed agreement. "But I am far more concerned by the abuses to my people."

"Patience wife, for we have come to end exactly that."

I swallowed down the demand that he end it immediately. Had I not seen him make things right with

Bluffroll in Pensmoore? Surely, I could trust him with this, too.

Instead, I cleared my throat. "All of this must have taken time to organize. And Coppertomb told me his Coronation Ball was to be in two days' time. Surely, that was more than two days ago."

"But only two in the Wittenhame." I glanced at him and saw his tight jaw and calculating eyes as his gaze swept around us and the certainty there brought me relief.

"I know you know all things as Bramble King, but how would he know that?" I asked, meeting Bluebeard's eyes. They twinkled at my admission that he was more than a mere man now.

"All the Wittenbrand will feel it in their bones. They are not of this world, but of another, and just as your mortal body tells you without fail when it is time to sleep and rise in your world, so their bodies do the same. It is the second night at home. And all present here know that."

"How nice for them," I said coolly.

He laughed but not in delight. This laugh was more an acknowledgment of all that was and it held a bitter mirth. We stepped together with that laugh, breaking the dancers apart with his inexorable strides. At first, no one seemed to notice except for the dancer he nearly trod on, but three steps in, the music stopped and a gasp tore from every throat at once.

And if there hadn't been enough proof before that I was married to the King of the Wittenbrand, all it would take was the looks on their faces to confirm it. I'd been there once when General Thistwaite returned from conquering the barbarians in the north and Svetgin had greeted him in estate. The General had marched his great white horse right into the throne room, its hooves still bloody with the deaths of our enemies, and the gasps in the court that day had been nothing compared to the gasps of the Wittenbrand now. They were like lazy children found out by their tutor, thieving servants discovered by their lord.

They knew a conqueror when they saw one. And I knew him, too. For he was my Bluebeard, the Bramble King.

CHAPTER TWENTY-SEVEN

"Ah, Coppertomb, my dulcet darling," my husband said, startling me even as his measured pace led us through the flowing water and toward the dance floor. "You've put yourself out on my behalf. To have crafted so generous a Coronation Ball on such short notice must have cost you great expense in both wealth and worry. Your endeavor is noted." He looked to me with mock admiration. "See how he has even kept my seat warm for me, wife. Has ever a manservant been so attentive or a vassal so abundant in generosity?"

Coppertomb came to his feet so suddenly that his throne fell backward, crashing into the feet of his statue with a clatter. His fist wrapped around his arrow-scepter and his mouth twisted into hatred. His face — so much younger than my husband's — was pale beneath the rib crown he wore, but his fine mortal clothing — fit for any king — looked plain and ephemeral opposite his true king.

Bluebeard's shadow, long and dark from where he stood before the central fire, was cast across the expanse and it shrouded our adversary so much that I could barely make out those with him.

"This is not *your* coronation ball, Arrow," Coppertomb said in a poisonous tone.

"Is it not?" Bluebeard said, looking around in mock surprise. "And do not call me Arrow, for the title belongs to another."

"Who inherited it?" Coppertomb spat the word "inherited" as if to remind us that Bluebeard had died at his hand.

"She who was once called Sparrow, now Lady and Ruler of the lands of Riverbarrow and honored by the title of Arrow."

"She will have to pay her tribute to me," Coppertomb said, hand drifting to the sword hanging from his waist.

"There will be no need for that," Bluebeard said, waving a hand. "She has already repaid her king tenfold."

"And yet I see no largess in my coffers," Coppertomb said, snapping a finger as a pair of winged Wittenbrand scurried to stand his throne back on its feet.

Though he was diminished in his mortal garb — and so were the rest of the Wittenbrand, I was conscious, suddenly, that we were surrounded. His court closed in slowly. They were armed — with any mortal weapons that weren't iron, but armed all the same. And there were thousands of them.

With the music abruptly ended, and the swirling bubbles and petals falling to the ground, with the eating and laughing paused, they seemed quite threatening. I looked around as subtly as I could as my husband led me closer still to his shadowed rival.

The Wittenbrand had been eating and drinking. And as was common for them at these events, there were some bearing bloody wounds and others with red-tinged blades. Some ran naked through the crowd laughing or growling. Some rode mortal beasts — tigers and boars who tore at any in their path, horses, of course, but also the grand fable elephantas of the jungle lands and the dusky camels of the deserts. And they bore on their persons trophies from the many lands the animals represented. Crown Jewels. Scepters. Prized pieces of armor and coronets.

I was looking, I realized, at a raiding party. But not a raiding party as I was used to in the mortal world, a raiding party that had *ravaged* the mortal world and rallied here with their slaves and plunder to spend a night in evil and debauchery.

And while I was not surprised at all to see that they were doing exactly as I expected Wittenbrand to do I was very surprised to find one notable person missing.

"Where is Grosbeak?" I asked aloud.

Coppertomb shot me an irritated look as he shifted, trying to move out of Bluebeard's shadow without being caught at it. My husband shifted with him, keeping the shadow in place, but the movement shed light on the figure standing to the left of Coppertomb's throne.

A centaur with a rotting yellow face and lank hair regarded me balefully.

"You ask, 'Where is Grosbeak?' but where were you when I was forced to wander the lands of Death bereft and alone?" he said, and for a moment I thought he hissed at me, but it turned out it was only a giant black mamba creeping down Coppertomb's statue and spooling around the base of it who was hissing, and when it thrust its head forward, Coppertomb placed a hand possessively on its head.

"I have many pets, mortal woman. Grosbeak is only one of them," Coppertomb said "And I fear you are too late. You were to come to my Coronation Ball."

"As I have," I interrupted. "And my dead is raised."

"Not by your power," Coppertomb said, smiling now as if he had won.

"He is not buried beneath the ground."

"But he was, wasn't he?" Coppertomb said smoothly. "And what was my ruling? That you, bride of the dead, would give yourself to me at the Coronation Ball."

"I cannot give you what I no longer possess."

"You were to be my bride."

"I am already married to another."

He laughed then. "At one time, such an objection might have stymied me, but I have now a worthy advisor. Your own friend and confidante. Is it not so, Grosbeak?"

And his gaze flicked to my old friend and mine turned to horror as I realized that Grosbeak was sweating so much that his face seemed to be malforming like hot wax.

"Feeling the effects of a geas, horrible revenant?" Bluebeard asked quietly, his fingers steepled under his chin as if he were considering something.

"I feel them," Grosbeak said and I swallowed because I remembered the geas Bluebeard had put on him — that if he betrayed me, he would feel the effects of his betrayal in his own flesh. Was that what was happening now? But how, then, had he betrayed me?

And then I saw her step from the shadow. Ki'e'iren.

Her eyes were narrowed and she smiled cruelly when they met mine. I felt my blood run cold as ice.

"I have found one who has a prior claim," Copeprtomb said, and his smile slowly grew as around us the silent Wittenbrand began to murmur in delight, and then — like an avalanche, a murmur grew to a chuckle and it turned to the kind of wicked laughter that takes its delight from cruel turnabout.

"But she was returned to her time," I said, feeling suddenly lightheaded. This woman had tried to kill me once — had, in fact, succeeded — and that was when she could benefit from my survival. How much more likely was she to try to kill me now?

"And offered a chance a second time to wed a bright Wittenbrand and live the life of grandeur promised her," Coppertomb said smoothly, and his smile was growing by the moment. He reached up and adjusted his crown with a look of triumph in his eyes. "Will you deny, Arrow, that she is your wife?"

"That's no longer my name," Bluebeard said slowly, but his expression was considering and he tapped his steepled fingers to his chin as if in thought.

"But will you deny that you married her first?"

"I will not."

The Wittenbrand calmed again, hanging on his words. They could sense drama in the air as a pike senses blood in the water.

"Or that she has a prior claim to you? To your wealth and your body?"

"I will not," my husband said, but he shot a look at Grosbeak that promised punishment later.

There was a murmur of excitement from the crowd.

I risked a glance at my old friend. Despite the warmth of the firelight, he looked green and grim and cracks were forming in his clay horse's body.

"Why would you betray me?" I asked him in a low voice.

"Why would I not?" he replied with an up-thrust chin. "What did I owe you? You, who paraded my corpse and humiliation through this world and the next."

But he would not meet my eye and I knew not what to do, anxiety rising in my throat until it seemed it would choke me.

"And if she is your living wife, you may not have another," Coppertomb said grimly. He spread his arms wide, addressing the crowd like a showman. "Look upon this would-be usurper, Court of Wittenhame! See how his weakness is exposed. Who can rule us who is ruled by a mortal? The dead fly in his perfume is this mortal wife of his — the error in his judgment, the flaw in his weave, the hole in his barque. It is this wife who claims him — this wayward mortal. She is usurper and fraud, a wife only in name, for she knew from the first of the existence of others, that they were not properly dead or buried and had prior claim to him. How could she lie to our court as she did and not face consequence? How could she lay claim to one of ours and not face punishment when we reveal she has grasped too high and risen too fast? This one's mortal wife, last of her kind, is incriminated in every way, and therefore is not his at all, but by right of the Wittenhame, ours to do as we please with. And we shall revel in her punishments. We shall feast on her terrors. We shall find joy in her screams. And he shall be made to watch all of them to remind him that he is but a vassal to us, but a supplicant before the throne of the Bramble King."

Coppertomb stepped forward, offering his hand to me as if he expected me to take it, but his eyes were on Bluebeard. And if he expected my husband to flinch or back up, then he was disappointed for Bluebeard merely tapped his steepled fingers against his chin and regarded us.

Coppertomb took another step forward as if trying to show his threat was serious.

I stared at Bluebeard, willing him to look at me. Had he not planned for this? Were we taken unawares after everything?

Behind us, someone began to beat a low rhythm on a hide drum and my heart beat in time with it as I looked between my accuser and my husband.

And I shouldn't have panicked. Not after all that had taken place. For had he not saved me again and again? Had he not planned all things for my benefit? But I could not help it. The threat was too near. The accuser too ... accurate. I had never deserved any of this, and by my husband's refusal to gift me with his gaze, how could I be sure he would ever look upon me again at all?

I swallowed hard and then I forced the words out — the only ones I could think of to save myself.

"I challenge Ki'e'iren. I will not have my place taken. If she wishes to displace me, then she will fight me."

There was a murmur of appreciation from the crowd. The Wittenhame adored a good challenge. I was counting on it.

"It is not your role to defend," Coppertomb chided.

"You have been found out. You have been exposed. And you will suffer your due."

"But the role of wife is mine if I take it by right of challenge," I pushed. "That is the Wittenbrand way. To take what you can by force or violence, is it not? And I will take it. I have walked the Path of Princes. I have wandered the lands of Death. I will not be cheated of my right now."

"You cannot deny her this," Bluebeard said to Coppertomb and when I looked at him his eyes were twinkling. "None of you can deny her this. She has issued her challenge. Let us see her make her play."

And the roar of approval that swept the Court of the Wittenbrand left me trembling, for I did not know how I was to defeat anyone, much less my savage enemy, but all our fates depended now on me.

CHAPTER TWENTY-EIGHT

"Meet on the dance floor. We shall observe the challenge there," Coppertomb announced, spreading his arms wide as if in a joyous announcement. I noticed his cheeks were brushed with gold dust. He looked young beside my Bluebeard as a willow whip looks beside a mighty oak.

Bluebeard cleared his throat, and I barely held back a smile when I realized that all who were gathered hesitated, waiting for his command.

"I rather think this dais a better place for a contest," he said mildly, still tapping his chin, but now with a look of devilry in his eye. "After all, if my wives are to battle, I think all deserve to see the result. Do you not, Wittenbrand?"

Behind him, another cheer rose up and Coppertomb flushed hot.

"The dance floor is just as adequate," he said firmly.

"But if we adjourn there, how will we admire … this?" Bluebeard asked, his voice dripping with disdain at the word "this."

He motioned toward the towering statue of Coppertomb and then he twisted his hand and as he did so the arms of the statue moved. They dropped the arrow scepter. It fell amongst the crowd, igniting screams of terror as it hit with a crunch that I was certain was not just rock on rock but rock with bodies smashed in between.

"He still has Wittenbrand magic," I heard a voice quaver and I shot a glance at the crowd where a horned woman leaned to whisper in the ear of a magnificent courtier whose face was pierced all over with golden rings. "Is it possible that he really is the Bramble King?"

"Tricks," the courtier sighed, but the sigh was a happy one.

And then Bluebeard twisted his hand to lay flat horizontally, and the statue moved to cup its hands at the waist.

"A better place to display a battle of the Queens, don't you think, Coppertomb?" he asked easily, swiping a drink from one of the trays passing by and toying with it.

The murmurs of appreciation around us were growing.

"You think to impress us by wasting what little Wittenbrand magic lies still at our disposal?" Coppertomb asked tightly. "We are not impressed. But I ask you this — man who is no longer the Arrow, Nameless One, Ghost of the Past — have you a stomach to gamble?"

"Always," Bluebeard said, downing his goblet with one quaff. He coughed. "Mortal wine? Were there no glow spirits? It's hardly a proper Coronation Ball without Wittenbrand draught, Coppertomb. We might as well be mortals. And here I had such confidence in you, I nearly had a mind to make you my steward."

Coppertomb's lip twitched manically and my eyes

widened. My husband was goading him to the breaking point, and while I should not have found that funny, I must confess that I did.

"We don't need dramatics," Coppertomb said firmly. "I have won my crown by right and trickery."

Bluebeard snapped his fingers and then Coppertomb's crown was in his hand. The Wittenbrand lord shook with fury but, impressively, he kept his face impassive.

"Cheap tricks. Go ahead," he said with a nod to me. "Use the last of her days on them."

Bluebeard smirked and then looked around at the crowd. "What say you? Shall I use all my magic on cheap tricks?"

The crowd laughed. Their eyes were bright and they'd abandoned their torment of the mortal servants to become spectators to the drama here.

"It's settled then, Coppertomb. I'll be displaying every cheap trick I know for the delight of my fellow Wittenbrand."

That garnered him another laugh.

"And I must confess, my young friend," my husband said, gliding around to where he could drape an arm over Coppertomb's shoulders. "You've presented me with an interesting riddle. Perhaps those assembled here can help us solve this. Who owns a thing? The originator, or the current possessor?"

"If you mean to ask if you are worthy of the crown because it's in your hand, then I shall tell you succinctly, no. The current possessor is not the owner."

"Ah," Bluebeard said, spinning the crown on his finger. "But I am the originator, for that is my pale bone thrust through the grip of the crown. How ... crass. Don't you think?"

"Then it does not belong to the originator, either."

Bluebeard smiled. "The first originator, then? He who made my rib? The Bramble King?"

"It belongs to me." Coppertomb clipped every word as he snatched the crown back and replaced it on his brow.

"But it bears no Brambles," Bluebeard said, looking confused.

I crossed my arms over my chest and looked at him wryly. He was delaying the inevitable. I would have to fight Ki'e'iren no matter how long he drew this out. One of my owls hooted as if to remind him of this and another made a powerful effort to fly away. He could no more leave my skirts, though, than I could leave this clever trap.

"The wager," Coppertomb said through gritted teeth.

My husband tugged him closer as if in a half-embrace. "Of course I'll gamble with you, dear Coppertomb. Nothing would please me more. After all, I could stand to win some of my own back after all your triumphs."

There was a murmur of appreciation from the crowd. They were loving every moment of this.

"Then offer me this," Coppertomb said, disentangling himself from my husband's brotherly affection. "Your most recent wife will stand as your champion, and your earlier one will stand as mine, and whoever loses, will leave the Bramble Court forever, never again to make a nuisance of himself."

"I would never call you a nuisance, Coppertomb," Bluebeard said sincerely. "All kingdoms need their flies or who else would dispose of the rotting flesh?"

"Take my wager, craven fool." Coppertomb's eyes sparkled and his mouth drew into a severe line. "I have plans for the Wittenbrand now that we own the world of mortals. We shall start the Games anew. But we shall start them without you and your onerous presence. You had not the good grace to die. At least have the dignity to leave when you are not wanted."

"Not wanted?" Bluebeard pressed his hand to his chest as if surprised. "I? Who brings with him such violent delights?"

There was laughter again and my husband winked at the crowd.

"Take. The. Wager." Coppertomb's eyes were bright.

"A bargain is struck," Bluebeard said and his eyes were dancing as he took Coppertomb's hand in his and grinned.

He had, of course, received exactly what he wanted but I wished he hadn't bet so high ... again. For now it was all resting on my performance and I was no warrior. I was not even as tall as my rival or as strong as she. I was certainly not so bloodthirsty. I had lost even my guide to the Wittenhame.

My guide.

Who had been suspiciously quiet.

I shot Grosbeak a mistrustful look and saw he had a mild, peaceable expression of slight boredom on his face. That was not right. Grosbeak, for all his terrible traits, was never peaceable. Never mild. Certainly, never bored.

I frowned, but before I could question him, Coppertomb waved a hand. "How are they to climb to the hands?"

Bluebeard flicked a finger lazily and steps formed leading up the sides of the statue to the hands.

"To every problem, a solution," he said, plopping down lazily on the throne and flinging his legs up, one over the arm and the other over the back as if he were a child and not a man.

I could practically hear Coppertomb's teeth grinding from here, but he did not bother to challenge my husband's right to sit on his throne. Or drape over it, as was the case now.

"Then no more delays. They shall fight, and as Bramble King, I have the right to determine their weapons. I shall choose —"

There was a loud clearing of a throat, followed by a hacking cough and all eyes turned to my green-faced former friend, lover of mermaids, traitor to all, Grosbeak.

"Need I remind you, my King, of the terms of our agreement?" he asked with a silky sweet voice. When was Grosbeak ever sweet?

"You need not," Coppertomb said tightly. "But, I pray you, remember who your sovereign is and who will remain your lord when this is past and you are nothing but a cracking clay horse with a Wittenbrand's head."

"Would that I could forget, my lord, and yet it is seared into every thought," Grosbeak said acidly.

"Care to explain, Coppertomb?" Bluebeard asked and his fingers were steepled under his chin again. I was starting to be skeptical of that gesture. It seemed to indicate that he knew what would happen next and when he caught my gaze, he winked at me, confirming that fear. He knew how I must fight, and like the rest of the Wittenbrand, he was longing to watch me acquit myself against my rival.

"It was the revenant who offered me the suggestion

that I turn to one of your former brides, and he who suggested that I drain the last of our residual magic to walk through the sands of time and draw her back to us," Coppertomb said and his smile was superior now. "And was I not correct to ask him — as I did — how to gut you? Was I not correct to assume you would crawl back here and try to take what is not yours? Was I not prescient to gather all I needed to defeat you one last time?"

"So prescient," Bluebeard said. "Perhaps when we are done here you may practice your visionary talents as an oracle to those similarly afflicted with poor planning and cowardly hearts. When I journeyed through the lands of Death I noted a pretty spot along a river of corpses that might serve you well."

"I'm glad you noted it, for it will be home to you hereafter."

"And what did our friend Grosbeak garner in exchange for this intelligence?" Bluebeard asked, smirking.

"He won the right to choose the challenge," Coppertomb said. "For he rightly guessed that your current mortal bride would wish to defend her position, and would gladly give of her last breath in your defense."

"Then perhaps Grosbeak should serve as oracle," Bluebeard said wryly.

Grosbeak sounded ill when he spoke. "I'll predict — accurately, I might add — that you'll father no children and live with no palace or lands."

"A grim fate indeed," Bluebeard said lightly, but his eyes were on mine when he said it for we both knew that whether Grosbeak mean to insult him or was truly psychic, his words were true. "Come then, my old enemy. What battle awaits my two wives in their quest to have me once and for all."

And there was silence as the Wittenbrand waited with held breath to hear what my former friend might say and his wicked smile told me that whatever it was, I would not like it in the slightest.

CHAPTER TWENTY-NINE

Grosbeak had always had a head for drama and he was not to be deterred by the mere fact that his body was now clay or that he had four feet instead of two. He clambered up the steps to the hands above us and looked out and over the assembled mass, his voice raised as he spoke.

"Lords and Ladies of the Wittenhame now in exile! Dukes and Duchesses, Counts and Countesses, fairy friends, centaurs, mermaids, and brownies, demonkind and angelic watchers, mortal dust and dreary human whelps — all who love tales of trickery and vice lend me your ears!"

"I see he's prepared a speech," Bluebeard said confidentially to me. "Your next pet should be voiceless, wife of mine."

"I'm certain you'll make it so," I murmured and he seemed to like that. His eyes lingered on me before he stole another glass from a passing tray and sipped it as Grosbeak carried on.

"We stand here together to determine a contest of wives — or Queens, as one of the competitors has suggested."

There was a general cheer at that.

"We all know the legend about the one who draws out the Wittenbrand arrow from the stone," here he gestured at Coppertomb. "He will bring milk and honey with him and we will all dance for ten years. He will shepherd in an age of glory. He will marry the finest woman who has been revealed through her actions to be pure in spirit, and all the land will see peace."

There was a silence after that. Perhaps his Wittenbrand kin were not so certain that they wanted peace.

"Who better to help find this worthy partner than I? I have plumbed the great depths where Death keeps his horde. I have been carried down the Path of Princes — for I am not one to walk, and my feet grow sore with any effort."

That garnered him a hearty laugh from the crowd. I noticed that drinks were flowing again and the people were merry as if this was going according to some internal script I did not know. The only individuals who did not look well pleased were Ki'e'iren, me, and Coppertomb.

"It was my pleasure to betray the Arrow to the Sword and make an attempt on his wife's life. And why should I not have? It was spoiling the game to see him take a new bride every time and drain her days, only to take another. The vampirian have always been a legend we despise in the Wittenhame."

"Hear, hear!" the crowd called back.

"But, I was caught in the act, my head taken, my will snatched. And I was bounced from place to place, passed from hand to hand — even dragged once by magic from Bluebeard's vaults to watch him as the Sword pried that very rib from his chest while he stood naked and bleeding. That was a grisly sight. And I don't mean the theft of a bone."

More laughter. He was nearly as good at this as my husband was.

"I won't explain or justify myself. I was a true son of the Wittenhame. I did exactly what suited me and bettered me at each juncture. And now here I am, gifted with twice the number of my original legs and with the great honor of declaring to you what challenge my former mistress will face ... oh and also Ki′e′iren who once I kissed while she was living and her husband was not looking."

Here he winked at Ki′e′iren and to my surprise her face colored and her eyes grew even harder. My gaze shot to Bluebeard, but he was drinking from his goblet, unconcerned at this revelation. I knew he cared not at all for his wives, but I did think he would care that Grosbeak close to cuckolded him. I was wrong.

"And with that revelation, and my assurance that I have thought long and hard on this matter and considered every possible battle a hopeful Queen of the Wittenhame might have need to endure, let me reveal the one I have settled on."

"This century, if you don't mind," Coppertomb said, drinking from his own goblet. His neck was almost puce, but he was still rigidly straight.

Grosbeak chuckled one of his evil chuckles. "Do not think I did not have you in mind, my darling audience, when I made my choice. For I know you. You are me. You have seen every possible physical and mental feat in your time. Arrows shot from horseback do not impress you. Nor does swordplay, nor do drinking games. Nor do knife fights, nor do bids of endurance where each member of the challenge slowly slices their own body parts off one by one."

Had that been an option? I was suddenly more worried than I had been. I glanced at Bluebeard and saw he was watching me with a hard, considering face. This was just like the hand. He needed me to go through with it, just as he did. And he would respect me if I tried, and suffer the consequences of my cowardice if I did not. Well. I was not giving up my place by his side. I was not backing down. No matter what challenge Grosbeak had settled upon.

"What we want, brothers, sisters, flesh of my own flesh," Grosbeak said, his voice rising in a crescendo. "We want novelty. We want drama."

I swallowed down a lump in my dry throat and shot my beloved a last look. There would be no help from him. I had made the challenge. He would watch me see it through.

"We want our competitors equally matched, equally likely to fall into the pit and never return. Equally likely to be humiliated and ruined. And we want them to do it to themselves!"

The crowd roared and my belly lurched. What would Grosbeak force me to inflict upon myself? What revenge would he take now for all the wrongs done to him while in my care?

"Ki'e'iren!" he called, "take your place here as the former of Riverbarrow's wives."

"You can't call me that," Bluebeard said calmly. "It is not my name."

"Fine," Grosbeak said, grinning hugely so that his terrible, leering mouth looked like a gash in dead flesh. "We shall call you by Izolda's name for you. *Bluebeard's* wives will join me here in the gracious hands of the Bramble King."

I felt my cheeks grow hot as Bluebeard laughed at the name I gave him but it was not a happy laugh, it was a sardonic one and he watched me as I ascended behind my rival. Would that my husband's moods were easier to read. Would that he were like mortal men in that, at least. But as ever, he was as mysterious to me as a fish of the sea is to a bird of the air.

I mounted the steps and I could see now why Grosbeak was grandstanding. From here, you could see all the land around. Fathoms and fathoms of moonlit islands, laced with the silver river and set off with blossoming trees. Between them, the Wittenbrand were gathered by the thousand, and all were watching me.

My palms grew sweaty and my breath hitched as I looked out over them. But why should I fear? Had they seen Death's lands and returned? Had they been made to watch everyone they love pass and their most beloved die before them? Had they survived all that and more? I did not think so. I would rip Ki'e'iren apart limb by limb with my own hands if I must. I would spread every drop of her blood over them like christening water. I would rend every one of them apart. I would do anything I must to stay by the side of my husband and confirm his choice in me. And I would not be afraid.

When I met my old friend's eye, here on the platform, it was with steel and determination and when he saw that look in my eye his own expression shifted to delighted excitement.

"We are ready," he said a little breathlessly. "Let the Game Commence. I name it for you now. The lives of these women and the fates of those they represent shall be determined by ... the Blind Man's Jape!"

The crowd gasped, and I did not know why or what I was to do, but their gasp turned to cheers and Grosbeak's grin grew broad and wicked as he lifted his hands in victory and reared in the air.

"You must be joking," I heard Coppertomb snarl from below.

But though I did not know what a Blind Man's Jape was, I knew one thing for certain. Grosbeak was not joking. And he was claiming his right and that meant whatever this terrible fate he'd chosen for us was, we must endure it or fail utterly.

CHAPTER THIRTY

"What is a Blind Man's Jape?" Ki'e'iren snarled as Grosbeak turned to us. "None of this is what was promised to me. I was promised little contest, if any. I was promised the right of supremacy!"

"You're trusting in promises now, faithless ally?" Grosbeak asked her wryly with a wink to me. He smiled like he was savoring this. "You were not content to stay in your old life. You had to crawl back to us little mousie mousie and you've landed in a trapsie. What else did you expect?"

She turned red. "You jest. When I was stolen by the Wittenbrand, that was a promise of power and riches to come. Or it should have been. Why should she inherit what was meant for me, merely because she's the last?"

"Precisely," Grosbeak said, his grin widening as he turned to me. "Why should she, indeed?"

"I'm the one he chose," I said coolly. "Does a man not have the right to choose his own wife?"

"And that is why Izolda is here," Grosbeak whispered confidentially to Ki'e'iren. "Because she lets other people do the choosing. You and I are better at seizing the reins, though if you win, it's not like you'll receive the power and riches you hope for. But that doesn't matter, does it mousie? It only matters that you are here right now to play with us."

"The Bramble King will wed me," Ki'e'iren said with a dangerous smile.

Grosbeak's laugh was delighted. "Did he promise you that? How delightful. I must admit that I'd enjoy the sight of him constantly humiliated by the presence of a mortal wife. So gauche. So terribly mortifying."

"Bluebeard took *her*," Ki'e'iren reminded him.

"Yes, well, he's mad even for a Wittenbrand," Grosbeak said, waving a hand. "Coppertomb is far too sane to enjoy that."

"We had an agreement," she insisted through gritted teeth.

"But did he promise you exactly that?" Grosbeak asked, leaning in as if imparting a great secret. "Because I'm willing to bet that he did not. Despite all my posturing just now, he is not looking for a bride, mortal or immortal. He is only looking to win."

Ki'e'iren's eyes widened and her jaw stiffened and she shot me a look of death. "Don't you have anything to say, usurper?"

I shrugged, trying to appear more detached than I was. In truth, my heart hammered and raced within me. I needed to stay sharp for whatever this contest would be.

"What is there to say, poisoner? You killed me once. You would kill me again. You would take from me all I hold dear for the entertainment of others. But I am not the mousie Grosbeak calls us. I will not scurry away in fear."

"Ladies," Grosbeak interrupted with a vicious smile, but he said the word slowly as if he wanted us to talk right over him. I shut my mouth with a snap. "We'll blindfold you now, and tie your hands behind your backs. There's to be no touching."

Below us, the crowd had begun to grow noisy again. I wished I could see those directly under the platform. It would have been helpful to pick up any cues from my husband, but he was entirely out of sight.

"No touching what?" Ki'e'iren made her objection sound like an Imperial decree. "How can we fight with no eyes and no hands?"

"It's a contest of skill," Grosbeak said leering at her, and there was something about how he did it that reminded me of something. My eyes narrowed. What was it? Oh yes! The time he'd told me about his harem of mermaids under the sea, he'd had that exact same expression on his face. "The Blind Man's Jape is as old and time-honored as a Three Day Bind. Did not Foinen the Terrible use the Blind Man's Jape to humiliate his wife Issarra? Did not Horace of Hagglesphere declare a Blind Man's Jape in his challenge to Surricus and win his entire wine store as the prize?"

"Can we get on with it?" Ki'e'iren asked testily.

She was remarkably irritating for one so lovely, though her white-haired beauty was so great that she nearly looked Wittenbrand. Perhaps she did fit this place better than I. Perhaps. But she would not win. I had fought for every inch of Wittenhame I'd tasted and I would fight for the rest of it, too.

"Let him tell his stories," I said dryly. "They are all he has."

Grosbeak offered a tiny bow in my direction and a nasty grin.

"The rules of the game are simple enough. Neither of you will leave the platform until a winner is chosen or that is a loss. You will not stop to eat or drink, or that is a loss. You will not remove the blindfold or free your hands or that is a loss."

"And then when she dies it's over?" Ki'e'iren pressed. "I do not object to killing my rival."

"Clearly not, since you did it once already," I agreed pointedly.

Grosbeak's eyes met mine and he laughed as if we two were having a marvelous time.

"This will be a delight," he said in a low, menacing tone. "Your funeral was not nearly long enough, Izolda. It makes the heart happy to see you back for a final showdown and a proper drawn-out death and burial. These pleasures should never be rushed."

"I couldn't agree more," I said dryly. Let him stew on that.

Grosbeak waggled his eyebrows but his tone returned to lecturing as he laid out the next part. "Your skill will be tested. She who finds her prize may claim it. She who does not, will receive her doom. I confess, I would dearly love to compete. I have the exact skillset required for such a challenge."

"Is it ugliness?" I asked. "Because I fear to inform you that I have the edge over my rival on that one."

Grosbeak scowled. "I will have you know that despite your husband's constant jests, I am glorious to behold, a delight of the eyes, a jewel among the Wittenbrand. I have been reliably informed on more than one occasion that my smooth wit and golden tongue bring delight to the ladies and I take every opportunity to practice and improve upon them. A skill you may soon wish you possessed as well."

"What are we testing?" Ki'e'iren asked as beneath us a song broke out among the Wittenbrand. It was the old "Fly with the Arrow" tune again, sung badly but with great enthusiasm from thousands of throats and Grosbeak half-closed his eyes at the sound as if reveling in it. "Is it the skill of means of death? I can kill a thousand ways."

"I'm sure you can," Grosbeak said, amused.

A Wittenbrand hurried onto the platform bearing four silk scarves. Two were white and two were black. Grosbeak held them up and looked back and forth between us before settling on white for Ki'e'iren with a wink for me. Yes, yes, very ironic to choose her as the innocent. I rolled my eyes at him. I was used to his antics by now and though I could barely suppress the storm in my insides, I thought I could at least manage to do this with dignity and a sense of humor.

The assistant, a Wittenbrand with long ears that ended in tufts of fur, and eyes so black they looked like night, deftly tied our hands behind our backs, making the knots so tight that they hurt.

I wondered if Bluebeard had stayed to watch. It would have been a comfort to see him in the crowd. That he held me so dear and yet with such light fingers hurt the heart just a little.

Can you hear me, husband of mine? I asked with my mind, but there was no response. Perhaps I'd lost the skill. Or perhaps he merely was not listening. Well. I'd chosen this. I'd have to see it through.

"... and she cannot manage a single one," Ki'e'iren was saying as they lifted the blindfolds to our eyes.

I stole one last glance at Grosbeak who cocked an eyebrow at me, and I could not tell if that was cruelty or kindness in his eye as mine were bound shut. With him, it could very well be both.

"And now the terms," he said when we could no longer see him. His growling voice sent shivers up my spine — and not good ones at all. The world seemed a madder place with my eyes and hands made useless. "You both claim to be the wife of one man. Who should know him better than you? You must choose him now from among all the Wittenbrand present. The rules state that none here may speak to you with their lips, nor touch you with their hands, so do not press them to do either."

"But how shall we find him then?" Ki'e'iren said and it was almost a wail. "This seems impossible!"

Grosbeak laughed, a cruel, delighted laugh. "Doesn't it? And that is the charm of it. Why did you think it was called a Jape? This is not meant to entertain you, but to entertain us. Whichever of the Wittenbrand who so will, shall parade themselves up to this platform and by their salutation, you must identify your husband."

"What does that mean?" Ki'e'iren asked, sounding irritated. A chill crept over me. This could not be as simple as it sounded.

"By their blandishment, they shall make themselves known."

Uh oh. I was starting to suspect ...

"I do not follow." She bit off every word.

"By presentation of endearment, so shall your fate be recognized."

When neither of us spoke, Grosbeak huffed out a frustrated breath. "Everyone gets a chance to kiss you and you have to pick which one is your husband or you lose. Is that so hard?"

"But which am I to choose?" Ki'e'iren asked. "The original or the Bramble King? He who was named Coppertomb before?"

"You tell me," Grosbeak said. "I'm no expert in matters of your heart."

And at our surprised gasps he laughed so hard that I heard him yelp as his hooves skittered sharply on the slick surface of the stone hands and his cry grew fainter as he — I was quite sure — fell from the platform to the crowd below.

I was not worried about him. It would take worse than that to kill my old friend and adversary. But my mouth was dry at the prospect of kissing half the Bramble Court in exile and my heart hammered in my head. What if I chose wrong? What if I did not know my Bluebeard by his kiss? So much depended on this.

I should have known that Grosbeak would choose something so ...icky ... as the means of our battle. I had seen Wittenbrand with the lips of serpents. I'd seen them with double layers of teeth. I'd seen Grosbeak's rotting mouth and tongue. My stomach heaved at the thought of kissing him. I was no mermaid to brave that. This was not the easy option. I could very well die of this. Slowly, from disease, rather than quickly from the edge of a blade.

Worse still, it would not be so easy to identify my husband for there were just as many angelic Wittenbrand as there were horrific. Just as many with thousands of years to learn to bestow perfect kisses. With no guide to who was who, I would be lost.

"I suppose you're feeling superior right now," Ki'e'iren said in an undertone. "But you should know that I have an advantage here. I have vision that exceeds that of most mortals and guess what? I can see through this blindfold. It's blurry, I'll admit. But I bet it's better than what you are bringing to this contest."

And she wasn't wrong, because I could see nothing at all. I was truly blind, and if I were to win this, it would take all the memories of all the kisses that I'd ever had to help me find my beloved.

CHAPTER THIRTY-ONE

I understood the drinking and singing now. And the sudden bursts of giggles. And Coppertomb's annoyance at Grosbeak's choice. And Bluebeard's amused steepled fingers. They had all known from the very start what this would entail.

More annoying than having to participate in this farce for their entertainment, was the blindness. I would have liked to see who reacted to what when it took place. As things stood, I was required to focus only on the task at hand.

The first footsteps on the stairs leading to our platform — or perhaps I should say the first hoof-steps because they clattered — set a spike of dread down my spine.

Someone laughed nearby and someone else said, "Look at the face the ugly mortal is pulling. She's practically green. Where's Bluffroll? He likes them green. He should be here."

"He'll not trouble this world again," I said precisely.

"And if you kiss me, you may find the same fate for yourself."

"She's cold as ice," the first one said, disapprovingly. "What was the Arrow thinking?"

"He's not the Arrow anymore. We can play with his toys all we like."

And then I was surprised by a very sudden, very wet kiss. I felt like I could hardly breathe, but I was certainly not going to open my mouth to draw in more air. Not after that. I swallowed, feeling ill at the smell of cheese that now wafted into my nose, and then I was kissed again, by someone new, I supposed, who at least smelled like wine and seemed to be less drippy.

I wiped my mouth on my sleeve and frowned. This was already horrible.

Beside me, I heard Ki'e'iren complain, "Don't waste my time. It's clearly none of you."

I opened my mouth to ask her how she knew and then my lips were caught by a pair that were petal-soft and caressed mine with loving gentleness. Like I said, it was going to be confusing, but I knew this was not my Bluebeard. This person smelled of honey and freesia, not mint.

Ki'e'iren seemed to like that kiss more, though. I heard her sigh.

But her sigh was cut off by a sound from below. Someone spoke in a low, menacing tone I could not quite catch, and then there was a scream that cut off suddenly followed by a second one that went on and on and then stopped.

I drew in a long breath — from my nose, I wasn't stupid — and steadied myself. There would always be violence where the Wittenbrand congregated. They were mortals with no veils, not bothering to disguise their peculiarities or passions. Where a mortal might kill your reputation, the Wittenbrand went for the literal throat. Where a mortal might silently plot revenge, the Wittenbrand plotted it openly, gathering support and offering riddles and challenges.

The next kiss thrust upon me was sharp and bold, as if the kisser were screwing up his courage to kiss me at all and then the one after that was hard and furious and followed by a laugh. I could almost have sworn that was Coppertomb.

There was a lull for me and I had the feeling that Ki'e'iren was receiving no lull at all. I heard wet smacks and moans from where she stood — in between screams and begging below us.

There was a metallic clash and the sound of sword on sword. Perhaps betting on the results had gotten out of hand. I'd seen that among them before.

And then a set of lips met mine that were tender in their touch but tasted of dead fish and rot and the teeth of the kisser nipped me as he finished his kiss. I spat to the side.

"I know that was you, Grosbeak. Are you happy to get it out of your system?"

He didn't break the rules by addressing me, but his laugh was as familiar as my own, and I frowned.

Honestly, how dare Bluebeard smirk and steeple his fingers knowing this was coming for me? Why did he not warn me if he knew, or stand to prevent it? How many times had he taken a blow for me and how long had I carried him pressed against my bare flesh, and now he stepped aside and allowed anyone who pleased to kiss me? It wasn't right, and I found I felt betrayal at his disregard. I had expected more from my husband. I had expected possessiveness and fidelity.

No one was kissing me now, and though I was grateful, it was not enough to assuage my fury. When I won this challenge — and I would — I would make him pay for not championing me.

Oddly, Ki'e'iren was still receiving kisses at a steady rate. They went on for some time and I was almost beginning to grow concerned — had I failed somehow already and been disqualified? — when a dry pair of lips met mine, but before the kiss could end, there was a strangled sound and a thump and the lips vanished suddenly from mine as another set claimed them, fitting my lips precisely, drawing mine into the embrace of his. I gasped and the kiss deepened, a forceful tongue sweeping between my lips in claim, and the roughness of an unshaven face brushing against my skin, and through the kiss I gasped his name.

"Bluebeard."

And his murmured laugh of victory was followed by a second kiss as a hand met my jaw and caressed it and then swiped the blindfold from my eyes.

My husband's cat's eyes met mine and I drank in the sight of him.

Behind him, Grosbeak was cursing. "You've ruined the whole thing. It's just like you not to be able to take a joke! You couldn't let it go on for a few hours, could you? No. Not Bluebeard. You couldn't just let a few Wittenbrand have a little fun, could you?"

"None other is to touch my wife," Bluebeard said easily.

"And yet several have kissed me," I said dryly, meeting his gaze with my steely annoyance.

"So they have, wife, but I suffered none to live."

"You ..." I looked down at the corpse at my feet. The one he had killed while the man was still kissing me. "Oh."

"He was courageous, that one. To kiss you when he's seen me kill a dozen others already for the same offense. Courageous, but foolhardy."

He reached behind me and my bonds fell away.

"Is this perhaps an overreaction?" I asked, chilled as I saw the bloody blade in his hand. How many had kissed me? How many were dead now?

I peered around him to where Grosbeak was nursing a black eye. His clay body was cracked and he was missing one hoof — likely from the fall. A sword stuck straight through his clay body, wedged in the hard torso.

"He stabbed me, too, in case you were wondering, and I'm already dead," Grosbeak complained. "I set the rules for this game. There was no mention of stabbing."

"I am Bramble King," Bluebeard said and as he said it he turned and drew me with him to the edge of the platform, looking out over the gathered mass below him. There was evidence of ... a battle among them? I was hard-pressed not to gasp at the sight. Bodies were strewn across the ground, red-flecked weapons in most hands and some were still locked in the conflict, breath heaving, arms grappling, their attention barely even on the platform.

This time his voice snapped like a whip. "I am your Bramble King."

He made a flicking motion and thorny vines began to grow from his hand. They tumbled to the ground and crawled across the surface, multiplying and blooming with white flowers which turned to dark berries, still growing and branching and tangling around the feet and legs of the crowd, forcing fighting Wittenbrand apart enough to still them. Their wide-eyed silence was all I needed to know that this act was his true win, not this game we'd just played.

"Challenge me with any wall to vault, any sea to cross, any army to fight, and I will show you again and again that I am your sovereign," he said but he didn't sound victorious, he sounded like he was threatening them. "But do not think to take or sully what is mine. I will have your respect — whether it is given freely, or whether I must take it with the edge of my blade. Choose today who you will serve. Is it to be me, or Coppertomb?"

And as he spoke, his winding vines rose up in the air, lifting Coppertomb, as if he stood upon the rising back of a sea monster. His teeth were gritted and his cheeks flushed and I realized that for the first time since I'd met him, there was uncertainty in his eyes.

"You thought to win by theft, Coppertomb," my husband said in a menacing tone. "You thought to steal my sacrifice and pretend it was your own. You thought to pull strings from behind the scenes rather than fight with your own hands. You thought to rip out my very heart and feed it to the grave. And you thought this would make you king."

He snapped his fingers and the silver arrow slipped from Coppertomb's hand, slicing his palm as it went and showering red upon the white blooms below his feet. It shot, as if launched from a bow, toward my husband and Bluebeard lifted a hand, and the arrow pierced into the gap in his palm created by the knife that had held him fast to the pillar of the sea. It stuck there, lodged in the ragged gap.

"This," my husband said, "Is mine. Bought with my deeds. Bought with my blood. Sign of my power." He turned back to his people. "And you are mine by the same merit. Now, choose. For those who choose to serve me will return with me to the Wittenhame."

Coppertomb scoffed. "There is no Wittenhame to which we may return."

"I have rebuilt it from the bones out," Bluebeard said, and as if on cue a swirl of pollen emitted from him like a cloud. "It will serve as home once more to my people and to their magic."

I heard a whisper then of, "magic" in the crowd. It sounded almost disbelieving.

"And those who will not serve, will go with Coppertomb to his fate."

"Fate?" Was the new whisper I heard echoing through the crowd.

"Fate?" Coppertomb said, crossing his arms over his chest and lifting one brow. "It is not for you to determine my fate. You have no authority over me."

"I am the Bramble King, he who was once the Arrow, Lord Riverbarrow, now your sovereign. All authority is mine for I have conquered Death," Bluebeard said in a low tone.

"Then what fate have you determined for me?" Coppertomb asked, annoyance in his tone.

"Patience," Bluebeard said, holding up a single finger to

him. He turned back to his people. "Decide, now, or go with this old serpent to his destiny. Any who would go with Coppertomb, raise now your token."

But though we waited in silence with nothing but the trickle of water and shush of the wind to answer, there was no response.

"Swear, then, before me," he said and the crowd looked at one another. One of them rose as if to come and kiss his ring but he said, "There will be no pomp and ceremony. Swear now, all together, or await your consequence."

As one, they fell to their knees, despite the thorny vines, and from the throats of thousands came the rush of their vow, like the sound of a waterfall.

"By height of night and light of moon, we give our fealty. Be ye our sovereign and dispense justice, sanity, and fated destiny to your people to the end of the Age."

And then Bluebeard spoke,

"By height of night and light of moon, I so swear to you. You will be my people and shelter within my bones until the end of the Age."

And Coppertomb's sigh was what told me it was finished. For I had never heard such a sigh of defeat before.

"And so it is done," he said bitterly as he plucked off his glove and revealed his missing finger for all to see.

CHAPTER THIRTY-TWO

"But not all done," Bluebeard said. And to my utter surprise, he slit his cheek with the tip of his sword to make his mark, and then, taking a drop of his blood on his fingertips, he flicked it out over the crowd and the ground shook, and the mortal world fell away and there was a feeling of being ripped from the earth and transplanted.

I reached for his hand and gripped it tightly as the almost-familiar madness of traveling between worlds gripped me, shook me, caved me in, puffed me out, and sent me spinning into the madness.

And when I recovered, we were once more within the Wittenhame, in that familiar place where the trees rose miles above the ground and the mushrooms were as large as houses, where the roots of trees were roads and the flowers could shade a whole family.

Everyone — the entire assembled crowd — had come with us, and they were arranged among the bramble vines exactly as they had been in the mortal world, but without their mortal servants or their weapons. Instead, between them, were banquet tables loaded with piping hot food and drink, covered in white cloths and piled with white flowers and dazzling with leaping sparks as if from a crackling fire.

It was day here — high noon, if I was any judge — and bunting was strung around the clearing, a strange kind of bunting made of clouds and shifting rainbows. Frogs the size of horses leapt from table to table with more good things borne on their sleek backs.

When my mind finished reeling and sanity began to trickle back in to join the memories that mixed with nightmares that mixed with hopes, I realized we stood at what must be a head table, placed on roots high above all the others. And to one side, was the glittering sea. It shone soft azure under the light of the brilliant sun and mermaids flipped up out of the water with porpoises beside them like huntsmen with their Hounds.

"Welcome," Bluebeard said, pollen swelling around him and tiny songbirds darting down to cover his shoulders and arms. The birds sang riotously. "Welcome, my folk, to my marriage supper."

There was a general cheer, though that was just as likely for the food as for anything else.

"Be at ease. Eat. Drink. Delight. For my bride is worthy of celebration, and she who bore me through death is worthy of your honor. But before I feast with you, it is customary for a new-crowned king to receive gifts, and the gift I demand is from my queen."

He turned his body to me, and I turned to him also, but with a raised eyebrow. What was this gift to be? Was I now to kiss all the mermaids in the sea and watch them be slaughtered for their trouble?

"Willst thou, bride of mine, pass judgment in my name, as your gift to me," he asked, offering me his hand. I placed mine in his.

"I will give whatever you ask of me," I said steadily. But I hoped this would be the last of the tasks, for I was tired and even the smells of roast chicken and peaches and honey rolling out from the supper table were not enough to tempt me. I needed sleep.

"Then stand now, in judgment of my enemies," he said, sweeping a hand to where I found Coppertomb, Ki'e'iren, and Grosbeak still embedded in vines.

"I have never been your enemy," Grosbeak said, pouting. "And have you not already run me through with your sword?"

But I could see that his outburst had directed the eyes of my husband's people toward him as if to question whether this would be tolerated, and an acid rose in my throat. I needed to get this right or my Bluebeard would lose the respect of his newly sworn people.

The Bramble King flung himself into one of two large oaken chairs at the head of the assembly — Wittenbrand thrones, I realized. His moved with a constant shifting that made the knots in the wood look like faces. No, not look *like* faces. They *were* faces. I caught sight of the former Bramble King within and my heart caught in my throat, even as my husband lounged with one leg flung over the arm of his throne and a bunch of grapes in his fingers.

He smirked at me, lifting a brow.

I was up for his challenge. So, with a pale face, I stepped

up onto the seat of the other throne-like chair. Fortunately, this one seemed to shift from flower to flower rather than face to face, though that still was unsettling in a piece of furniture.

"You cannot mean for her to judge us," Coppertomb said in a low, throaty voice. He sounded like he might growl at any moment. "She is mortal."

"No more," Bluebeard said, pausing to suck a grape from the vine before seeming to remember that he was speaking. "I have granted her equal share in my days."

There was a gasp from the crowd. And I will never understand the Wittenbrand because, as if this declaration were a signal, they all seated themselves and began to dig into the spread, watching me from time to time as if I were their entertainment.

"Do go on, wife. I am burning with curiosity to see what fates you will find fitting for my enemies."

"You have already defeated your enemies, my Lord," I said clearly. "You have stood on the neck of Death." His pleased laugh made me bold. "But under your authority, I will speak so that each here receives what is fitting."

"I have every confidence in you, as do we all," Bluebeard said and then winked dramatically at the crowd. They laughed, but it was a nervous laugh as if they were afraid they might be caught up in "receiving what is fitting." They had good reason to be worried. They had been complicit in all of this.

"To Ki'e'iren who tried to usurp my place," I said forcefully so that all would hear, "I assign this fate: go back to your time and place and dream no more of the Wittenhame. Be mortal in every way, and remember forever how you betrayed us."

"Ooohhh," the crowd whispered together. To them, the fate for forgetting this place was a fate far worse than death.

Ki'e'iren gasped, clearly unhappy, but then the vines drew her in and she disappeared, sent to her fate.

Bluebeard quirked an eyebrow at me and I felt the blood rush to my cheeks. Had he thought that too harsh, or too light? I could not tell. Or perhaps he found it too predictable. The Wittenbrand did not like things to be predictable. He flourished a hand as if bidding me to continue.

"To Coppertomb who conspired against my husband and tried in every way to make him stumble and fall, who, at the end, stole his beating heart and gave it as a feast to the barrow. Execution is too good for him. One death can only be enjoyed once." There was a murmur of approval from my husband and a mirror murmur from the crowd. Better, then. They turned their sparkling eyes on me, ready to see what torture I would gift to the one they had followed into tormenting the mortal world. "Coppertomb, I condemn to banishment." There was a disappointed sound from the crowd and I saw the man in question begin to smile. Until he heard my next words. "I banish you to the lands of Death to wander until you succeed in walking the Path of Princes." My heart was racing as I uttered his judgment in full and my voice rose as it gained confidence. "Languish there among so many whose fate you wove. Drink deep of despair with them. Make friends with Death — your only companion. And learn the lesson hubris teaches all of us: that in the end, we are all equals. Rich or poor, mortal or immortal, in the dark of despair, there is no great and small. We all are lowered even into the dark embrace of death. And how shall we bear up under his crushing weight?"

"I hardly think," Coppertomb began with an easy smile, but his words choked off and he gasped and the crowd gasped with him, freezing, as a white figure in long robes strode forward.

Death's beard and hair flowed delicately in a wind that was not there, and he walked over the waves of the sea without his feet so much as getting damp. In one hand, he held my severed hand, and he twisted it so that it beckoned to Coppertomb, and with a look of horror, Coppertomb looked down at his feet and when he saw that they were moving of their own accord to follow Death, ignoring any will of his own, they danced a complicated step as they went. And in this moment, he was no higher or greater than those poor mortals who were made to dance until their feet were in tatters. He let out a choked cry that cut off as if he'd bit his own tongue.

And when he had danced half down the aisle, following the white specter, his breath hitched into panicked short breaths, he threw a look over his shoulder and spat. "I will see you again, mortal Izolda. If not in this life, then in the next."

"I'm counting on it," I said. "For my husband bid me dispense justice and so I have. But if ever I lay eyes on you again, I shall dispense injustice and that to fulsome measure."

And my husband's barked laugh was the last thing

Coppertomb heard for Death leaned in, kissed him, and he was no more.

I swallowed and we all took one long minute to breathe before Bluebeard slurped his wine noisily and startled us back to reality.

"More judgments, wife?" he asked with a lifted brow.

"Yes," I said in a shaky voice, for Bluebeard was looking at Grosbeak, but this next judgment I planned to go elsewhere. I turned in place again and looked out over the feasting crowd. "Folk of Wittenhame," I said clearly. "I judge that you, too, have wronged my husband, uniting under his rival." I risked a look at Bluebeard and saw him frozen, regarding me warily. "And so I sentence you with this. For the duration of my husband's reign, you shall not cross the barrier into the mortal world. You shall not harry those made without magic, nor reward them, nor use them in your schemes. You shall not know them at all. They shall be insulated from you, and you from them, for an age and half an age."

And the silence that met me was far deeper and far more sober than even the silence that met my judgment of Coppertomb.

"Wisely said, Bramble Queen," my husband said in a low voice.

The murmur that followed his was part resigned despair and part awe, and I felt I needed to swallow to go on.

"But there is more," Bluebeard said, nodding toward Grosbeak. My old friend had his rotting chin thrust up into the air, his clay arms crossed over the jutting hilt of the sword sticking from his chest. "Loathe though you may be to judge he who was once your ally, he is enemy to me, and he shall be punished. Doom him now, with your own tongue."

I reached down to the table and drew up a goblet and drank, and then I turned and I strode to Grosbeak and offered him the cup and to my surprise, he met my eyes silently, his twinkling with humor, and he took the cup and drank it to the dregs.

"Think not that you can best me, Izolda. For I know all your secrets and all your lies." His voice had an edge.

"This much is true."

"Strike then, your harshest blow. I shall drink your cup of wrath."

It took great courage for me to meet his eyes then. For though he may have been enemy to my husband, I owed him as many thanks as I did punishments. And so I took a long breath, tossed the cup aside, and turned to the crowd.

"To Grosbeak, treacherous ally, betrayer of plans, criminal of heart and mind, I give this punishment. Lose now your clay body and be delivered to the sea in the flesh you wore before you were dead and buried. And the sea shall have you until she tires of you. And you shall be our ambassador to both her and her kind. A punishment and a gift knit together for both the good you did and the evil, that you may know the emptiness of great power and find, perhaps, at last, what love might exist still for those who seem beyond all redemption."

And when I looked back at my old friend he was laughing and as he laughed, his clay body fell away, and his face crumpled to nothing and out of the wreckage of what had once been Grosbeak a man rose to full height and stepped out, his skin perfect and unmarred, naked as the day he born and — to my shock, for I had forgotten his face from before death — surprisingly good-looking.

He bowed to me once, folding at the waist, and then a great wave rose from the sea and splashed over him, sweeping him away, and for a heartbeat, I thought I saw four mermaids, two holding each arm, one cradling his head and a third tangled around his waist and they carried him off to the heart of their mistress.

And the last I saw of him was a wink.

I could not claim I would not miss him sorely, or that I was not sad to see him leave, and I do not know how long I stood, looking out to sea, only that after a time, my cheek was tickled by whiskers and warm breath and arms wrapped around me from behind, and my beloved's voice purred in my ear.

"And now, fire of my eyes, I think it is time that you, also, receive your just reward."

CHAPTER THIRTY-THREE

My Bluebeard swept me up in his arms and carried me, hooting owls and all, out across the azure waves as if it were no more difficult for him to walk on the rolling surf as to walk on the sand, and I should have been caught up by the silver gleams of the wave-tips or the soft deep blue of the cloudless sky, or the pollen that still followed my beloved in a golden swirl, stirring up new life in his wake. But it was not these things that I dwelled on. Nor was it the white sandy beach of the island he took me to, nor the great leafy fronds of the trees there that cast the cool relief of shadows over the sand.

No, it was the depth of the world held in his shining cat's eyes and the hungry longing that hovered just beneath the surface of them. It was the warm arms that held me safe in their embrace and the gust of his breath as he carried me, the quirk of the edge of his smile as we drank each other in wordlessly. Those were what caught my heart.

"Is this to be my reward then, or yours?" I whispered,

my breath caught slightly in my throat for in all the wild, tangled fairytale we'd woven together, I'd had little time to dwell on what "after" might look like and I found myself to be almost overwhelmed now that it was upon me.

"Can it not be both, bride of my heart?" He murmured to me, his voice pitched only for my ears.

"I suppose it could," I said, considering, but I would not be myself if I were not practical and as he set my feet down on the white sand, I could not help but press him with what still troubled me. "But I must confess, I find I am still quite grieved by your actions before your folk. You allowed me to be kissed again and again against my desires. Am I to expect that treatment in the future."

He paled slightly as he looked at me as if the thought of what had happened wrung some emotion from him.

"I killed each one who set his lips to thine."

"So you did," I said, lifting my owls — who had gone to sleep with their heads tucked under their wings — so that I could wade into the foaming surf. I was trying to appear confident, but I was deeply troubled. "And yet, you allowed the violation. I agreed to the challenge, but I had thought it would be some contest of merit. It did not occur to me that you would leave me to such an exercise in humiliation without preventing it."

And when I turned, he was standing before me, and he had stripped off coat and weapons and jerkin as if he planned to bathe in the sea. The great gaping hole in his side distracted me for a moment. He wore that for me. For always.

It was hard to be angry at a man marked so.

He froze, biting his lip and looking at me intently.

"And is this your last doubt of me, my wife? I have given you my flesh, my bone, my death, and my fidelity. I have honored you as my queen and made you secure in that position forever. I have invited you into partnership with me, into a share of both sufferings and reward." He paused, eyes blazing and I felt a small quake of fear. "But you harbor one last doubt, hmm? Will I uphold your honor in the future? Will I never again suffer a violation to your person? Is this the last question that must be answered before you can find happiness in my arms?"

"Yes," I said, lifting my chin steadily. "It must be answered. For how can I trust the rest of my future in your hands without an answer to that?"

He nodded, looking down and his expression was thoughtful as he waded into the sea with me. When he reached me, he took my hands in his and my owls hooted and tried to fly away when I dropped my skirts. They made such a protest that I was forced to hold my skirt in one skeletal hand to keep them from the sea and his hands in my flesh one.

And when his gaze met mine I felt myself swallow at the purity of the emotions I saw there. His eyes radiated finality.

"You know the old hymn. You've heard it sung. You followed it onto the Path of Princes."

"Yes," I whispered.

"Sing it for me." He stepped nearer, leaning in so that all I could see was his dear face and his parted, wanting lips. He drew in a breath like a backward sigh.

"I sing very poorly," I said, cheeks heating.

"Sing, all the same." One of his hands left mine to caress my cheeks with the back of his hand, drawing my attention to the holes in his palms which he bore even as Bramble King, and would bear now forever. He gave me that. Could I not give him this?

My lips trembled, but I sang for him.

"Fly with the Arrow,
Dance with the Sword,
Give Your Heart to the Barrow,
Die with your Lord

AND IF EVER YOU be broken,
And gasp on the ground,
Hold up your fine token,
And join with the sound.

SING FOR YOUR SOVEREIGN,
Bow to your Dream,
Make Haste for the Fallen,
Rise in Esteem.

AND IF EVER YOU be broken
And gasp on the ground,
The word may be spoken,
And salvation found."

He tilted his head so that his lips brushed my cheek as he whispered, "There's more to the song."

"But that's the Path of Princes," I said, leaning back so I could narrow my gaze and meet his. "The whole of it."

He smirked. "So it is. But the rest is the Way of Kings."

And my lips fell open and I felt as if I could not catch my breath as he sang to me, sweet as any songbird,

"From the Kiss of your Enemy,
Your Home Restore,
Bring each one to Justice,
Fairness Adore.
And if ever you be broken,
And troubles abound,
Know vow is Unbroken,
For your King is Crowned."

"But how," I gasped. "How did you know."

"I've always known," he whispered, leaning in to rest his forehead on mine. "While others walked the Path of Princes, I was walking the Way of Kings and you were walking it with me."

"It might have been nice to know," I said wryly, finding it harder and harder to resist his charms as he kissed down my neck and buried his lips in the flesh where my chest met my shoulder.

"Mmm," he murmured.

"But now there will be no more surprises?" I asked

His head whipped up in that odd lightning-fast way he sometimes had.

"Well," he said, smirking mischievously, "maybe some surprises."

And then he spun me gracefully around to show me what was fluttering down from the sky and onto the island

— our old Grouse House. A black raven was nestled in the thatch and it croaked at me balefully.

I gasped. "I thought that was lost forever."

I turned enough to see his glowing smile directed at me.

"And I thought you said you could have no home. I thought a life with you would be sleeping in tangled tree roots and eating wild berries."

"The Bramble King has no home," he agreed. "But who is to say that the Bramble Queen may not have one? Perhaps, my dearly beloved Queen of my heart, you may see fit to invite me within, to share your sup and fire ... and perhaps even your bed."

He paused and I loved how he held his breath to hear my answer.

"Oh, so now is reward time," I said dryly. But it was hard to be cool and dry on the outside when on the inside my pulse thundered and my blood ran hot.

He smiled so sweetly that his eyes went crinkly around the edges and his dimples showed. I could barely breathe with the beauty of it.

"I hope so. I hope it will be reward time for a very long time. An age and half an age, perhaps."

"And what is to be *your* reward?" I asked, quirking my lips to tease him.

His smile washed away and he fell to his knees in the surf but I would not let him bow before me, so I threw myself to my knees with him while my owls coughed and sputtered, half-drowned and furious.

He took my face between his palms and his eyes were

deep and dark, his voice full of longing. "Be my reward, Izolda, fire of my eyes and flame of my heart. Be everything I gave myself for."

"I will," I gasped. "But only if you will be my consolation in return, for I love you, my Bluebeard."

He leaned in then, gathered me in his powerful arms, and drew me to him, until I was clasped tight against his chest. He leaned in tenderly to kiss me long and deep. And then, he leaned back to lie in the shallow water, bringing me down over his chest in a tangle of wet cloth, foaming water, and glittering pollen. And there, as I lingered over his warmth and strength, he kissed me and ran his fingers through my tangled hair, until my poor owls begged for mercy and had to be set free. And when they were released, he made up for the moments spent freeing them with kisses upon kisses as if he would gift me all those he stored up over the ages of his great quest.

The Law of Greeting stole me away. The Law of Love brought us together. And kept us together.

And if Happily Ever After is how a fairytale ends, then ours ended here. But truly, it had only just begun, for love is like that. One peak is crested only to reveal another. One depth plumbed, only to uncover greater depths still, and a thousand years from now, when we are nothing more than terrifying legends to the mortals who were once my kin, we two will still be learning our love as one learns the heights of music, the breadth of art, and the deep deep depths of the written word.

And if my old friend Grosbeak saw me from his place within the sea, then he may very well have noticed that I had a very bold imagination after all — one that might have put even him and his mermaids to shame.

It certainly made my Bluebeard laugh and sigh, and it is for his happy sigh that I live — for an age, and half an age, and forever.

THE END

AUTHOR'S NOTE

Bluebeard's Secret is my heart and everything I love about fairytales laid out on a platter. It's a story dear to my heart with characters who are alive in my mind and will continue to remain alive whispering to me. I think the best stories have the same heart — one of love, sacrifice, and seeking restoration. And if they can have some humor and a nod to how dark things can be before that restoration takes place, then all the better.

If you enjoyed the series, you will likely enjoy the series of stand-alone paladin fantasy romances that I'm planning for 2023. That world is already shaping up in my mind. (You should follow me somewhere so you don't miss news on this.) You'll also likely enjoy my Fae Hunter series and my Mayfly World stories which are featured as short stories in various anthologies and also published as short novels (*Stolen Mayfly Bride* and *Married by War*). You'll find links to all of that at www.sarahklwilson.com.

Thank you for reading and being part of this journey

with me. We are friends now in heart, even if we never meet.

Special thanks to Grosbeak. Without him, I'd never have found my way through.

And to Melissa who loves all this as much as I do.

HEED THE CALL!

Sign up for my newsletter for
new-release alerts and all the
latest on my art.
I'll give you a free
audiobook just for signing up and
you can leave at any time.

www.sarahklwilson.com

Try one of Sarah K. L. Wilson's other kissy & stabby ROMANTIC FANTASY books.

A stolen-bride fairytale with bite!

A monster hunter with a fierce bodyguard!

A trickster fae and the seer he can't stand to see suffer..

A blind hunter playing a deadly game against all of faerieland and her dangerous fae captive.

A girl with powerful magic destined to fall for the brother of her enemy.

"SARAH K. L. WILSON WRITES VIVID CHARACTERS WITH HUGE HEARTS. IT'S IMPOSSIBLE NOT TO FALL IN LOVE WITH THEM."
- A. L. KNORR

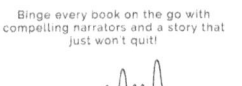

LISTEN TO THEM ALL ON AUDIO!

Binge every book on the go with compelling narrators and a story that just won't quit!

www.sarahklwilson.com

BEHIND THE SCENES

USA Today bestselling author, Sarah K. L. Wilson loves happy endings, stories that push things just a little further than you expect, heroes who actually act heroic, selfless acts of bravery, and second chances. She writes young adult fantasy because fantasy is her home and apparently her internal monologue is stuck in the late teens

Sarah would like to thank **Melissa Wright & Eugenia Kollia** for their incredible work in beta reading and proofreading this book. Without their big hearts and passion for stories, this book would not be the same.

Sarah has the deepest regard for the talent of her phenomenal artist KDP Letters who created the gorgeous cover art that accompanies this book. Without her work, it would be so much harder to show off this story the way it deserves!

Thanks also to the Noble Order of Female Fantasy Authors who keep me sane – sort of. And for my beloved husband, Cale and sons Neville and Leif who are endlessly patient as I talk to them about bookish passions.

And a HUGE THANK YOU to my patrons, **Mike Burgess, Jennifer Wood, Victoria Churchill, Ken Baker,** and **Carly Salsbury** for their support. I couldn't do this without readers like you!

Visit Sarah's website for more information:
www.sarahklwilson.com

Milton Keynes UK
Ingram Content Group UK Ltd.
UKHW022119140823
426865UK00004B/20/J